CROWNED

GATEKEEPERS OF THE GODS

JENNIFER CHANCE

For Mona
May true love find you wherever you go.

Queen Catherine mounted the steps to the Temple of Winds, her shoulders back, chin high, and her practical yet still elegant sandals clicking on the polished marble. She could hear the thrashing seas below her, crashing against the gateway rocks. She didn't miss the building storm clouds on the far horizon, either.

Good. Both the mighty Aegean and the coming storm matched her mood. As one of the highest ranked gatekeepers of the gods who'd been pushed too damned far by the insolence of certain members of the Greek pantheon, she was powerful...and she was *pissed.*

Catherine strode quickly through the achingly beautiful temple, taking in every detail. The Temple of the Winds was one of Oûros's most well-kept secrets, a two-way conduit between mortals and the pantheon of gods. As its keeper, she adored every inch of the structure, from the smoothly carved white columns, to the eternal fire burning in its ceremonial maze, to the richly painted interior of its pristine dome. How many times had she come up here to dream a little, give general thanks for her blessings, and listen to the wind whistling up the cliff, without a care in the world?

Today, she had a different sort of offering to give. And different demands to make.

She moved with single-minded focus through the familiar routine of tracing the maze's path to the eternal fire, lighting the taper, and then moving to the three permanent ceremonial offering bowls placed on the temple's ledge. The first bowl was closest to the Aegean, which frolicked far below this cliff-side idyll, closest to Poseidon. And it was Poseidon to whom she owed the greatest debt today.

She paused only long enough to scoop her hand into one of the pockets of the bag she carried slung over her shoulder. She pulled out several small shells, a few tiny shattered pieces of metal from her son's downed plane, and a precious handful of iridescent scales, the molt of a sea nymph, which had been recovered from the royal underwater equipment just few days ago. She laid the pieces in the offering bowl, then added several scoops of dried flowers from a different pocket. Hydrangea for gratitude, rose petals for love, wild gladiolus for power.

"Thank you, Poseidon, for bringing Ari back to me—to all of Oûros. Thank you to your nymphs who helped point the way."

She lit the pyre with her taper, watched the flame shoot up quickly, the stream of smoke straight and true. Her offering was accepted, and she sagged a little in relief. She owed many gods for the gift of Aristotle's return. Eros, of course, as the kingdom's patron deity. Zeus and Hermes, absolutely. But it was Poseidon's sea nymphs who had brought the intelligence that had drawn the royal family to look in Turkey for the lost prince. Those same nymphs had helped the American adventurer Nicki Clark as she'd risked her life to rescue the prince. "I will give you *anything* I can in return."

The crashing sea below boomed in response.

She turned to the second bowl. Another scoop into her bag yielded the same mix of flowers, but her questing fingers also gathered up three Greek coins, which she dropped into the offertory vessel. Two fell with Zeus's profile visible, the third with his mighty eagle. She added another eagle's feather to the mix and set the small pile aflame.

"Thank you, Zeus, for your strength and your protection," she said, her voice turning harder. "And for your aid in the coming battle. Ari is back, but with him come the whispers of deception by one of the gods. Typhon arrays his monsters against us. We cannot let that stand."

Far off to sea, the storm crackled and raged, but the smoke from this second offering scattered in the breeze that kicked up off the Aegean.

Irritation sparked within Catherine. Zeus wasn't convinced? He wouldn't help her? Or was he waiting to see what Typhon would do—how far the gates could be pushed before they burst open? She knew the gods of Olympus could get restless behind their gates.

A puff of wind put out her flames, and she stared at the smoldering pile, her eyes narrowing. Her taper remained alight, but her offering? No. "You'll help, mighty one," she said grimly. "But not yet, hm? Not yet."

She turned to the third offertory vessel, and dipped her hand back in her sack—but save for a few more handfuls of dried petals, nothing remained for her to give. The only other item she'd carried with her was her journal. And that couldn't...

Suddenly, the second pyre, Zeus's offering, crackled back to cheery life. Catherine jerked back so sharply she almost dropped her taper.

Slowly, carefully, she set the still-lit wand on the edge of the third shallow bowl. Then she pulled out her journal, opening it to the last entry. A dream she'd had, not four nights back, after she'd witnessed Ari via a closed-circuit camera—he was alive! Boldly, brilliantly alive, for all that he had no memory of who or what he was. He was thin, haggard, exhausted-looking...but he lived. That night she'd dreamt of sea nymphs and starlight, but she couldn't remember anything else.

Leaving the journal on the ledge, she pulled out two heaping handfuls of flowers, scattering them into the vessel. "Who shall it be, then?" she murmured. "Hermes, do you wish to whisper in my ear while I'm awake? Morpheus, do you wish to walk in my dreams...or in Ari's? I welcome—anything. All of it. Whatever aid you can give us to take on this battle and keep the gates strong."

Catherine carefully set the taper into a notch on the bowl, and picked up her journal. She ripped out a blank page, folded it, and tented it on top of the pile of flowers. Then, in one quick movement, she recovered the taper and set the offering to light. "Speak to me, god of Olympus, however you will," she breathed.

A whistling wind gusted up from the ocean, briefly scattering the smoke rising from the third bowl. The column snapped back into place a moment later. Both of her offerings to Zeus and Poseidon continued to burn tall and steady from their bowls. All offerings were apparently now worthy.

The wind gusted up, sending a whirl of debris into the temple. Catherine watched with wide eyes as two feathers skidded onto the ledge by the bowl. A gift from the gods, perhaps, but the iridescent blue of the badly frayed kingfisher feathers were dull, their brown undertone muddy.

Her brows lifted. The kingfisher was a bird of Morpheus's. But it had been an old bird and a sick bird who had contributed these feathers. The sight of them laid a chill on her heart. What secrets needed to be revealed? What did age and death have to do with her family's struggle?

With a steady hand, she dropped the feathers into the bowl, and studied them as they caught fire.

"Keep us safe, Morpheus," she murmured. "Tell us what we need to know. All who love Aristotle, who love this country, will pledge themselves to you in return."

The flames curled the feathers up cheerfully enough, but the fire looked to burn out too quickly—and she had nothing left to give. She sheltered the flame from the wind with her cupped hands. "I swear, any member of the royal family would be honored to serve you, should you help keep us safe."

The flames leaped higher, and the trees surrounding the temple of winds murmured and sighed with almost human voices as the wind sailed through them. She smiled, her heart lighter. Zeus's offering had burned clean away now, and Morpheus's quickly followed.

Then Catherine turned her attention back to her offering to Poseidon. The flames in the first bowl were finally dying away. All that was left at the bottom of the bowl was the indestructible scrap from Ari's plane and the shimmery sea nymph scales.

"If anyone born of the sea can help my son, I beg of you, Poseidon—*help* him," she implored as she leaned close, her hands dropping to grip the sides of the stone bowl. "Do this, and I swear to you, our families will be joined evermore."

A boom of far off laughter danced upon the wind.

One

The roaring speedboat smashed headlong through the white-capped waves of the Aegean, apparently deciding today was the day it would pick a fight with the open sea. Fran Simmons knew exactly how it felt.

"Isn't this *great*?" Beside her, Nicki Clark gripped the side of the boat, her bright red life jacket more a formality for her than any sort of needed protection. Nicki lived for any ocean-adjacent adventure—the more outrageous, the better. "The island is even more gorgeous—you'll see!"

"Great!" Fran echoed, glad the gale-force wind meant she didn't have to carry on a conversation with Nicki. She needed the time to think, to plan. To figure out how she was going to unravel this newest vacation tangle that had wrapped up her and her three best friends.

A vacation! That's how this trip had been described to her originally. She wouldn't have agreed to it otherwise. A few weeks traveling through Europe, ending in Paris and starting with the tiny seaside country of Oûros, nestled between Greece and Turkey. The aquatically challenged Fran hadn't even minded the idea of them all vacationing next to the ocean—as long as *next to* never ever meant getting *in*.

The trip had offered the perfect chance to reconnect with the three women who'd become Fran's rock. Six years ago they'd all helped Fran become the person she was today in more ways than they'd ever know. She'd lost a bit of that person over the past year. Her grad thesis work with traumatized soldiers had shown her exactly how much she could help others, but it had also revealed some cracks in her own hard-won self-concept. She needed to re-establish her base before she could launch herself into her next challenge: life after grad school.

But the relaxing girls' trip through all the tourist meccas of Europe had gotten derailed almost immediately once they'd set foot in the idyllic seaside kingdom of Oûros. Within what had seemed like thirty seconds, Emmaline had fallen in love with the newly minted crown prince of Oûros. Then Lauren had taken out her whack-job ex-boyfriend with the help of a gorgeous captain of the Oûros National Security Force. After that? Nicki had set out on a grand rescue adventure with the royal family's icy cool ambassador. The fact that one of these men was royalty and the other two were straight-outta-Greek-mythology *demigods* was just icing on the crazy cake. Their entire adventure now felt like a wild delusion brought on by too much tsipouro and too little sleep. Except every morning Fran kept waking up to the *same* delusion.

Now, apparently, it was her turn to get roped into the chaos, and she had to play it smart. The royal family wanted her help for a very legitimate reason, and she would give that help. But only on her terms. She couldn't afford to make any mistakes.

"Oh my god, Frani, look! Dolphins!"

Terror seized Fran's heart, and she gripped the side of the boat so hard she thought the rail might break in her hands.

"Wow!" she shouted back, fixing her gaze on a point far beyond where the pair of shark-like mammals leapt out of the sea.

She could not—*would* not—betray her abject fear of freaking dolphins, of all things. Dolphins! Possibly one of the most beloved sea animals on the planet, and they made Fran's legs buckle whenever she so much as thought of the creatures. Her baseless horror of dolphins was so absolutely, unforgivably ridiculous, she'd never breathed a word of it. Today didn't seem like a great time to start.

The engine throttled back abruptly. Fran flinched as a spray of water splashed over the deck of the speedboat.

"Man! We were flying." Nicki beamed at her. "Hey, don't be nervous. I'm telling you, there's nothing serious you have to do here, other than, you know, help."

"I can't truly add value here. I told you that already." Fran tried to keep the sharpness out of her tone, but at least this wasn't a lie. "I'm not anywhere close to being licensed to work with anyone, and from everything you've said, Prince Aristotle—or Ryker, or whoever he thinks he is—needs the care of a medical doctor. He's the king and queen's oldest son! Surely they can afford the best medical care in Europe."

"He has plenty of doctors. And neurologists and shrink people too," Nicki said, her grin not dimming a fraction. "But they're all a hundred years old. The queen thought, you know, maybe having someone his own age who at least had some background in PTSD would be good. Someone who wasn't a doctor. Or about to die."

Fran quirked a glance at her. The idea sounded no less lame than when she'd first heard it. "So she wants me to be his playmate."

"His *companion*," Nicki corrected. "And come on! You'll be great at this. Ari has been through hell this past year, and you've worked with tons of guys like that. With this job, you're not really working. More like, you know, hanging out. How hard can it be?"

Fran grimaced. A hundred distinct faces slid through her mind...haunted faces, worn and weary and forlorn behind their forced smiles. Soldiers with falsely cheerful expressions that seemed to have been carefully taken out of a box and worn like a mask until at last, these men and women could hide again from the real world, returning to the place inside that both soothed and tormented them.

Nevertheless, Fran suspected she could help Aristotle Andris. If she'd learned one thing from her year-long study of traumatized soldiers, it was that sometimes merely sitting with them in comfortable silence, letting them know they weren't alone, was the best gift you could possibly give.

She could do silence, right? Anyone could do silence.

Especially someone with so much to hide.

Fran stared at the private island they were puttering toward and reviewed her story again. She was a grad student: true. She had a year of working with military personnel enduring Post-Traumatic Stress Disorder under her belt, as part of a psychology thesis program for which she'd earned a scholarship: true.

She'd met Lauren, Nicki, and Emmaline during her under-grad years, and they'd all struck up a friendship that had profoundly strengthened over the years: also true.

Then came the rest of her bio. Her name was Francesca Simmons. She'd spent an idyllic childhood in suburbia. She had a cozy middle-class blended family back in Michigan with her father, his wife, and Fran's two step-brothers, basic cable, hot dogs on the deck every summer weekend, and absolutely no run-ins with the law.

False, false, and false again.

"You said Prince Ari had been held prisoner?" she asked finally. She turned back to Nicki who bounced on her toes, her satisfaction at winning obvious.

"Yup!" Nicki glanced at the dock as the boat cruised in. When she spoke again, her words were lower, more hurried. "I'm sure you remember that he'd taken off from the municipal airstrip in Oûros one night last June and crashed his plane in a storm somewhere off the coast of Turkey. Well, he washed ashore, delirious. Then he got caught in some vagrant round-up and put into a work camp. He still has no idea he's the heir to the kingdom of Oûros. He thinks he's some pilot. But according to the doctors, his prognosis is good. There's nothing physically wrong with him. He's just sort of...forgotten who he was."

Fran couldn't help her half-choked laugh. "Sometimes that isn't so bad," she said wryly. "Though maybe not when you're a prince."

"Hey!" Nicki waved furiously at a new target, and Fran pivoted as well, shielding her eyes from the brilliant Aegean sun to take in the rapidly approaching dock, and the two men standing on it. She recognized the Oûrois ambassador Stefan Mihal, of course. He and Nicki had been charged with traveling to find the errant prince.

Fran didn't like Stefan much, but it wasn't because of anything he'd done to her. The man—*demigod*—was simply too smart. He'd run dossiers on all of them when Emmaline had been in the middle of her whirlwind courtship with Prince Kristos, Ari's younger brother. Fran hadn't been able to breathe for a few days until everything on her had checked out. She'd covered every base imaginable to create her new life, and it appeared that hard work was paying off.

She knew more than most, however, that it could all be yanked away in a heartbeat. The faster she got out of Oûros and back into the rhythm of her own anonymous life, the better.

Stefan caught one of the tie ropes at the prow of the boat, while the second man grabbed the edge and stabilized it. With a delighted "thanks!" Nicki accepted the second man's outstretched hand and mounted the step halfway up the side of the speedboat. Then she leaped out of the boat, clearing the short distance to the dock like she'd been born to the sea.

Fran, on the other hand, widened her stance as the boat rocked, then clutched the back of the passenger seat to steady herself, rigidly not focusing on the water surrounding their craft. *Breathe in...breathe out.* She just had to step out of the boat and on to the dock. If she fell into the water *where the dolphins lived,* she was going to drown. She knew she was going to panic and drown; there were no two ways about it. So she couldn't fall into the water. She could only step off the fucking boat and onto the deck, without falling or drowning. There was no other option, so that's what she'd do.

The unfamiliar man turned toward her and she steeled her nerves, unable to look at anything but the dock.

"Easy there, it's just a short step," he said with a thick Mediterranean accent. The boat tipped precariously again and Fran's balance shifted. She flashed a grateful smile in the man's general direction, focusing on the step in front of her as she lunged for his hand.

The moment the man's rough palm closed around her fingers, a zip of awareness rushed through Fran, sharp enough to make her forget her fear for a split second. She glanced up and found herself staring into the face of quite possibly the most gorgeous human she'd ever seen—which was saying something, since Oûros was chock-full of beautiful humans. But this one was tall, broad-shouldered and intense, his dark hair streaked by the sun. He had a deep tan, dark chocolate eyes and high, sculpted cheekbones above a neatly trimmed beard.

His face broke into a broad grin as she stared.

"You good, miss?" The impossibly gorgeous man asked as another wave rocked the boat.

She blinked, recalling herself. "I'm good, I'm just a little—"

Before she could finish, he tugged her up out of the boat... and into his arms.

Two

R yker Stavros couldn't help it if he pulled the American a little more forcefully than he'd intended. There'd been such terror in the woman's eyes, barely covered by her bravado, that he would've wagered serious money she'd never willingly entered a body of water bigger than her bathtub in her entire life.

What he hadn't planned on was the shock of pleasure that'd rippled through him the moment he'd touched her hand. She'd clearly felt it too, and that surge of interest had made it easy for him to shake loose her death grip on the passenger seat and liberate her from the speedboat.

The American was surprisingly compact beneath her bulky life jacket, and for one blessed moment she was a warm and vibrant bundle of energy in his arms. He hated to let her go. But he also hated the sudden flare of wariness that skated over her features, displaying a rushing parade of emotions that whisked past in a blink, leaving a breathtakingly beautiful and serene face behind.

He righted her, then stepped back once he was sure her feet were stable on the deck. "Not so bad, eh?"

"Thank you," she said, with a smile he would swear was genuine, despite the caution flags she'd thrown up. She was flat-out stunning: flashing golden-brown eyes, sun-warmed skin and rich dark hair tucked under a scarf. She could almost pass as a Mediterranean herself until she spoke. Her accent was classic Northeastern American.

Ryker frowned. How did he know that?

"Sorry," she said now, coloring a little under his gaze. "I'm afraid I'm not very good with boats."

"All the better you're on dry land now." He turned to Nicki Clark, the red-haired green-eyed American he'd met only a few days earlier. She stood next to his own countryman, Stefan Mihal. The two of them had rescued him from a Turkish hell-hole. He was still trying to figure out why he'd merited a diplomatic intervention from the royal family of Oûros...but now he had a more urgent question for the athletic, exuberant Nicki. "Why did you force your friend to come all the way out here if the ocean makes her nervous?"

"What are you talking about?" Nicki scoffed. "The ocean doesn't make her nervous." She wrinkled her brow, shooting her friend a startled glance. "Does it?"

"Not at all. I simply don't like to fall into it." The words were smooth and measured, the way Ryker suspected every-thing about this woman was smooth and measured. Straight-ening further, she held out a hand. "Francesca Simmons," she said. "Thank you for your gallant rescue."

"My pleasure." Automatically, as if he'd performed the gesture a million times in his life, Ryker reached for her hand and bowed over it, grazing her knuckles with his lips. Even her knuckles were perfection, soft against his wind-chapped skin, and he found his mouth unexpectedly watering at the thought of kissing her more deeply. *What the hell?*

He straightened abruptly, flinching a bit as he realized the three of them were staring at him. "Did I do something wrong?" They couldn't have picked up on his flash of lust, for gods' sake. He'd barely brushed the American's hand.

"Not at all." Stefan Mihal stepped forward, clapping him on the shoulder. This man felt like someone Ryker knew...*had* known, anyway...but he couldn't place the tall, elegantly built man, with his blond hair and blue-gray eyes. Still, he recognized Stefan as an ally he could trust. That would have to be enough for now.

"Your manners are better than mine, for certain," Stefan said, then turned to Francesca. "Miss Simmons, allow me to introduce Ryker Stavros, our guest here on Asteri Island. Much like you, he's been gracious enough to keep me company while Nicki and I recuperate."

Stefan's phone rang, and he fished for it as Nicki shifted toward him, the two of them moving in uncanny synchronicity for two people who'd apparently only recently met.

Francesca's laughter tugged his attention toward her again, and he took in her wide smile and bright eyes. "Well, I'm glad to see I'll have help keeping Nicki from scaling the walls." She surveyed the tiny marina, her gaze climbing past the thick knot of trees until she registered the buildings clustered higher up on the mountain. "Is that the guest house?"

"One of them," Ryker said dryly. As her startled gaze dropped to his, she grinned, and he found himself smiling with her. "Stefan is a friend of the ruling family of Oûros, it would appear. This is their island. The whole thing. Though you know that already, yes?"

"I do...but standing on the actual island still takes some getting used to." Her gaze shifted back toward the promontory, and he realized she hadn't met his eyes for more than a second, as if he made her nervous. Now she shielded her brow with her palm. "You should see the royal palace," she said. "It has so many rooms, you could get lost in it."

The moment seemed to freeze for Ryker, the way it'd been doing since he'd arrived on the island. He sensed there was something he was missing in her casual words, something important, a breath from his grasp. As it usually did, the flash of pain that accompanied the almost-memory wrenched him all the way to his toes.

This time, however, a soft hand touched his bare forearm, gentle and soothing. He glanced up and saw Francesca regarding him intently, her green eyes soft and considering. "Do you like island living?" she asked, as if nothing had happened.

He glanced quickly at Stefan and Nicki, but they were bent over Stefan's phone and arguing about something in low, urgent tones. Probably proper sailing angles in high wind or some other equally ridiculous measure. He'd never seen two people so certain they were right about so many things—particularly if the other person asserted the opposite.

He shook his head, refocusing on Francesca. "Honestly? I don't know. They've told you my story I assume?"

To his surprise, she frowned. "Nicki hasn't told me much of anything other than she's going through a battery of tests after she overexerted herself."

Her name must have broken through Nicki's competitive haze, because she scowled over at them. "It's not a battery. It's, like, three."

"Let's head to the car." Stefan took advantage of Nicki's distraction to turn her toward the vehicle, and it was only then that she reached for her life jacket.

Belatedly, Francesca did the same, her lips dropping at the corners as she surveyed the jacket with bemusement. "I don't suppose there's a quick-release?"

Ryker laughed. "It's not too hard. Here." He pulled the

catch on the waistband, then freed the top snap as well, unzipping the bulky garment and helping her out of it.

"Oh, hooray. I can breathe again," she said as he tossed the jacket into the speedboat. Nicki's went sailing after it, and Ryker reminded himself to head up the dock with the others instead of staring at Francesca.

It didn't work. Freed from the heavy jacket, Francesca's figure could have been sculpted by an Italian master, sensually curved beneath her lightweight summer clothes. The breeze kicked up, plastering her tunic top to her breasts, and Ryker's mouth went dry.

Fortunately, the American didn't seem to notice. "How much longer will you be here?" she asked Nicki brightly. "You told me on the trip out here that you were all right."

"I am all right," Nicki insisted. Still, her explanation of the complicated round of medical tests Stefan insisted she undergo after her recent fainting spell lasted all the way to the edge of the dock where a limo waited. As he listened, Ryker felt marginally vindicated. He'd also been undergoing a roster of testing since he'd come to the island, the equally onerous work-up ordered by Stefan. Ryker didn't know how much pull the diplomat had with the first family. Apparently, it was a lot.

One thing was certain; they were making damned sure Ryker was no danger to himself...or, he suspected, anyone else. They also weren't telling him anything about his life or his past, although Stefan clearly knew. Ryker supposed it made sense— he should try to remember on his own rather than simply accept what others told him. Still, he couldn't stop the feeling of apprehension that was building with each passing moment. He was missing something here...something important.

"Fran asks a good question, though. How much longer do you think we'll be here?'"

Nicki's question cut across Ryker's thoughts, and he

followed her gaze to Stefan. The man's aristocratic brows arched as he regarded Nicki.

"You have somewhere else you'd rather be?"

"Well duh, yeah. All of us girls have the entire continent of Europe to explore. Sooner or later, you'll have to let us all get back to our vacation."

"We've all been *languishing* without her," Francesca put in wryly. "Sunning by the pool, gorging on three gourmet meals a day while we wait. It's been a terrible hardship."

"See?" Nicki crossed her arms and stared pointedly at Stefan. "How long?"

Stefan set his jaw, and Ryker watched him with interest. The stoic man was clearly concerned about the American beyond simple camaraderie. "Another week, perhaps." He shrugged. "Possibly longer."

"Ugh," Nicki groaned, flopping back in her seat. Ryker swallowed his own grimace. He wanted to resume his life, reunite with his family on the mainland, and start rebuilding his world. As much as he appreciated what the royal family was trying to do for him, he had to get back to work. Stefan had told him he wasn't married. But he had to have had a life, a job. It was time to find it.

They wove their way up the mountainside, and his attention moved to Francesca again. She sat almost motionless in the luxurious limo, her face in profile as she studied the road. Her main focus seemed to be mapping the route to the marina, carefully noting each turn. It was as if she already was as stir crazy as he was, and she'd barely been there a half hour.

He settled back in his seat, his mind spinning. Perhaps he could do something with that. Maybe the serene, careful Francesca Simmons would be his ticket off this rock.

Three

The royal apartments on Asteri Island were every bit as luxurious as those in the palace. There was neither more nor less security here, for all that it was a bit more spread out. Still, Fran couldn't fight down her anxiety as she paced the sumptuous bedroom that had been prepared for her. Nicki had dropped her off with an eye roll and foul words about another heart monitor test, but Fran hadn't missed the way she and Stefan had sparred with each other the entire way up from the marina.

It didn't take a psychology degree to identify that there was a definite energy between the two of them. It also didn't take one to deduce the same between her and Ryker—or Ari, as she really should refer to him, at least to herself. Though he was undeniably more weathered, once she got up close to him, she realized the prince was undoubtedly a match to the dozens of pictures of him scattered throughout the halls of the royal residence. She hadn't made a particular study of them, and she regretted that now. Especially since the queen had some misguided belief that she could help tug Ari back toward his memories.

Fran wasn't an expert on memory loss by any stretch. Sure, it wasn't completely uncommon for victims of traumatic events to lose portions of their past—particularly those memories directly connected with the violence they experienced. But a full-scale amnesiac response following the crash had to be somewhat unusual. Ari had taken the further step to become an entirely different person, too. According to Nicki, he'd adopted the persona of the childhood avatar he'd chosen when playing with his brother Kristos.

What did Ryker Stavros mean to Ari that he clung to that persona in the wake of the crash versus the person he truly was?

Not my problem, Fran reminded herself for the fiftieth time. And it wasn't. She knew it wasn't. Nicki had been clear on that score, too. No one was expecting Fran to provide some kind of psychological evaluation of Ari. They simply wanted her as the token companion. Someone who could tag along with the prince without irritating the bejesus out of him, she suspected, and maybe help him be more willing to take his medicine.

She grimaced. They wanted her to be Mary Poppins.

A brief knock at the door startled her. "Miss Simmons?" called a voice from the hallway.

She hurried to open the door, nodding at the uniformed maid. The woman appeared as sunny and cheerful as every royal staff member back on the mainland. Fran wondered if it was an act.

Stop it. Not everyone fakes their way through life.

The maid beamed at her. "Queen Catherine has arrived and requested your presence in the receiving room, if you're refreshed from your trip?"

Fran lifted her brows. That was quick. Nicki had told her the queen had returned to the capital city for some reason or another, but here she was, already back on the island. "Of course."

She followed the maid down the long, sumptuously decorated hallway, all of it wrapped in marble and hardwoods, with gilt-framed mirrors and lush ferns breaking up the opulence. No pictures, but this villa seemed like an offshore guest cottage, not an official palace residence. She snorted, then coughed to mask the derisive sound. What would it have been like to be Ari, growing up in this sort of household?

Her childhood with her dad hadn't been bad, not really. Not until the end. But it hadn't been anything like this.

The maid stopped before a large door and gestured Fran inside, but Fran hesitated a moment.

"How many of them are in there?" she asked.

The woman dimpled at her with almost conspiratorial understanding. "The lot of them. King Jasen and Queen Catherine, Prince Kristos, Ambassador Mihal and Captain Korba. Also Dr. Lessing, I believe." She brightened. "And Miss Clark. So you're not without friends."

"Never that," Fran said. Then she straightened her shoulders, her script set in her mind, and sailed into the room.

The maid had missed two additional doctors who sat at the edge of the chamber—or at least they looked like doctors—but otherwise, she'd been right on target. Fran registered sweeping views of well-manicured grounds, the wide sea beyond, and an achingly blue sky. Then the royal couple turned toward her as a single unit, and Queen Catherine Andris stepped forward with her hands outstretched.

"Francesca, thank you so much for coming on such short notice." Real gratitude rang in her voice, so earnest that Fran couldn't help but thaw a little. She allowed the queen to clasp her fingers and returned her regard steadily. "It means so much to me to have someone Ari's age here while he's being analyzed by all these strangers."

"Catherine," King Jasen murmured, but the queen dropped

Fran's hands and shifted toward him, the sweep of her glance taking in the older man standing at his side.

"Tell me I'm wrong, Dr. Lessing," she said majestically. "That it's a bad idea to have a companion who can help Ari reintroduce himself to his former life, someone who can't stir up memories because they don't know each other."

"You're not wrong," Dr. Lessing responded with a polite nod. "A young member of his own country might have been better, but I do understand your need to keep Ari's presence here a secret."

"No one can know he's back until he's ready to be back," the queen said severely. "Francesca neatly avoids the issue. She's Nicki's friend. That's enough to explain her presence here. And Nicki and Stefan's testing protocol is generating enough media coverage to keep the public satisfied."

"*Media* coverage?" Nicki demanded. "Are you serious?"

That set off a lively debate, allowing Fran to step back from the knot of people and glance out the window again. Her gaze drifted over the distant waves, and she was surprised to feel an almost visceral tug toward the water—as if the ocean wanted her to step closer. She twisted her lips. *Not a chance, my friend.*

A distant flash caught her eye, and she blinked. Thick, angry storm clouds bunched up on the horizon, heavy and threatening, where before there'd been clear blue skies. Yet another reason to avoid the deep blue sea, she thought. The weather could change in an instant. She swiveled back to the others as Nicki's protests ran out of steam.

"Has Prince Ari's recovery progressed to your satisfaction?" Fran asked, her tone easy. She pointedly did not glance Stefan's way. So far, he didn't seem to pick up on her hyperawareness of him.

Dr. Lessing's expression became sterner. "It's not an exact science, I'm afraid. It could be months."

What? Fran kept her face composed, but Nicki squawked on her behalf.

"Months!" she protested. "No way. Fran can't stay here that long. None of us can." Fran watched as Stefan sent his cool regard Nicki's way, but Nicki didn't waver. "And we definitely can't remain much longer cooped up here on this island, no matter how awesome it is. I swear I've already been over every inch of it and we've barely been here a full week."

Dr. Lessing spread his hands. "Actually, Ari may do better with a gradual reintroduction to his former stomping grounds."

"These *are* his stomping grounds," Queen Catherine retorted. "He's been to this island a hundred times over the years."

"But not recently." Prince Kristos Andris shifted against the table where he was leaning. "The last few times you announced you were coming here, Ari always managed to be fooling around in his airplane or on some diplomatic trip, entertaining foreign visitors, that sort of thing. We haven't been out here for, what—" Kristos glanced at Dimitri Korba, captain of the Oûros National Security Force. "Three years? Four, I think."

"At least," Dimitri said. His voice was a sonorous boom, and Fran smiled despite herself. Lauren had missed the hulking captain since he'd come to the island to watch over his best friend. Of course, Ari didn't realize that the occupants of the island's primary guest house were his own family and closest comrade. "And the island was given over to friends of the state more often than not."

"True, but—"

"Your Highness." Stefan straightened, his hand at his ear. "Ari is approaching the main house."

The queen whirled on Dr. Lessing. "Should we see him?" she asked, her tone so pleading that Fran's heart twisted. "Can we talk to him yet?"

The doctor frowned. "I don't think that would be wise, Your Highness."

Even as he spoke, Fran's resolve to get off the island and out of Oûros was dealt a mortal blow. All these people wanted nothing more than to have their son back, their son, their brother, and their best friend. They weren't thinking about her. They weren't interested in prying into her background and revealing all her stupid secrets and missteps. They were thinking about Ari.

And she could help them with that. She could help him, maybe, walk the path back to his memories—or at least give him someone to talk to as he found his own way.

"I'll intercept him, if that's helpful?" she suggested as the queen turned to her, obvious in her urgency. Fran pointed. "I think there's a door to that garden, right? I could go out that way."

Queen Catherine nodded quickly. "He loved that garden as a little boy," she said. "He hasn't been there yet that we know of."

Stefan's words set them all on edge. "He's at the front drive. We can send a diversion."

"I'll go out now." Fran offered up the same warm smile she'd used to win over drunks and ball-breakers from the time she'd been five years old, her hands lifting in the same conciliatory gesture that had allowed her to back away cleanly from pushers and pimps alike.

The audience in the royal receiving room of Oûros's island idyll was different, sure...but they relaxed all the same.

"It'll be fine," Fran said, hoping desperately she was right.

Four

"It'll be fine," Ryker muttered, surprised he wasn't wringing his hands like an idiot teenager. He knew Francesca was staying at the main house along with some other VIPs, but there was no reason for him to think she'd be randomly strolling through the gardens on her first afternoon. Still, he couldn't stay away.

The door opened at the front of the main house and he instinctively shifted his direction, angling around the long drive toward the western gardens. He'd scoped the whole building out already—its exterior, anyway. He'd also wandered down every path and access road in and out of the compound. The place had impressive security, but the workers seemed to be doing their best to stay out of his way. He appreciated that. Stefan may have thrown a gauntlet of doctors at him, but he'd tried not to make him feel like a prisoner.

Ryker had barely cleared the house when he heard Francesca's voice, high and clear—and talking to someone.

"Yes, I know. That's fine," she said as he quickened his pace, passing the final row of bushes to move into the garden proper. "I can't wait to see you too...right, absolutely. You too."

A pang of jealousy struck Ryker so hard it made him scowl, and he barely blanked his expression in time as he rounded the corner and saw Francesca. She disconnected the call and was pocketing her phone when she saw him.

"Ryker," she said. "I was just about to ask where I might find you. Nicki's last time trial is going over and I'm on my own for a few hours. So I decided I didn't come all this way to sit in my room."

"Then I'm glad I can be of service." He frowned, though, uneasy in the shadow of the big house. Something seemed off about Francesca's manner...or maybe it was the place that seemed off. He tilted his head, focusing on the fountain. Was it that? It seemed oddly familiar.

"I guess I could simply sit out here." Oblivious to his sharpening attention, Francesca walked over to the bubbling fountain, a wide basin with a cluster of twirling sea nymphs in its center surging through a spray of water. "I didn't realize how big this garden was."

"There's another garden closer to the sea, if you'd like to see it," he said. "More fountains, but also flowers, trees—and a view." He nodded at the house. "Not that this isn't an impressive view. I've done a thorough study of the island over the past few days, and there's a reason they chose this site for the main house."

"It sort of looms over us, doesn't it? But these flowers are enough to take my mind off anything but their fragrance." Francesca laughed, and more of Ryker's unease cleared away. Everything was catching him at odd angles on the island—like he should recall more of it, and he simply couldn't. Or he almost thought he did, then it slipped away. Francesca pointed out a particular flower growing in a bright purple cluster. "I think those are my favorites."

"Borage," Ryker said without hesitation, and she repeated

the word as if to commit it to memory. "And you choose well. It usually grows wild but—"

A bolt of pain seared through him, practically splitting his temple, and he staggered forward a step.

"Ryker! Are you okay?"

At once, Fran's cool hands were on him, one at his temple where his own hand gripped his head, the other braced on his arm. This close, he could smell the scent of lavender on her, adding to the sense of peacefulness she seemed to weave around him. His headache abated as quickly as it started. He sagged in relief, then offered her a rueful grimace.

"Sorry. I had the most powerful image of something important attached to those flowers, but..." he shook his head. "It's gone now."

Francesca pulled her hands away, but not in a manner that implied she was shy or embarrassed. More like he no longer had a need for her soothing touch, so she removed it. He didn't agree with that assessment, but since Francesca remained beside him, he wasn't going to argue the point.

They strolled out of the garden, down one of the carefully tended cobblestone paths that seemed to run riot over the entire property. The silence between them felt natural, as if they were old friends. The sudden thought struck him sharply—but with no pain.

"I didn't...know you, did I?" he asked. "Before?"

"Oh! No, you didn't," Francesca said, her smile doing little to ease the spike of disappointment that flared through him. But he knew he shouldn't be surprised. There was no attendant flare of pain when he regarded the American, and he sensed there would be, had they been close. Before the incident with the borage, the only truly searing pain he'd felt was the first time he'd met Stefan. Then again, he suspected the man gave everyone a headache.

"What do you know about me then?" he asked Francesca as they continued walking. "Other than I'm stranded on this island without my memory?"

Her manner was easy and unaffected. "Nicki said you'd been in an accident quite a while ago—a plane crash," she said. "That you lost your memory then, and they'd recently found you. That's all I know."

"Some friends I have, it would seem," Ryker nodded. "To send a diplomat and an American to find me. It makes you wonder how little is going on in the country, eh?"

"I get the feeling that the royal family would do as much for any Oûrois citizen they thought they could help—especially one stranded in a foreign country," Francesca said, scanning the ocean in full view from the stone paver path. Fragrant flowering bushes swayed around them in shockingly bright starbursts of pink and purple, and Ryker once again was certain that they knew each other, somehow. Or that at the very least, he was supposed to know her. "I mean, I'm sure there are plenty of times they can't help, but your situation was one where they could. So they did."

She glanced at him a little shyly, he thought, the stiff Aegean breeze tugging at her soft curls. "I heard the queen offered petitions to the Greek gods to bring you back."

"She would." He said the words with such finality, they both blinked. A faint headache skated through his mind, but no genuine pain. "You see? There are some things I do remember, and that is one of them. The royal family believes in honoring the old traditions. I...I should like to meet the queen, I think. Have I met her before?"

Francesca's eyes widened in curiosity. "I don't know, actually. But you're apparently sure that her making an offering to the gods is no big deal, so that's something."

"Ah! That, yes. In Oûros, we're fiercely proud of our

connection to the gods. Our..." he drifted off, gripped by the sense that he was about to say something he shouldn't. To cover his confusion, he lifted a hand to his brow, as if sighting something far out to sea. "Our history has long been tied to those, ah, legends. They're very important to us."

"Are they truly just legends?" Her question was asked lightly, but Ryker tensed, once again wary.

"What do you mean?"

She waved a hand. "I mean—well, the way some people talk, you'd almost believe the gods were real. Like, that they're legitimately walking around somewhere, wreaking havoc—and that their great, great, great, great half-human grandkids are still rolling around the countryside."

"That...would be something," Ryker allowed, more certain than ever that this was a topic he needed to be careful about. This was something he needed to keep safe. But *why*, exactly? He believed the gods did exist—still existed—and still had some sway in the world. But he also knew without a doubt that he couldn't admit those beliefs. Not out loud, anyway. His role was too important.

What role, though?

Francesca still regarded him almost hopefully, so he gave her an easy smile. "Have you met any of these demigods yet?" he asked teasingly. "Maybe they could help return my memories. There's got to be a goddess or two for that."

"Oh, wow—I hadn't thought of that, but you're probably right!" Francesca's laugh rippled out like sunshine. "You gotta admit, the whole Greek mythology connection makes for great tourism." She sighed, gesturing out to the Aegean. "Not that you need it, though. It's so beautiful here."

"Safer ground, Ryker thought, but he welcomed the diversion. "You're visiting on vacation?"

"The very beginning of one, yes. It just sort of got...

extended, unexpectedly. And then Nicki needed these tests done, so we'll be waiting a little longer." She tilted her head and peered at him. "She told me the story of finding you. I'm so sorry for everything you went through."

"So am I," he said gruffly. "Your friend risked her life for me. I'll never be able to repay her for that."

"You gave her an adventure," Francesca countered with an easy smile. "So I'd say you're even."

He laughed, another boulder of tension loosening and falling away. "Well, I can at least repay her by moving forward. I'd like to find my family. To be walking around healthy and as whole as I can be, knowing that someone out there is waiting and wondering what happened to me...that doesn't sit well. It's not honorable."

Francesca nodded, but this time, she didn't dismiss his concerns. When she glanced his way, her eyes were steady and kind. "I think Stefan wants to be able to give your family as much information as possible regarding your health. You've lost your memory, but that doesn't mean it's gone for good," she said. "If there's a way to nudge it back into place while you're under a doctor's care, then so much the better."

Ryker grimaced. "They've done no end of nudging, but it's led to nothing so far." That wasn't true, of course. But he'd had his guard up every time he'd gone before the panel of doctors who seemed to be watching him every time he turned around. He supposed they were probably watching him now.

Nevertheless, walking with Francesca improved his mood considerably. The wind blowing up over the promontory caught at her hair, pulling it from its pins, but she didn't seem to mind. Her manner was easy as they climbed the stone staircase to the terraced garden, her delight obvious as she took in the mani-cured gardens, the bright flowers vibrant against the brilliant sky, and the crashing Aegean far below. "This is incredible!" she shouted.

"Windy too." He laughed back at her, his heart suddenly lighter than it had felt in over a year. Right then, he was no longer a stranger without a family, a home, or a place in the world. He was simply a man standing on a terrace with a pretty girl, surrounded by flowers, sunshine, and sea.

"Oh!" she gasped as a strong gust of wind battered them. He pointed to a low copse of trees. She nodded, her hands to her hair as she made a run for it. He kept pace with her until they'd reached the trees, then let her take a few steps ahead. Her laughter warmed him in a way that made him realize he'd been cold for far too long.

Get a grip on yourself, he ordered, but the command fell on deaf ears, especially as the American faced him again, her expression as full of light and life as the Aegean itself. There was something different about this woman, something powerful and true. It was as if the gods he was so certain existed had brought her to him—and only to him.

"Francesca," he whispered, stepping toward her.

Warning bells weren't merely ringing in Fran's ears, they were klaxon-blaring for a three-alarm fire. How had Ari gone from disarming candor and grins to the intensity that now set his face into almost a scowl?

And why didn't she know nearly enough about this man, other than his name and position and the barest skiff of information about the trauma he'd endured? She'd known way more about her PTSD study participants, and *they'd* never looked at her like this.

Even as she scrambled for something to say, Ari stopped, his body going rigid for a long moment as he studied her face.

"I've frightened you," he said abruptly. "I'm sorry."

Fran stopped herself from immediately crying out "no!," though that was her first impulse. The truth was, Ari *had* been about to overstep, to push past some invisible line in the sand. She couldn't afford to let that happen.

He wasn't her patient, no. But he was someone's patient. He was traumatized, vulnerable. She needed to respect that. Not give into her own pathetic impulses because an incredibly gorgeous man had stared at her with such an overpowering yearning that her knees went weak.

Oo-kay. Deep breaths.

She wasn't an idiot. She knew that attraction could spark quickly when someone was lost and hurting. That's all this was, and she could handle it. Handle it, not think it was real.

She realized Ari was waiting for her to speak, and she gave him a reassuring smile. "It's okay. I'm feeling a little marooned here and I've been on the island barely one afternoon. It must be much more difficult for you, with so many questions left unanswered." She scanned the protected grove curiously. "How is it the wind is so much calmer here?"

"The trees help. And this grotto has a hidden pathway that trails all the way down to the sea. Or at least...I think it does."

As soon as he spoke the words, Ari winced and took a step back, his hand once more lifting to his temple. Fran could have kicked herself as she moved quickly toward him. She wasn't trying to make him recall facts of his former life, she was asking questions. The same way any tourist would ask questions of a native.

But this native had lost a good portion of his memory. The strands of his past were tangled up so thickly, there was no telling which might lead to an easily recalled piece of information, and which to an area riddled with pain.

Clearly, she'd touched on the latter.

"I'm sorry. I shouldn't ask so many questions. It's a terrible habit of mine, one I've always had..." Her words dropped into a soothing patter as she helped Ari to the bench beneath the trees. The space was warmed by the sun and protected from the worst of the wind, which, as Ari had said, was deflected by a thick stone wall. He grimaced, both hands pressed to his head, but he let her sit him down and peel his hands away from his temples.

His hands shook, she realized. Not violently, but with a tremor that didn't stop even when she clasped them tight.

"Ryker, are you in pain?" She studied his face, which he'd tucked in tight to his chest, his muscled shoulders now shaking as well. "I can—I can go get help."

"No," Ari gritted out. His head came up then, his eyes almost wild until they found hers. His hands shifted. She firmed her grip on them, the fury of their trembling not subsiding. But his gaze was steadier as she met it, and she willed every ounce of strength she had into him as she waited for him to continue.

"No," he said again, more slowly this time. "Please, don't call for help, or ask for a doctor, or tell anyone about this, if you don't mind. It'll stop—soon." His eyelids drooped and his brow knotted as he appeared to focus intently. "It always does."

Fran longed to reach out to Ari's forehead, to wipe away the trickle of sweat that glistened on his brow, but she said nothing —did nothing overt but hold his hands tightly. She regulated her breathing, drawing in air slowly and steadily, pushing it out in a calming cadence. Eventually, the rhythm of Ari's breathing found and matched her own. She saw the tension loosen first in his shoulders, then his brow...then, finally, his hands.

His eyes flickered open. He spoke a word in Oûrois, then seemed to recall himself. "Sorry," he said, blinking at her. "I didn't expect that to go on so long."

"Don't apologize." She continued to hold Ari's hands. They'd finally stopped trembling. They were now loose and relaxed in her grasp, but at least not limp or clammy. They were the hands of a man who worked, she realized suddenly, the finger pads rough and calloused, the palms thick with old scars. Not the hands of a prince, but of a prisoner condemned without trial to a work camp.

Who knew what other scars Ari bore, either on his skin or far beneath it? Scars he'd received without knowing anything more than a fictitious name and a made-up occupation? "The doctors don't know any of this?" she asked.

He shrugged. "Oh, I'm sure they know some of it. When the week began, I was still having the nightmares."

Fran's heart shimmied as Ari sighed wearily and continued. "Those were quite a show, from what I understand. I shouted a lot—angry at those gods you mentioned, I suppose. Angry at myself for not remembering more. I don't remember any of the details of them. I forgot each one the moment I clawed my way back to consciousness."

"You've been through a great deal."

"I suppose I have." But Ari's voice sounded almost mocking. He focused on her with a sudden intensity that put her once more on her guard. "My captors kept me in a cage. Did Nicki tell you that?"

At her mute headshake, he swung his gaze away, staring at the far ocean. "A cage like you'd put a big dog in, except we were men, not dogs. We didn't quite fit. Mine wasn't so bad—I could move, almost stretch out. I did stretch, too, different muscles at different hours every night, like clockwork. Some of the other prisoners..." He shook his head. "They didn't know the value of doing that. And I couldn't tell them. Their language was different enough that I couldn't make myself clear. Or they weren't in any mood to get advice from an outsider."

He slanted her another glance. "There were animals too, I think. Monsters—or they looked like monsters to me. Misshapen beasts like something..." He smiled bitterly. "Like something out of myth and legend. That's when I realized we had to be drugged when we were in the cages."

At her startled expression, he laughed, but the sound was grim. "I know. But I'm telling you, I saw inexplicable creatures on the regular, dragged past our cages in the dark, when most of the other men were asleep. Heard them too, sometimes." He shook his head. "They had to be pumping us full of hallucinogens. There's no other way to explain it."

Fran bit her lip. Nicki hadn't mentioned anything about caged animals—but then again, maybe she'd been sworn to secrecy. And maybe there hadn't been anything in Ari's prison but other men. Drugs could do terrible things to the mind.

She squeezed his hands, afraid to speak and even more scared to let go. Ari didn't seem to notice her hesitation. His gaze dropped, and he stared at their clasped fingers. "All that time in the cage, and I couldn't remember what I'd done to get there. I figured I must've done something, though. No one imprisons a man for a whole year for no reason, right? I don't care where you are."

He seemed to be waiting for her to say something. Fran chose her words with care. "It sounds like you weren't imprisoned by actual law enforcement," she said. "They probably didn't need a reason."

"But they needed an opportunity." Ari met her gaze again, and his eyes were clear. Lucid. "I'm not saying what they did was right, for me or those other men. But we had to do something to put ourselves in harm's way. We had to do something to catch their attention. If I can figure out what that was, if I understood a little more of what had led to my capture...I think it would help."

Fran watched him critically. He was talking of real memories here, without question. His brow was once more furrowed, his expression intent. And yet, there was no indication that he was in pain. He wasn't flinching away from her, and his words remained steady, untroubled. How could he probe these recent memories so easily, yet the most innocuous mention—a flower, a buried memory of the details of a royal estate—literally drove him to his knees? That made no sense to her, but it had to be significant.

"How far back do you remember?" she asked.

He blinked, considering the question. "The morning after my crash. That happened at night, I'm pretty sure," he said, and his voice held a slight tremor, but she didn't look away. His hands had started trembling again, too. "It was morning when I washed ashore, and I was—clinging to something. That's the kind of memory I have. Broken up." He shrugged again. "I wasn't broken up, though. I remember being proud of that. That I'd managed to come out of the water more or less in one piece. Nothing too badly damaged."

He shivered, though it wasn't cool. The afternoon sun was warm on Fran's back. His gaze fixed on a new point over her shoulder, and didn't waver. "I traded some junk from the airplane for a boat—a terrible boat but I didn't care. I had to get to the mainland. I had to hide."

Hide? A shiver of apprehension slid through Fran. She was out of her depth. Had someone been hunting for Ari? Threatening him from the start? No one had said anything about that. But there was no time to consult the official history of Aristotle Andris before the crash. All she had to work with was Ryker Stavros here and now.

And he needed her.

Six

Ryker knew he should shut the hell up, that he should pull his hands away from Francesca, but neither of those options appealed right now. Sweat dripped cold down his neck, but he didn't care. He didn't want to stop, didn't want to let go when he was so—close, he thought. To a breakthrough. A relevant memory. Something.

"Once I got into the open water, I spent as much time rowing as I did bailing. Couldn't trust the motor. I was taking on water too fast to move at any speed." He turned away from Francesca's beautiful face but didn't see the softly swaying trees behind her. Instead, he saw the long rocky shoreline that had marked the mainland. There'd been heat, he remembered now. So much heat.

"I landed, made it to the outskirts of a city. The local squatters helped—or tried to. Tried to keep me quiet, anyway. Out of the way. But they found me."

"Who?" Francesca prompted, and he couldn't stop the smile that creased his lips. The word was steady and quiet, but cautious too. Like everything about her was cautious. When he'd said her name so roughly, his intent to kiss her obviously clear, wariness had been Francesca's primary response. Not fear. Not revulsion. But caution. As if she had to proceed carefully, bit by well-considered bit.

He didn't mind answering her, though. "I don't know who. Someone new, different. That I understood. Someone I'd evidently managed to piss off. And hell, maybe I had committed a crime. It seemed like I could have, the way I was so—I don't know. Guilty, really. I felt guilty. Over what I don't know."

He shook his head, knowing how all this must sound. "Believe me, I already laid all this on Stefan. Not the timetable —that was a new memory. That I'd landed at night and all that. But the guilt..." He chuckled now, recalling that memory clearly when everything else was in such a fog. "I asked him if I'd committed some sort of crime. He stared at me like the idea was insane. So I asked him if I was a priest."

Francesca's eyes flashed wide, a snorting laugh sneaking out despite her clear attempt to remain dispassionate. "A priest?"

"I didn't know! I was looking for answers. The way Stefan reacted made me laugh. But he said no, in the end. They'd checked. There were no crimes committed the day I'd disappeared. No warrants for my arrest. No one asking for my head on a platter. No missing priests." He grimaced. "And if anyone would know about my past, it'd be Stefan, let me tell you."

"He seems thorough."

Francesca's voice sounded a little wan, but Ryker knew she understood—anyone could see Stefan Mihal would stop at nothing to get answers. "Yeah, thorough would be how I'd describe him, too." And a few other words that Francesca didn't really need to know, he thought. He'd rather avoid the aristocratic diplomat going forward.

And he could avoid the man a lot more easily if he wasn't tripping over him two hundred times a day.

"Anyhow, I'm apparently clean. I have no criminal history,

and I *don't* seem to have upset the wrong men at the wrong time." Ryker breathed a long sigh, finally working up the strength until he could finally let go of Francesca's hands. He felt their loss like a physical ache and focused on clenching his own into fists. "Of course, that hasn't gotten me any closer to getting free of this place. Maybe now that you're here, things will move more quickly."

Though he hadn't intended the words as some kind of negative, Francesca drew herself up sharply. "How do you mean?"

Ryker could have kicked himself. The layer of frost edging Francesca's tone was gossamer thin—but it was definitely there.

"I mean, it's been silent as a tomb here for the past week. Other than Stefan and Nicki, nothing but me, the docs and the VIPs in the big house, who must be here for political asylum or something because they are seriously hiding out. I haven't caught a single glimpse of them. Now that you're here, however, and it seems like your friend Nicki is about to climb out of her own skin, it feels like...I don't know. Like life can start up again."

To his relief, though he hadn't realized he'd been nervous, Francesca winked at him. "I'm glad you have such belief in my abilities to move the indomitable mountain of Stefan Mihal," she said wryly. "I honestly think Nicki suspected he'd say no to having me drop in, so she zoomed over to the mainland before Stefan guessed what she was up to. Now that I'm here, he's not sure what to do with me, either."

"You don't believe she truly needed you for moral support?"

Once again, Francesca appeared cautious. "I'm not saying she didn't," she hedged. "And of course I was happy to come when she asked, regardless of what she needed."

"You two are that close?"

She shrugged, but her manner changed subtly again, becoming more confident. "It's more a point of knowing we can rely on each other. Nicki is a big believer in the mental side of recovery from an injury, and I'm interested in that too."

Her last words tugged at him, and he frowned. "The mental side," he repeated. "You're a doctor? A trainer?"

Francesca's easy laugh should have soothed him, but he was getting the sense that such reassurance came easily to her, a tool she used to give comfort and relief. Not that it wasn't authentic, but there was something intentional about her every response that made him itch to know the woman below the surface.

First, however, he had to understand the woman on the surface.

"I'm a student, I think is the most accurate way to put it," she said. "I'm training in psychology, but I've worked with athletes many times throughout my coursework. Soldiers too."

A psychology student, he thought. That explained a lot of her careful manner. "Soldiers?" he prompted.

"A bit," she nodded. "I was part of a several-month study to help injured service men and women recover from Post Traumatic Stress Disorder. As you can imagine, there's no shortage of candidates for that."

He stared. "You didn't go to a war zone, surely."

"No, one of the allied bases in Europe. There was a hospital there that received patients from multiple places." She was being deliberately vague, but at least this he understood. He had served in—

The shock of pain was almost reassuring this time, even though it gripped him in a crushing vise.

Once again, Francesca was there, her hands gripping his, her murmured words soothing as he bent toward her. He convulsed, and agony raced through his brain. Then everything went black for a short while, and there was nothing but Francesca's voice, steady and even, telling him that everything would be okay, that the sun was bright and warm, that the borage had never bloomed more brightly, that the sea seemed to be calling them, though they were far up on the mountain. Silly words, nonsensical words, yet they formed a pathway that held comfort for him. A pathway leading him home.

When Ryker came to, he was sagging against Francesca on the bench, his heavy body almost dwarfing hers. He struggled back to a seated position. She let him get his bearings, shifting slightly so he could stretch out his legs and tip his head to the full sun.

But she didn't move away from him, he thought, as his thoughts slowly re-ordered themselves, his pain fading back. She didn't move away.

And perhaps more importantly...she didn't let go.

Seven

Fran climbed back up the stairs to the main villa much later, having finally convinced Ari that she was capable of returning the fifty yards across the courtyard by herself, especially given the patrolling guard.

He'd come out of his episode exhausted but stable, and once again had begged her not to tell the doctors anything. But how could she not? He clearly was enduring tremendous pain every time the past struggled to make itself known. And the fact that he could remember everything up to bits of the trauma of his accident—yet nothing before—seemed significant. She'd need to talk with the doctors to fully understand his condition.

Then again, she didn't want to probe too deeply. It wasn't her job to get entangled with Ari, merely to make sure he had company until wiser minds determined his next course of action.

Which argued for—

"Francesca."

Fran stopped short, startled as Queen Catherine stepped out of one of the sumptuous sitting rooms of the guest villa. The queen beamed at her, setting her instantly on her guard.

"Your Highness," Fran said carefully.

Catherine immediately waved off the honorific. "I beg you, dispense with that. You missed dinner. You should eat." She practically tugged Fran into the room with her, and a quick glance around the space confirmed no one else was there. "The others wanted to go fetch you, but it would have seemed odd, and there's enough oddness on this island already. Ari might pick up on it, and we can't allow anything to damage his recovery potential."

"What is his recovery potential, exactly?" Fran asked as she seated herself on the couch. A collection of small, stuffed pita-style sandwiches on a gleaming tray sat in front of her, and she realized she was hungry. She hadn't noticed when she'd been walking with Ari, the two of them close enough to embrace... although they hadn't. He'd let her hands fall away as soon as they'd left the terraced garden. He hadn't stopped touching her at every reasonable opportunity, though—her shoulder, her waist, her arm. They were bonding, she suspected, but not in the way of patient and doctor.

In a far more dangerous way.

"We don't know, which is more frustrating than I can possibly express," the queen said, her hands shaking slightly as she poured water from a large carafe into a tumbler on the coffee table. "According to the doctors, Ari's brain is healthy. His body, though clearly recovering from the privation of his long stay in the work camp, is healthy. They predict he'll have joint pain when he's older, but who's to say anything about that? I have joint pain."

Fran smiled, but she caught the queen's underlying nervousness. "You don't believe what they're saying?" she hazarded.

"Oh, it's not that." Catherine sat back in the large wing-backed chair, holding her glass of water with both hands. "I think they're exactly right. I don't think there's anything wrong with Ari's body or his brain. But his mind—well. You make a study of the mind. You know how complicated it can be."

"I do," Fran nodded, though suddenly all her textbooks, journal articles, and reports seemed woefully inadequate in the face of the queen's pain. It was one thing to consider mental challenges in the abstract—or with strangers. But this woman was Ari's mother. His recovery was intensely personal to her, and she needed answers, not theories. Answers that Fran couldn't give.

Catherine regarded her now over her drink. "What did he tell you?" she asked. "You two talked, right? He used to love to talk. It was one of his best skills in managing all the drama with the royal families and foreign delegates." She swallowed, then leaned forward to trade her glass for a linen cloth. As she sat back in her chair, she lifted the cloth to her cheeks, whisking away the tears that had appeared there.

Fran watched her, her heart squeezing. She'd become a good reader of people over the years, and there was nothing in the queen's manner but authentic sadness. Hope and loss and fear all entwined together, a constant chokehold on emotions that gave way with each scrap of positive news, only to clamp down anew with each setback.

She made a decision. She wasn't a doctor or an assigned caregiver. She was a friend giving aid where she could. The queen wasn't a doctor either. So what she did with the information was her own decision.

"Ari is trying to remember things," she said. The queen went very still. "Not in front of the doctors though. In fact, he specifically asked me not to tell the doctors of his efforts."

"Why?"

The question was sharp but reserved, and Fran nodded. She could trust the queen not to endanger her son, but also not to put him through unnecessary pain.

"He's resisting it—remembering," she said. "His hands shake, he sweats, and he has terrible, blinding headaches. A searing pain that shoots through his head, is how he describes it. Like a flash migraine."

"He's never had headaches before, not like that." Catherine sat forward. "What does he recall that brings them on? Anything? Was he in some distress?"

"It's anything before the crash, it seems. If he struggles to remember something during or after the crash, he's calm. Frustrated, because those pictures aren't always clear either—but calm. However, even happy memories from his past bring on the negative reaction." She demonstrated, putting her hands up to either side of her face and screwing up her expression with a wince. When she glanced up again, the queen was staring at her.

"That poor boy," she murmured, and despite herself, Fran smiled. Ari was in his late twenties, a grown man. But she'd never had children. She supposed that for a mother, children never grew up, not really. They were always a source of worry.

For some mothers anyway.

"Why didn't he want you to tell the doctors this?" Catherine asked, recalling her.

"I don't think he wanted to be treated like a lab experiment," Fran said, which made the queen snort. "But there's something more to it, too. I think he's afraid of something—something he saw. Something he believes is dangerous—if not to him, then to his family."

She nodded as the queen's brows lifted. "Don't think he's not doing everything he can to make his way back to you," Fran continued. "Family and his obligation to family is probably his driving force. He's convinced they're on the mainland, and he's getting anxious to go back there. To find them." She waved her hand in front of her face. "But he's also nervous that whatever is keeping him from remembering is important. So he wants to continue trying to figure it out—but not in a way that might keep him stuck here. So that's why he doesn't want the doctors to know."

"Typical Ari," the queen said, but she'd taken hold of her emotions once more, and stared across the room—not at Fran, but at some far, fixed point, echoing what Ari had done only a few hours before.

Like Ari, she made decisions quickly, too. "Let's not tell the doctors this. You're under no obligation to do so, of course, and neither am I. If the episodes increase in frequency, or his reactions worsen, tell me. But for now, we can honor his wishes to work through this on his own." Her lips twisted. "He would have preferred that, anyway. He was always fiddling around in that infernal airplane of his, tweaking the electronics, testing new gear. But—" Her fingers tightened on the linen cloth in her lap. "I never thought that he would do anything truly foolish. Anything that might put himself in danger. He had so much responsibility—too much, perhaps. It simply never occurred to me that he might be unable to meet those obligations week in, week out."

She sighed a soft, broken sob. Fran knew the queen wasn't really talking to her. She was talking to the ragged pieces of her own heart, working through her pain as best she could.

"He fully plans to meet those obligations again," Fran said gently.

The queen blinked at her, her eyes bright with unshed tears. Then sorrow morphed into irritation. "I don't care about that—"

"Oh, I know. I know." Fran lifted her hands in a soothing gesture, never stirring from the couch. "But Ari does. It's a motivator for him. He may not know what had been required of him before, may think he simply needed to get onto the next job in his soldier-of-fortune list of things to do." The queen's glower crumbled a little. "That doesn't change the fact that he wants to get back to it. He's champing at the bit."

"Now that truly is the Ari I remember," Catherine said, more color flooding back into her face. Color, and a hint of relief, too. "Has he said anything about taking a boat? Leaving?"

"A boat? No." Fran's focus sharpened. "That would be bad, I think. He'd be recognized in the capital city."

"Yes and no." The queen tapped a long finger to her lips, regarding Fran shrewdly. "If he was traveling with us, then yes, of course. He'd be noticed immediately. But his hair is far blonder than it was when he left, and his skin is darker, almost swarthy, after a year of working in the sun. He trimmed his beard when he first arrived, but it's already growing thick again. If the two of you went into the city—it could be the break-through he needs. And, should something go awry, the entire Oûros National Security Force would be there as well as the palace guards, all the doctors and our entire extended family."

"The two of us—into the city?" Fran lifted her brows at her. "Your Highness, you barely know me."

"Nonsense," Catherine flapped her hand. "You and your friends were all carefully vetted by Stefan ages ago." She beamed at Fran as she warmed to the idea forming in her mind. "I know everything about you I need to, dear, don't you worry about that."

It was hours before Fran could settle down enough to sleep, hours she spent in front of the wide windows of her bedroom, staring out at the Aegean. The sunset had been glorious over the water, of course—undoubtedly fulfilling some long-ago royal command. Now the ocean was burnished by moonlight, with pinpoint stars puncturing the indigo darkness.

She stared at that ocean until she couldn't keep her eyes open any longer, knowing that the nightmares would come this close to the water. Nightmares always threatened when she slept this close to any body of water larger than a swimming pool—and she'd never been so surrounded by the wide open sea as here.

She pulled a pillow close, praying for an easy night.

She didn't get one.

The dream came stealthily, still managing to catch her by surprise despite her nervous anticipation. But it started quietly, simply. She was at a party in an enormous room, all bright lights and chandeliers. There was no water anywhere. It was a party, and it was fine.

She moved through the chattering and laughing crowd, searching for familiar faces and finding none. Everyone looked dressed for a wedding in the tropics. The women wore fancy dresses of filmy, flowy fabrics, jewels glittering at their ears, necks, and wrists. The men wore cool, lightweight suits. As delighted as they seemed to be with each other, they didn't notice her. She was happy to be ignored. Music played over the throng, or there seemed to be music, but it was nothing she recognized, and the ballroom where everyone milled about seemed to go on forever. There had to be walls, windows, or doors somewhere, but she couldn't see them—there were too many people.

Somebody jostled her on one side, and another woman's arm grazed hers, so Fran pulled her lightweight shawl closer around her body, glancing down to note her shimmery tight dress. Was it her nerves, or did that dress seem to shrink tighter against her body, cutting off her breath? She wanted to get away, but it was a distant feeling, a jittery one—not a sense of real danger, more an inkling of concern.

The crowd ebbed and flowed around her, and when a space opened, she eagerly stepped into it, only to realize that she was now on the front lines of a corridor of people who had cleared to allow some sort of dignitaries to walk through. She leaned past the row of people, staring at the retreating figures. Two men stalked up toward the head of the room, large and imposing even from the back. They also wore suits, but they were darker, heavier. The man on the right had thick, flowing salt and pepper hair, and his suit was a stormy gray. The other man had shorter ebony hair, and he wore midnight blue. But that's all the time she had to focus on them before another man hurried by her. She blinked and peered at him. He was no over-large, muscle-bound male, but a thin, ascetic looking old man, with thinning white hair, an aristocratic nose curved like a hawk's beak, and hollow cheeks. He wore a well-cut black tuxedo that looked as old as he was. He stared around as if looking for someone, and his eyes lit on her.

She'd never seen him before, but he clearly recognized her. He smiled wide and knowingly. "*Monster*," he whispered, then he turned back and Fran could see he was not alone. Another male stood just behind him, and he seemed wrong to her eyes. This one was built as big as the men who'd passed ahead, and he wore an iron-gray jacket and pants, a deep midnight shirt, and a golden tie. His skin was as pale as the old man's, his hair thick and jet black and...moving?

Fran gave a little gasp as she stared at the writhing hair, whipping around his head like tiny snakes. She stepped back into the crowd as the man's eyes found hers. They were large, black and glistening, as reptilian as his hair, and no sooner did she think that, he smirked at her, hissing. "*Mine*," he taunted.

What? No! Even as Fran jerked back deeper into the crowd, the snake man tilted his chin up and laughed, and everyone around her laughed too. It was a horrible cackling sound, sly and dark, that spread across the crowd of partygoers like a poisoned tide.

She turned to push her way through them, to escape, and panic swamped her, choking her scream in her throat.

Everyone had changed. There were no more humans in the room, only *creatures*, jittering, stamping animals on two legs and four, with spikes and scales and large gaping mouths. Some had wings, some had the heads of humans on the bodies of birds, and some were lizards with thrashing tails and grasping talons. It was a herd, she realized. A herd of monsters shoved into this ballroom and she was trapped. She was one of them! She was—

"No!" she gasped. Shoving and pushing, she ran through the crowd. Her clothes were ripped at by unseen hands, her hair pulled. She swung and kicked out, sweeping the smaller creatures out of her way, evading the bigger ones. She used every trick she knew to escape, to flee. She'd been escaping her whole life. She knew how to do this.

At one point, she looked up, toward the front of the room where the two large normal-looking men had disappeared at the head of the open pathway. Were they up there, on some dais, watching her flee?

"Help me!" she pleaded, her voice hysterical, and another voice rang out, older, heavier.

"Mine," it boomed.

"No!" Fran plunged back into the crowd. There was an opening, she saw finally, a wall! She angled toward it, picking up speed, rushing—rushing—then skidding to a stop as she realized the floor ended and an open pit began. She gaped. A twenty-foot wide murky moat now stretched out between the edge of the floor and the distant wall. It churned and boiled, frothing, and something floated on the surface of it, iridescent and flat. Fish? But no. It was too big to be a fish, too long, too wrong. Not moving. Dead.

She couldn't go any further, and she still needed to escape. But as she turned back to fight her way along the edge of the moat, the crowd around her pressed close, pushing and poking, shoving and twisting her up in her own shawl, pressing her tight. She couldn't breathe, she couldn't move, and a terrifying almost human-like creature with blue skin and writhing hair and snakes that hung from his arms reached for her, grasping at her.

She backed up, terrified now, and felt herself tipping back, back...

Back.

She crashed into the water. This horror was more familiar—the churning, twisting, horrifying plunge into the deep. She was in the lake again. She was dying. She couldn't swim! Her legs were like concrete, her arms thrashed and flailed, and she couldn't, she *couldn't—!*

Fran burst awake.

Her sheets were tumbled and twisted around her, her pillows flung across the room.

And outside her window, stretching far into the distance, the mighty Aegean tumbled and rolled.

Eight

The morning of a new day was now several hours old, and Francesca hadn't yet made an official appearance. She was close by, though, so that was progress.

Ryker watched from the rooftop of the guest villa he'd been given, using the stargazing telescope affixed to the decking to focus in on the trio well up the cliff-side walk. Francesca was there, appearing slightly frazzled as she waved her hands, clearly in some argument with Stefan and Nicki. From the mildly amused expression on Stefan's face, she wasn't telling him anything of great import.

She definitely wasn't making any gesture that would indicate she was telling them that Ryker had spent most of the previous afternoon hyperventilating in her arms.

That lunacy needs to stop, he thought grimly, swinging the scope around to the second location of interest for him: the marina. As usual, there were only a few vessels docked—two large speedboats, a mini-yacht, and a sailboat. In the time he'd spent on the island, he'd seen only one man working on that sailboat, and he was there again now.

And damned if Ryker didn't think he knew him, somehow.

His reaction to the sailor was similar to the one he'd had with Stefan. There was an immediate headache and pain, followed by a curious surge of panic. But it was nowhere near the intense agony he experienced when he tried to focus on far more innocuous memories, like flowers or...well, his family.

He focused again on the man cleaning the sailboat for what Ryker thought was easily the fifteenth time. He was burly, heavily muscled, but he worked with a focused efficiency that made Ryker think of the military. Had he met the man there? He didn't think he was a direct relative. They didn't look enough alike.

It would make sense that Stefan had called in one of Ryker's friends, though Ryker couldn't imagine why he hadn't brought them face to face. This morning's round of doctor visits had gone exactly according to his plan. He'd been affable, upbeat, and had responded to all the doctors' questions with his full attention, neatly steering them away from questions about what he recalled of his family.

Any questions about the accident were easy enough to handle. He simply focused on what had occurred after he was in the water once he'd ejected from the plane. That was also a hazy murk, but there were no attendant headaches with such thoughts. It was only when he tried to remember what happened immediately prior to the accident or malfunction or mistake—whatever he'd done to lose control of his plane—that his mind went sideways on him.

"What are you looking at? Is that a telescope?"

Francesca's bright, sunny call startled him, and he took his eye off the scope to peer over the roof railing. Sure enough, she was standing in front of his small guest villa in a light-colored tank top and short pants, her hands forming a sun visor as she gazed upward.

"The marina," he said, keeping his tone friendly as he

glanced up the road. Stefan and Nicki had disappeared over the ridge. He wondered if they'd realized he'd been spying on them. "Want to take a walk?"

"Of course! Nicki and Stefan apparently are going to test her rock climbing abilities on sheer walls over open water, and that's not something I need to see." Francesca frowned, examining the side of the villa. "Actually, I wonder if there are bikes here..."

She was still rooting around in the small shed by the house when Ryker exited the villa. One bike already leaned against the stucco wall. He regarded it dubiously. "That looks older than I am," he said, and she laughed from inside the shed.

A moment later she emerged, pushing a second decrepit bike. "I get the feeling visitors to this island aren't big on cycling."

"Too hilly." He peered into the shed and his brows lifted. "There's a motorbike, though. That's probably a better option for the return trip, anyway."

He strode past her as she stepped out of his way, then she backed up several steps when he pushed out the bike a minute later. It was a newer bike but meant for sturdiness, not speed, with a long, heavily padded seat. "You ever ride?"

Francesca nodded, but there was no denying the immediate wariness in her expression. She didn't glance his way, but focused on the bike. "Long time ago, yeah. Not usually on the back though. I may not be a great passenger."

Her words struck him a little oddly, but Ryker didn't have time to puzzle out why. He didn't know how long the man on the sailboat would be there, and if he was someone who remembered him from his old life...

"You up for a ride, then?"

"Sure," Francesca said, easily enough. Had he imagined her reluctance before? He didn't think so, but now she appeared content as she pushed the old bicycle back into the shed. She leaned it against the wall, then moved out of Ryker's way as he pushed the second one in. For a moment, they stood in the shadows of the small shed, the two of them too big for the space. Before he could capitalize on the opportunity, however, Francesca ducked around him and stepped into the sunshine, strolling away with deceptive casualness.

Had he made her nervous by standing too close to her? Yesterday she'd seemed completely at ease with him, but today she seemed nervous, distracted. Then again, yesterday she'd been cast in caretaker mode because of his memory flares. He wasn't in pain today, and he didn't need her help.

Not yet anyway.

Silently, Ryker shut the shed doors, then returned to the bike. Though he needed Francesca for what he planned next, he didn't like the idea of her thinking that she was some babysitter. Because that's certainly not how he saw her. He'd much rather imagine her viewing him like a man, not a charity case.

One thing at a time, though.

"Wonder when this thing was ridden last," he said, leaning the bike away from him. He checked the tank. "Plenty of gas."

"Kick start, so easy enough to find out." Francesca considered him, her expression assessing. "I assume you can ride?"

He considered that. "Feels like it," he said. Then he shot her a grin. "Wanna see?"

"I'm serious." She laughed. "No headaches as you imagine the process to start the bike or shift gears? No anxiety?"

"Nope." Ryker swung his leg over the bike smoothly, then braced the bike with his right foot and leg while his left foot found the kick starter with an unerring sense that it was the right move for the bike. Almost like he'd ridden it before, though nothing else on the island felt that predictable.

Sure enough, the motorbike roared to life, and he scooted forward slightly on the seat. "Can I give you a lift?"

"You sure you have your license?" Francesca teased, but re-opened the storage shed and a moment later returned with two helmets. She handed one to Ryker, ignoring his rolled eyes, then donned hers. She arced a leg over the seat, settling in behind him. "It sounds a little rough."

"God only knows how long it's been since it's been ridden," he nodded, twisting to scan the back of the bike and the smoky exhaust. Everything looked more or less right and sounded more or less right, though. So he supposed he could trust it. And he didn't want to wait another minute up on the ridge, when the man with the boat could finish his chore and leave. "Hang on tight," he ordered.

Francesca did without complaint. She slid her long, slender arms around his waist, and locked hand and arm together. "Warn me when you—hey!"

Ryker gunned the motorbike, and Francesca's laughter matched his as the thing took off in fits and starts, smoke blowing percussively out of the tailpipe for a few yards until the machine evened out. Then he was rolling down the street, gradually picking up speed until Francesca's hold around his waist tightened in earnest.

"Roads are easy," he called over his shoulder. "Not too steep."

"Focus!" she shouted back. He grinned, then opened up the throttle a little more. This high on the ridge, the wind was strong enough to blow the sun off their skin, and he roared down the narrow access road, past the primary guest villa.

If his doctors were watching him from inside, well...let 'em look, Ryker thought. He wasn't doing anything wrong. He was simply a man taking a spin on a motorcycle with a pretty girl and no particular place to go.

If he played his cards right, they wouldn't know he was gone until he'd reached the mainland.

# Nine

Fran allowed herself to relax a fraction as Ari proved that, amnesia or no, he could manage a motorbike that was little more than a souped-up scooter. The wind in her hair was doing a good job of clearing away the last of the exhaustion she felt from her rocky night's sleep. As always, she hadn't remembered anything from the nightmare, but based on the destruction of her bed, it'd been a doozy. There'd been water, she was sure. There'd been drowning. There always was.

But now she was outside, in the sunshine, zipping down an asphalt road in the middle of an island paradise. This was better. This was good.

The baby motorbike wasn't anything like the muscle bikes Fran had grown up with at her father's bar, but the sound of its revving engine still took her back to those days. She focused hard on the rocky landscape and open sky, so different from the concrete, grease and corrugated metal that had surrounded her when she'd last heard motorcycles roaring to life.

She'd left that life behind a long time ago, as well as a half-dozen other lives in quick succession. Each new reinvention of herself had served its purpose, getting her farther away from her past and helping her convince others she could do more, be more. By the time she'd entered college as an independent student on a full-ride scholarship, she'd done everything necessary to become Francesca Simmons.

She wasn't about to screw that up now.

The queen might trust her to babysit Ari as he struggled to find himself again—literally—but the return of his memories would happen sooner or later. Probably sooner, if her sense of Ari's progress was right.

After she'd remade her bed and restacked all the pillows, she'd curled up under a blanket on the couch and spent the rest of the night and part of the morning reading the documents the doctors had provided to the royal family. Ari was healthy, his mental and physical responses all in line. He didn't yet remember who he was because he didn't want to remember. That, coupled with his strong feelings toward protecting his family, indicated to Fran that he had a specific memory he was afraid of remembering. A memory he firmly believed would threaten those he loved most once it was revealed. He'd keep chipping away, though. He was too stubborn not to keep trying, from all accounts.

She straightened as they cruised around the last corner of the long road, and the rocky tree-lined hills gave way to the marina, with its white-washed buildings and cheerful boats bobbing on the now-gentle waters of the Aegean. The prettiest craft was a sailboat with a tall mast, and with a thud of panic Fran recognized Dimitri Korba, captain of the ONSF, half-hanging off the boat, scrubbing away.

Ari stopped the bike, and Fran leaned forward quickly. "The road keeps going around the bend." She pointed. "Why not see where it leads?"

"Maybe in a few minutes," Ari said. He moved to get off the

bike, leaving Fran no choice but to hop off first. He dropped the kickstand and headed toward Dimitri.

Fran's first instinct was to try to haul Ari out of harm's way, but she instantly rejected that idea. She didn't want to seem like she had an agenda and besides: Dimitri Korba was a decorated, battle-hardened military officer. He should be able to think on his feet.

Even coming face to face with the best friend he'd thought was dead.

"Hey!" Ari called, or at least that's what it sounded like, though the inflection was slightly different and she got the feeling it was an Oûrois word. It did the trick, though. Dimitri immediately glanced up from where he was leaning precariously over the side of the boat and waved. Not an overly friendly wave, either—more an acknowledgment.

He called something back and hauled himself to a standing position, and Fran noticed he stepped out of view for a moment. When he looked down again as they neared, his expression was carefully neutral. "Good morning," he said—in English, for her benefit. She and the gruff Oûrois captain hadn't had many occasions to talk, but they were on friendly enough terms.

Ari wasn't having any of it, however. He launched into a quick stream of Oûrois that made Dimitri blink, then lift his hand to his chin, as if to consider a proposition. He shook his head, and Ari redoubled his efforts, gesturing broadly.

Dimitri lifted his own hands as if to ward off the verbal barrage, laughing now. He swung his gaze to hers, but despite the mirth in his voice, his gaze was full of warning. "You put him up to this? You're American, yes?" he asked.

Fran didn't hide her shock. "Put him up to what?"

"Return trip to the mainland—for free, he says, at least for now. And I know, I know. You'll pay me when you find your family." He waved off Ari's irritated scowl. "Seems to me you'd be missing out, leaving such a pretty girl behind."

"I'd go with him," Fran said immediately, though her stomach knotted at the idea of getting back on the ocean. She didn't miss Ari's quick, triumphant smile—and the queen's orders were loud in her ears. If Ari was determined to get to the mainland, he'd find a way. Fran would go with him simply to keep tabs on him. She could alert the royal family to his whereabouts soon enough. "I have money, too—enough for transport, I think. So you'd get paid for your time, if you can spare it."

"You've been working on the boat for three days now," Ari put in, speaking English. "Surely you want to take her for a run."

"Surely." Dimitri glanced away quickly, staring up at the mast as his throat worked. Something about this exchange smacked of a familiarity that was probably not lost on the captain, even if Ari couldn't see it. Dimitri focused again on Fran. "You can leave now? Or you need to go back?"

"Now," Ari answered for her. He flashed a winning grin at Fran. "You have money, yes? You Americans always carry every-thing with you."

She chuckled ruefully—he wasn't wrong. Her passport and money were securely around her neck in a long-strapped pouch. "I do."

"Good. You can call Nicki when we land—and Stefan, if you feel you must."

Dimitri barked a laugh. "Stefan Mihal!" he said. "If you're trying to escape him, good luck, my friend. I'll have no part of that."

"I'm not a prisoner," Ari snapped back, and Fran stiffened. There was genuine steel in his voice, and she could see a glimpse of the man he was beneath the confusion. "Mihal has been a good friend to me, but his hospitality cannot last forever. I need to find my own way."

Dimitri shrugged. "Very well. I can leave in fifteen. You any good on a boat?"

Ari blinked, and Fran watched him closely. There was no pain in his gaze though, merely contemplation. He nodded. "I think so."

"Then climb aboard and get your friend up too. Be careful with her. She's got the money."

Dimitri disappeared over the side of the boat and Ari regarded Fran soberly. "I apologize," he said. "You don't need to come to the mainland with me. I just—I'm done with this place." He gazed back up the mountain road. "I've been a prisoner for a year, and I can't wait any longer to break free. To relearn who I am."

"I understand," she said, and she did. If Ari was starting to associate his stay on the island with captivity, there was no point in him remaining here. And with Dimitri standing watch over him at least all the way to the mainland, the royal family would have time to figure out a game plan.

They boarded and Dimitri stood at the head of the gang-plank, handing them into the boat. When he gripped Ari's hand, Ari visibly flinched. He said nothing at first, though, just hopped lightly onto the deck and confronted Dimitri. Fran held her breath, certain he'd ask Dimitri if he knew him, but Ari surprised her.

"Ryker Stavros," Ari introduced himself. "What should I call you?"

"For today, you can call me captain." Dimitri grinned at him. "And help me get this girl out on the sea before anyone notices you're gone."

Ari laughed, the sound rich and full, and the two of them set to work. Fran stayed out of their way, scanning the deck nervously until she found the bin of life jackets. She'd made her way over and had secured herself into one by the time they set sail. It was a far less choppy mode of travel than the speedboat, she realized quickly, but that didn't keep her from gripping the railing tightly as she surveyed the surface of the water. Were there sharks in the Aegean, along with the terrifying dolphins? Probably. She should get a second life jacket.

"You're doing a good thing here." To her surprise, Dimitri stood in front of her, and she blinked up at him, then shifted to see Ari at the far end of the boat, manning the wheel. "He needs to regain control of his own life, see places more familiar than here."

"He recognized you, I think, at least on some level," she said. "I'm surprised he didn't grill you."

Dimitri shook his head. "I'm not. Ari was never one to reveal his thoughts without being absolutely sure of himself. If he recognized me, but didn't know how, he wouldn't have wanted to tip his hand. I agreed to take him to the mainland, and that's his primary objective."

"But what are we going to do once we get there?" Fran asked.

"I've thought about that," Dimitri said. "The royal family has a number of residences throughout the capital city, a few of which they've acquired since Ari's accident. He won't know them. I can call ahead and have one made ready for you, and you can pass it off as your flat while you're staying in the city."

She considered that. "You think he'll buy it?"

"Probably. Either way, he's not going to borrow trouble. He needs a base of operations in the city, a place where he can get his bearings. We'll give him that. Where he goes from there is up to him. It's a good plan, yes?"

Fran bit her lip and glanced back out to the rolling ocean. After her nightmares last night, anything that got her away from the ocean was a good plan in her book. "Let's do it."

Ten

Ryker watched the captain and Francesca from the corner of his eye as he stood at the wheel, though his attention remained focused on the beautiful sailboat. It was a luxurious craft—far too extravagant for the average sailor. Then again, the man in charge of it was no ordinary sailor, he was almost certain.

Ryker was sure he'd known him before the crash, and equally sure the man realized it. The captain had to know Stefan Mihal as well, or he wouldn't have been allowed to dock his boat in the pricey marina of the equally pricey Asteri Island.

One thing was for sure: both Stefan and this man were treating him with kid gloves, just like all the doctors. At first, Ryker had thought it was to aid in his recovery, but now he wasn't so sure. Now he wondered if they wanted to *manage* his recovery.

Which meant they had questions about what had happened the night he'd crashed his plane as well.

Ryker scowled. He knew without a doubt that his family was in danger. As long as that family thought him dead, they would remain safe. Stefan hadn't told anyone of his existence, he thought, and he felt in his soul that this sailboat captain was trustworthy enough to keep his mouth shut as well. As long as Ryker followed their script, anyway. He wondered if he'd be tailed the moment he set foot in the capital city.

Probably.

His gaze shifted to Francesca again. He shouldn't have involved the American, but she had friends in the city, and he could lose her quickly enough.

Except now that they were underway, he didn't want to lose Francesca. She calmed him even though sensed she was hiding something as well. Maybe because of that fact. Two people with something to lose made good partners.

Ryker hailed the captain and handed over the wheel, noting how the big man remained polite, almost distant, for all his easy manner. He also didn't look into Ryker's eyes. Definitely, this man knew him, and definitely, he didn't want to push.

Perhaps this man was also in danger because of him, but Ryker didn't think so. There'd been that flash of pain, but it was definitely milder with the captain than with Stefan. Why?

Too many questions, he thought. Nowhere near enough answers.

Bracing himself as the wind picked up, Ryker made his way over to Fran. She looked up with the searching concern he was getting used to seeing on her face.

"How are you feeling?"

"Good," he said, dropping down beside her on the built-in bench that curved into the side of the sailboat. "When we land, this captain will be watching us. I think it best if we split up—you go on to your friends at the palace, and I'll find my way."

"I have lodging..." Francesca began, but Ryker cut her off. Honesty came more easily with this stranger than with the doctors, and certainly more than with Stefan.

"No," he said. "I need to find my way without Stefan and

whatever agents he may hire following me. Your lodgings may be safe, but they'll be monitored. I need to blend into the city."

Her eyes narrowed slightly. She considered him with a shrewdness that seemed too sharp, too experienced for her normally calm, compassionate manner. "Do you want to hide in the city or leave it?"

"I can't leave." He spread his hands. "Something happened to me here that affects my family. Something that occurred immediately before I boarded an airplane that crashed into the Aegean." He gave her a devil-may-care wink. "I'm a very good pilot, I'll have you know. I may not have my memory, but I do know that. I don't simply crash planes."

She seemed unconvinced. "There was a storm."

"And storms don't occur out of the clear blue sky," he said. "There's always a predisposition, even if the weather patterns are erratic. I would have been prepared for that. The fact that I wasn't..." he shook his head.

She shrugged. "Well, you know, I've heard a lot about the Greek gods since I got here. Maybe Zeus sent one without warning."

He blinked at the sudden spasm of pain in his temples, and he stared at Francesca. "Zeus..." The word sounded like a benediction on his lips. His heart leapt in recognition, his blood practically pulsed with new energy. "What do you know of Zeus?"

More to the point, what did *he* know? His certainty went deeper than a few colorful passages in a tourist brochure. To him—or at least to the person he was before the crash, certainly —the Greek god Zeus was a real, living being. He was sure of it.

He lifted a hand to his head. *Had he gone insane?*

"I'm sorry," Francesca said hurriedly, flushing. "It's just in Oûros, you have such a rich tradition—I'm sorry. I didn't mean to seem flippant, truly. I think people should believe whatever they want to believe."

"Believe..." Ryker frowned, peering at her more closely. "Believe in what?"

She blinked at him. "Never mind, I'm just being silly. I'm so sorry I upset you."

"You didn't." He grimaced. "I have to learn more. Remember more. And I can't do it if my family knows I am alive. With me essentially disappeared, Stefan will not notify them."

"True..." Francesca made a face, her gaze raking over his face, his clothes. "You're very tan right now, and your beard is growing in again. I don't know what you looked like before you crashed—"

"I was clean shaven." He nodded as her brows went up. "I remember being surprised when I realized it. My clothes were very nice, even soaked as they were from the sea. I ditched the heavy flight jacket, but once I finally understood that I'd survived an accident of some kind, I took inventory. I had an unusual watch—very expensive, custom made. Good for trading. Bits of the plane washed ashore with me, all of it looking top-of-the-line. Whoever I was, I had money as well as skills."

"Well, if you really want to disappear, you need to reverse that," Francesca said, surveying him critically. "Cheaper clothes, scruffy face, low-rent lodging. Lodging is the most important. You need to get off the streets to avoid being found, and move around at night." She frowned at him. "What about ID?"

He spread his hands. "I have none of that."

"I know, but—how necessary is it in Oûros? In the US, you need a driver's license if you're driving a car or getting a legit hotel room, but if you're not..." she shrugged. "No big deal. Especially if you buy things with cash."

"In Oûros, it's law for everyone to carry identification at all times," Ryker said automatically. Then he gave Francesca a broad wink. "You see? I'm remembering things—simple things, with no headache. I suspect greater understanding will come to me once I touch the stones of my homeland with my own feet and walk along her streets."

Her smile matched his, but her manner didn't lose its intensity. "My point is, you'll need a fake ID."

"Ideally. If I cannot find one, though…" He shrugged. "A victim of a mugging, a man down on his luck. I could pass, I suspect."

"I'm American," Francesca offered. "If you were some boy toy I picked up, and I was paying the bills, would you be hassled?"

He quirked her a smile. "A boy toy?"

"You know, like you were some guy I met on the beach. I decided you were cute, so I'm willing to pay for your meals and drinks or whatever while you hang out with me."

"Is this something you do on a regular basis?"

"We're talking about you, not me." She laughed. "What're the odds you can get away with no papers for a few days if you're hanging out with me?"

"A few days?" He considered. "Good, but not excellent. If I have to get into someplace official, or I look too much like a vagrant, there could be trouble, much like in Turkey." He shook his head. "But I don't know where to get an identity card anyway, so it doesn't matter."

"That, I'm not worried about." Francesca studied him. "Straight up. How much *do* you actually remember? Not the bullshit you're feeding the doctors and Stefan, but for real."

Her shift to more direct language took Ryker by surprise, and he didn't temper his response. "I know more than I realized at first," he said. "The basics, anyway. How money works, the kind of jobs that people have—jobs I probably had at some point, though I have no recollection of specific work. What foods I like and what I don't. The music I prefer. I know the names of popular performers, stupid and useless information like that. What I don't know is anything to do with my friends or my family—or about my actual life."

He didn't tell her why he thought that was, and instead continued. "I can recall street names, places I expect to find in the capital city—all of them in what I know to be the high-rent district though, which also makes me think my family is wealthy. I'm almost certain I'm not married and have no children. Stefan said as much, but nothing more. I know I live in the city, that I've lived there my whole life." He spread his hands. "But I don't know who I am, or what happened to me the night my plane went down. If I learn one, I suspect I will learn the other."

"So you need time," she said.

"Time, money, freedom." He smiled wryly. "And apparently, false papers. To become someone I'm not until I can figure out who I am."

"Fake it 'til you make it." The expression on Francesca's face made her seem far older than her years. "A new identity for you, Ryker Stavros, isn't going to be a problem."

$$Eleven$$

It took only a few minutes of discussion between Dimitri and Ari to get the ONSF captain to see the wisdom of letting them go ashore in the sailboat's small dinghy versus cruising into the bustling marina. This way Ari and Fran would seem like a happy, carefree couple, and could pull the boat ashore literally anywhere along the beach, then carry it out or leave it. They were less than a half mile from shore, and the water was calm enough.

Dimitri certainly didn't seem to care.

"I won't be returning to the island," he said quietly to Fran as she counted out American dollars into his palm, keeping up with the charade of him as ferryman. "You need me, you call. You don't need me, call anyway. I'll be close by."

She glanced over to Ari, scowling down at the dinghy as if it caused him personal affront. "He may give me the slip."

Dimitri grinned. "He's thought of it, I'm sure. But not right away. He's no fool. He's figured out that he'll buy himself a few more days if his keepers think he's with you."

"True," Fran said. She kept her manner light, but the words cut a little more deeply than she expected. Of course, Dimitri was right. Ari didn't want Fran with him because he was over-flowing with affection for her—merely to dupe his benevolent captors.

Well, she could at least help him go the extra step toward his recovery by creating an identity they couldn't crack until he was ready to let them do so. The sooner he remembered everything, the sooner her own life—and those of her friends—could return to normal.

Dimitri handed her down into the small boat and tossed down a third life jacket, which she held to her knees as Ari began to row. They hadn't gotten more than a few yards from the sailboat when Ari cocked a glance at her. "You're that worried I'll dump you in the water?"

"Never learned to swim," she said, and with a wince, she heard the flat Midwestern twang in her voice. When she got scared, it always surfaced—which is why she'd done a good job of ensuring she didn't place herself in frightening situations. But it was tough to avoid the ocean on a vacation of beach lovers, so she'd sucked it up. Sitting on the white sand of Oûros's Royal Beach had been one thing, though. Bobbing in the water with a man who only had a scant year of actual memories was another.

He continued rowing as she stared out over the open water. Was that a *dolphin* she saw out there? No. No, it was not. It was a...flying fish or something. Completely different than a dolphin. Exceptionally un-dolphin-like. She peered hard, defying the creature to surface again. It didn't, which saved her from having a full-on meltdown.

Ari waited until she returned her attention to him before speaking again. "You didn't have lakes or rivers where you grew up?"

"Both," she said tersely, though she was happy to focus on him and not on the acres of rolling sea surrounding them. "Small river, pretty big lake. But we didn't have a boat, and I didn't have a lot of free time to play in the water, so swimming lessons weren't a priority." When she and her dad did go out to the lake—which happened nearly once a week in the summer— it was to run a bar truck for the local bikers. From the time she was maybe ten years old, there was no way she was wearing a swimsuit around that crowd.

"Then how do you know you can't swim? For some people, it comes naturally."

Fran snorted, but between her nerves and her embarrassment, it was easier to talk than to keep it bottled up. "Yeah, that's not really a thing for me. When I was twelve or so, I was, um, carrying some groceries for a group of boaters out on the lake. I went down the dock and made the handoff, no problem. When I turned, though, I slipped and fell into the water. Even though I technically didn't know how to swim, I knew what I *should* do to get over to the dock ladder. But I just—couldn't. It was like my legs were stuck together and weighed about a thousand pounds, and every move of my arms churned up so much more water than it should. You'd think I was an outboard motor. I sank like a stone, completely freaking out the whole time. I nearly drowned in that damned lake not three feet from the freaking dock. It was horrifying."

Ari's eyes never left hers. "What happened? How did you get out?"

Fran winced. "The kindness of strangers. It took nearly a half-dozen men doing their best not to get punched in the face to get close to me. They jumped in after me and somehow stopped me from spinning around long enough to haul me over to the ladder. Once my butt cleared the water, my legs could work again, but I was so incredibly weak...and seriously mortified. They all just laughed—but not in a mean way." She shook her head ruefully. "I was just a kid who needed help."

From that day forward, she'd seen the silver lining of the

Black Megadeath Motorcycle Club—and, truthfully, most of them hadn't been bad men. They'd taught her a lot, too—like how to talk her way through her fears and how to fight when talking wasn't enough.

That's what she needed to focus on, as Ari got them closer to land with each self-assured stroke.

He'd fallen silent again though, watching her, so she smiled at him brightly. "You know how to row, so that's something. Maybe you're a fisherman?"

"I don't think so." He shook his head. "Figured that out when I had to row ashore in a leaky boat after the crash. My hands are calloused now, but then—no. I didn't work as a laborer before. I don't think I managed a trade either." He quirked his lips. "I had to be a pilot, or I was a kept man, which seems unlikely."

Despite her nerves, Fran laughed. "I could almost see it. You're a little scruffy now, but with another nice shave, a haircut..."

"Perhaps you should reconsider your earlier offer. I could make an excellent boy toy." Ari waggled his brows, and Fran's heart quickened a bit. Despite the haggard look that dogged him, she could almost see the man who'd beamed out of the news photos from a year ago. That Ari had been untroubled, earnest, and seemed so much younger than the man leaning into the oars in front of her. But there remained glimmers of him.

"We're getting close to the main beach," she said, her attention drawn to the wide swath of sand. "You should...I don't know, turn?"

"Turn." He laughed again and glanced over his shoulder, sighting their position. As he did, his expression brightened so abruptly Fran nearly dropped her life jacket.

"What is it?"

"This...I know this place," he said. He craned his neck,

peering up as his powerful strokes took them away from the Royal Beach, and near a rocky promontory that jutted out into the water, and soon became a cliff nearly thirty feet high. "There's something high up there, beyond the cliff's edge. You can't see it from below by design, but...I absolutely know this place. The water is very deep here. Very deep. But it levels out in a hurry, just around the bend."

His voice was warm, his eyes dancing as he maneuvered the oars to take them at an angle to the beach. "Once we get through these deep waters, there's a beach with shallow water where we can land relatively easily. We can take the boat and hide it in the trees. We used to do it all the—*aigh!*"

The convulsion shook Ari with such violence that his hands jerked high. The oars jacked violently in their rings, the boat immediately rocking as Ari clapped his hands to his head. Forgetting the life jacket on her knees, Fran scrambled forward, wrapping her arms around him.

The force of her motion sent him falling backward as well, but instinctively he grabbed her, holding her against his body as the boat tipped precariously first one way then the next. As Fran dipped toward the water and she lost her grip on Ari—two sets of hands erupted from the water and latched onto her, then yanked her clean off the boat and into the water!

"No!" Fran barely got the word out before she clamped her lips shut, plunging deep. She whirled around, her arms windmilling and her legs churning. And just like it had been in the lake all those years ago, she didn't seem to have any control over her own body. She spun and whirled, her arms spinning her in a circle, her legs like concrete poles, fused together, flapping, writhing—

Wait. *Flapping?*

Desperate and panicked, she froze in the water—but somehow stopped sinking. She opened her eyes wide and stared all around her, whirling fast, shocked and confused at everything she could see. It was as if the underside of the water was as bright and vibrant as the sunny day above. She could see the hull of the rowboat, the shadow of Ari surging up. She could hear the faint cry of him calling her name from far away.

"Francesca!" he bellowed.

"Fran, Francesca, Frannie, Fran, Francesca, Francesca—" a new, chirruping chorus assaulted her ears. Fran spun around, automatically drawing in a startled breath—which made her brain stutter and her lungs seize with renewed panic. *How was she breathing? How was she—*

Her eyes flared wide as she saw the unmistakable flap of a row of tails rapidly disappearing into the darkness. Instinctively, she moved to chase after them. Then a shadow streaked overhead and the water exploded in a violent frenzy around her. She saw Ari plainly as he entered the water, a thin line snaking through the water behind him. He turned and she whirled back toward the boat, easily seeing the ladder now dangling in the water. *The ladder!*

With one powerful lunge, she willed her body toward the boat—and barely stopped herself from crashing into the hull.

Suddenly, Ari was right behind her, grabbing her arms, thrusting her up. He wrapped her hands around the sides of the ladder, then gripped her waist, but she couldn't get her feet to work—her feet!

She scowled, looking down, but all she saw was churning water. Then Ari's hands clamped at her waist—shoved her high—

She burst out of the water, lungs heaving, somehow snagging the ladder and hauling herself up. The moment her ass cleared the water, her legs seemed to regain their ability to move again. She scraped, hauled, and pulled herself over the side of the boat, flopping to the far side to weigh it down as Ari scrambled into the boat as well.

"*Francesca*," he cried. He pounced on her, shoving the hair out of her face, his long, strong hands skimming her arms, her legs. "Are you hurt? Did you take in water? Can you *speak*?"

He shook her, and she gasped out a choked and gargled breath. "Ar—Ryker, I'm fine! I'm fine!" She tried to flail away from him, setting the boat into a frantic rocking motion again, but Ari's strong grip held her fast.

"Steady! Steady," he ordered, his voice low and tight. "I'm okay, you're okay. The boat will be okay too, but you must stop moving."

Fran's heart thundered loud enough to drown out any other thought but that she was once again on the verge of imminent death. She couldn't go into the water—she couldn't! She'd just had her second near-death experience—this time in the fucking ocean and there hadn't even been dolphins around!

Unless... She squeezed her eyes shut, trying to remember what she'd seen underwater. Had those been actual *tails* that she'd seen rushing away from the scene of the crime? *Were* dolphins trying to kill her? And how had she ended up in the water in the first place? How had she overbalanced that badly? Everything was fading in her mind, blanking into shadows as she wheezed.

"You're okay, Francesca." Ari pulled her to him, hard. She tried her breathing exercises, struggling for control, for her center. But her center was cartwheeling dangerously, and the only thing controlling her was Ari's powerful arms around her, pinning her to his chest and torso as his legs spread wide. His non-stop, soothing patter never faltered.

"You're okay, yes? You're fine. I've got you. You won't fall in again. You've got your life jacket and me and the boat and the oars. The oars float, did you know that? They float. The boat has a ladder. You climbed up the ladder. The boat has a tie line. I'm tied to it by the tie line. The Aegean is our cradle and Poseidon keeps us safe. You are fine, you are safe. It's okay…"

Fran dragged in a choked breath, glad her face rested against Ari's chest. The thin cotton of his shirt did nothing to block the heat of his skin, damp from the exertion of rowing and the splash of water. She'd originally moved forward to protect him, but now she burned with embarrassment. *She'd fallen into the freaking ocean! She'd nearly killed them both!*

"You didn't nearly kill us." Ari's words were soft, his chuckle quiet. "It was hot, and I was glad for the swim. And now you are safe, beautiful Francesca. Safe and out of the water." Ari's hands were moving slowly up and down her back—comforting her, quieting her. But his body was firm and muscled beneath hers, and she couldn't deny how good it felt to be held in some-one's arms…even in such an awkward position.

For another precious few seconds, she allowed herself to indulge in the security of his arms. She hadn't allowed herself to indulge in any serious relationships before she'd been accepted into college. After that, there'd been grad school to study for and an endless round of jobs to pay the bills. She hadn't had time for a relationship, and she'd never found someone who she trusted not to ask too many questions.

Funny how it took her nearly *drowning* to accept the touch of a man again.

But the moment was passing. She needed to regain control of herself…and to let Ari get control of the boat.

She breathed out a long sigh. "We're not going to die?" she ventured.

Ari's laughter shook them both, sending the boat to bobbing again as she clutched at him.

"We're not," he assured her. "I'll need you to sit up as I sit up, then to move back to your seat. Once you've done that, I'll get the oars back in line, which will set us rocking again, but it will be okay." His voice was quiet, like she was a fawn about to bolt. "Can you do that?"

She considered it. "Maybe." She lifted her head off his chest to find him looking at her, his chin tucked down, his gaze steady. His shoulders rested on a storage crate behind him, and though his entire body was locked to provide her support, he didn't seem to be in any discomfort. Soaking wet, yes, but not uncomfortable.

She braced herself against his chest, then edged back. "You...threw me out of the water at the end, didn't you."

He barked a laugh, smiling widely as seawater still dripped from his hair. "I did. You didn't seem able to climb."

She winced, but it was only the truth. "Yeah, well...That must have been some work camp you were in for a year." She stared at his arms, his shoulders. How had she not noticed before how *built* the guy was? Muscles strained beneath his soaked shirt, and his broad chest still heaved as he drew in steadying breaths. "You sure you weren't a water polo player on top of being a pilot?"

"Always a possibility. Now easy does it, back you go." Still grinning, Ari watched her as she straightened, nodding with reassurance as she slowly edged back to her own seat. "You good?"

"I'm good," Fran managed, straightening her jacket with one hand as the other gripped the side of the boat. "You can relax now."

Twelve

Ryker wished it was as easy as that. He sat up, wincing slightly as his body compressed, the pain serving to clear his head as he struggled to get his body to ignore the fact that seconds ago a woman had been sprawled over him for the first time in a year. Soaking wet, terrified, and wearing the world's bulkiest life jacket, but a woman all the same.

He reached for the anchor and pulled it up, then leaned forward on one knee to reset the oars as Francesca clutched the sides of the boat. When she'd burst toward him, her arms flailing, he'd barely had time to register her movement before she knocked him back. She'd done it out of pure instinct, clearly seeing the shock of pain that had rattled him, but the woman had obviously never been in a boat before and she'd nearly capsized them both before he got his arms around her. And then...

"How did you end up in the water?" he asked, and her eyes flared wide, panic filling them.

"I..." she swallowed and glanced away. "I swear to God, I didn't mean to."

"Well, I would think not. But I thought I had you secure."

"You did—it wasn't your fault," she said hurriedly. "It was almost like...I mean..." she frowned and glanced away. She had the weirdest fragmented memory of hands reaching out of the water, but—no. That was patently impossible.

"I don't know what happened." She gave another coughing laugh. "I just sort of fell. And then, when I landed in the water, I...I mean, it was almost like I could see everything so clearly, like I could *breathe*. I wasn't so scared at that point, just confused. I saw...I mean, I thought I saw..."

She flashed him an embarrassed glance. "I know that's not possible—breathing underwater, feeling like I wasn't going to die—but maybe it's because you jumped in so quickly. Everything was so confused."

"It didn't feel quick to me." He grimaced. "I may not know who I am, but thank the gods, I've had some rescue training." The oars felt good in his hands, and he focused on the movement, trying also to recall what had happened in the water with Francesca. He'd thrown the anchor, dropped the ladder, and attached the line to himself. Then he'd gone over the side to find her. "By the time I got my bearings, you were already snugged up beside the boat, so hoisting you up was that much easier." He winked at her. "It appears you can swim better than you thought."

"Yeah..." If anything, Francesca seemed a bit more distressed. "Did you see—I mean, could *you* see underwater?"

"Not easily. But you did?"

"I mean..." she blew out a distracted breath. "What I saw made no sense. First off, that I could see at all was weird—and then there were, like...I don't know. Giant fish or, um, maybe dolphins swimming away from me. And I wanted to *follow* them, which makes no sense. Then you jumped into the water and I realized I pretty much had to be drowning and I needed to get the hell out of the ocean. So I tried to move toward the boat and boom, I was there. All of that happened in, like, a few seconds."

"Yes." He shook his head, dismayed that even his few snatches of memory were fading with each long sweep of his oars. "I entered the water to find you, there was some churn, and then you were at the boat and the ladder was there. I mostly went by gut instinct at that point."

"At which point you saved my life and held me when I continued to freak out." She groaned audibly. "Um...thank you for that. I'm so sorry."

He glanced up to see her blushing furiously, her hands still clutching the side of the boat. Instantly, he flashed back to the pure, unmistakable pleasure of feeling her in his arms.

Fortunately, Francesca's heavy life jacket had kept her from becoming too intimate with his body, or she would have discovered exactly what he'd thought about having her pressed so closely against him. As it was, he still could barely breathe when he thought of it.

"No apologies necessary—and you're welcome." He watched the sailboat in the distance as he began rowing toward shore again. Had the captain noticed their brief disruption? Probably. But it was so quick, the man might have mistaken it for an intentional dip in the water.

No doubt he was waiting to see precisely where they pulled this small row boat ashore. But if they moved fast, he and Francesca could disappear into the city before any agents of the well-meaning Stefan Mihal could find them.

Francesca's quiet words recalled him. "Before I landed us in the water, you remembered something. It caused you pain."

He grimaced. "A lot of pain. I recognized some of this shoreline and my brain wasn't too happy about it."

"And now? You're recalling it again, right? When you have an episode like that, does the pain come back?"

Ryker chuckled a little derisively. "No. Once it happens the first time, the trigger disappears. The memory doesn't get any clearer, but the pain goes away." It had been the reason he'd been able to bear being around Stefan. "Almost like I'm still fishing, but I've lost the hook entirely."

She nodded. "I'm glad of that, in a way. It would make it more difficult to land if everywhere we went made you flinch."

"Fair enough." He peered at her. "How about you? You safely got out of the water—would you go in again?"

"Oh, hell no." She made a face that had him laughing again. "Not if I can help it."

"Really? So you're not a fan of spas or pools, either?"

"Yeah, well...weirdly enough, those aren't a problem. I mean —not the deep end, let's not get crazy. But hot tubs and chlorinated pools? I can totally deal with those—except for the swimming issue. Any body of water with actual living things in it? At least if I can't touch the bottom? Freakout city. And don't even get me started on dolphins."

"Dolphins?" Ryker asked, trying and failing to keep the shock from his voice. "But—"

"I know! I know." Fran waved off his surprise with irritation, her cheeks flushing. "I have recurring nightmares of them spiriting me away into the depths of the ocean, never to return. It's ridiculous."

"Not ridiculous," he said solemnly. "Perhaps you should make an offering to Poseidon to ensure you're safety. You are in Oûros, after all. Such things carry more weight here."

She smiled at that, and he was struck again by her beauty— and her isolation, he thought. Francesca Simmons was used to making her way on her own. Probably the only time she ever allowed herself to be helped was...if she was drowning.

The remainder of the trip was uneventful, and they found the rocky inlet exactly as he'd expected it to be. It was deserted this morning, and he ran the boat up close to shore as Francesca shot him a nervous glance.

"I'm getting out," he warned her as he tucked the oars inside the boat.

She squeaked in protest, slapping her hands to the sides of the boat, though they weren't moving at all. "You'll get all wet again."

"I'll dry. Here we go—"

He lifted himself up and stepped out of the boat in one smooth motion, grabbing it to steady the craft as it bobbed upward without his weight to ground it.

"Oh," she said, peering over the side. "I guess it's pretty shallow." She looked up at him expectantly. "I can get out now too?"

"I can lift you if you don't want your feet to get wet."

"I'll manage. The ocean isn't so bad if it's just my feet."

Still, Francesca didn't move, and Ryker grinned as he stepped to her side. "Give me one hand. When you're braced, I'll have you even if the boat tips. Deal?"

She nodded tightly, but it took two tries before she would lift her hand to his. He gripped her forearm, and when she stood and the boat tipped—as he'd known it would—he swept her into his arms.

"Feet up," he ordered, splashing through the shallows until he reached the shore. "Okay down."

"The boat—"

"I'll get the boat."

Disrupted by their movement, the boat had slid off its rocks, but Ryker caught it easily enough, pulling it to safety and then further up onto the shore. As he remembered—and this time without the pain—there was a natural indentation in the brush that easily accommodated the small craft.

Francesca frowned, however, as he stepped back from it. "Won't it get stolen?"

"That's not going to be a problem," Ryker shrugged. "We were watched by the sailboat captain the whole way into this inlet. I'm surprised we didn't have Stefan's agents waiting to hand us out of the boat. As it is, we should hurry." He reached for her hand, tugging her onto a well-worn pathway.

She let him pull her along. "How far are we from the city?" she asked. "I need to get to a bank."

"Fifteen minutes, more or less, if we hurry. It's straight up this promontory, but not far."

"No hurrying." Francesca's words were sharp enough to make him slow, and she shook her head as she surveyed him critically. "We need to look as chill as possible. Unbutton your shirt and roll up your sleeves—maybe your trousers, too? I want to look like we just took a dunk in the water, but now we're totally chill. The more people who can dismiss us as tourists, the better."

As he complied, she pulled her own outfit apart, tying her shirt at her midriff and rolling up her trousers farther, exposing toned calves above her sandaled feet. She also shook out her hair and let it fall around her shoulders. It was longer than Ryker had realized.

"Why don't you wear it like that all the time?" he asked as they set off again.

"Too out of control," she said, her voice clipped and final, her attention no longer on him. "Let's make time here."

Agreeable enough, despite her change of manner, Ryker led her through the forest, moving quickly until they reached the edge of town. Then they angled through the city streets that sloped gently toward the ocean again. "There's a beach access— there," he said, and tugged her down another alley until they stepped out on the wide expanse of Royal Beach.

Francesca was watching him curiously. "So...is this familiar?" she asked quietly.

"Yes—and no," he said. "I don't have any sense of threat here."

She laughed. "Good. I've got enough for both of us. Walk beside me now, if that's okay."

They fell into step together, and her words came low and fast even though she swung her arms and laughed, the epitome of a vacationer in love. "We need to get to a bank, get euros. You'll have to handle the transaction. The less I say the better. I'm more noticeable than you are right now."

He nodded and she kept going, walking him through the next step. When she asked for whatever dive bar was closest to the marina, though, he hesitated. "The marina is almost certainly going to be watched," he said.

She shook her head. "Not if they're searching for us at my rented villa," she said. "We go behind them and they won't think to double back."

"Fair enough."

After they'd visited the bank, the bar district was next, and it was exactly as Ryker remembered it. But he had no attachment to this place either, other than knowing it was where men went to pick up dock work, boat work, and supplies. "It's not a safe place for women, I'm ashamed to say," he murmured as they approached the second to last tavern from the water, a seedy place with bars on the windows and crude, hand-painted signs on the door.

Francesca stopped. "This is totally the right place."

"You sure?" he eyed the bar dubiously.

"Oh, yeah. So you go in alone. I'll wait in the street, but close, wringing my hands," she said. "We've been mugged, and I'm your girlfriend. Announce that right as you go in. Tell them you have lost your papers and see how they respond. If they indicate they can help, tell them straight out that you want the cheapest papers they can get you fast. Pay..." she blew out a breath. "I don't know what the right amount is. Not too much, though. You've been mugged, and this was money I had hidden in my clothes. In fact, tell them that up front. No more than maybe seventy-five euros. You simply want to get home with no trouble." She firmed her hand on his arm. "They won't believe you, but that's not the point. The point is to give them a story they can remember and recite believably if anyone shows up later with a problem. Make sense?"

He frowned at her. "How do you know all of this?"

"Not important," she winked. "Now kiss me like you're about to do something that makes you nervous. They're watching inside."

Ryker studied her, but not for too long. Francesca's face had changed completely. She seemed frazzled, anxious as he squeezed both her hands, kissing her hard on the mouth.

As it had been the day before, the touch of Francesca's lips against his was electric, but Ryker forced himself away, pleased that her eyes had gone wide. Was that an act, though, or was she reacting to his kiss?

The question sent a flair of irritation through him, which he carried into the dark confines of the tavern. The place was just the way Francesca had explained it would be. A bar with several men in clusters and tables at the back. After he made his plea to the bartender, the man gestured him to the back where a few men sat with their bags beside them. He sputtered out the story again.

To his surprise, they didn't look at him. Not close anyway. "How much d'you have?"

"I—we were mugged. My girlfriend..." Ryker cast a longing glance outside, relieved that Francesca was there, talking to a squat older woman in the street. "We were mugged. She—this is all she had left in her pockets. If it's not enough, I..." he reached for his pocket and the men tensed.

"How much?" the one closest asked him again. Something had shifted in the man's hand, and it was Ryker's turn to stiffen. A knife gleamed beneath the edge of the table.

"Seventy-five euros," he said.

The knife disappeared. "Buy us a round. Come back with the rest."

Without asking any other questions, Ryker went to the bar, where the barkeeper already had the drinks lined up. The man didn't look at Ryker either, merely accepted the money he gave him and gestured to him to take the three drinks. By the time he returned to the table, a folded piece of cloth was beside one of the men's elbows.

He sat the drinks down with the rest of the money tucked between the glasses, then reached for the thick cloth packet. An oily hand lifted and clamped over his until the second man pawed through the euros.

"Good luck to you," the first man grunted, then lifted his hand.

Ryker pocketed the cloth packet.

Getting identification papers shouldn't be this easy. Regardless, he did feel better knowing he could at least produce papers should the police stop him—which they might, if only because of his disheveled appearance. He couldn't deny the sense of relief as he stepped once more into the sunlight. Francesca had been right—getting false papers had been the right decision.

And now that he was a whole new person, he had a whole new agenda, too.

Where he needed to go and what he needed to do couldn't happen until nightfall. That left him hours to see exactly what else he'd been missing from life for the past year.

Thirteen

"You—give money? Give money."

Fran blinked at the old woman standing too closely in front of her. "I'm so sorry," she said automatically, though her nerves tensed. She sometimes gave to panhandlers, but aggressive ones scared her, especially those who had such a flat, hard expression on their faces.

"I gave all my money to my boyfriend—my boyfriend!" she said more loudly when the woman poked at her, hard enough to bruise. This was no trembling waif sent into the streets to beg for her supper. This woman was sturdily built, her mouth set into a fierce scowl. "I have no money!"

"Bah!" The woman pushed at her, and only then did Fran see a child darting past on one side of her, felt the brush to her side. Her pocket! There was no money in it. She carried everything in her neck pouch. But the sudden shot of fear that raced through her tipped all too fast into anger. The way it always had, since she'd been a little girl and had learned the hard way that fear was sometimes worse than whatever faced you. Fear made you stop when you most needed to act, pouring sludge into your veins when you needed fire.

Her anger served her better than her fear now, too. Especially when the woman pushed her again.

"I said stop that." Fran didn't shout or threaten. Instead, she stepped forward forcefully and pushed the woman back with equal strength, hard enough to make the woman grunt. The panhandler's gaze whipped up to her, her mouth tight in an ugly snarl, but Fran's chin jutted out, her fists came up. She wasn't Francesca Simmons now but a different Fran, a Fran who was small and scared and tired and so, so angry that she couldn't think straight anymore. *You want to fight me, you—*

The woman didn't give her a chance to finish the thought.

With a sharp, dismissive curse she wheeled around, loudly proclaiming something that Fran guessed wasn't complimentary to Americans. Instantly, Fran's anger cleared, her sensibilities reminding her where she was, what she was. Though her pulse hammered, she quickly unclenched her hands and lifted them to smooth her hair in place.

After that, no one said a word to the crazy American girl standing in the tiny alley next to the broken-down bar. But no one else bothered her either.

Fran's nerves had almost settled by the time Ari rejoined her within fifteen minutes of entering the seedy tavern. He walked with a jaunty step—too jaunty for the cover of a man who'd recently been mugged—but she supposed the men he'd bought his identity from were not paying too much attention to anything but the amount of money they'd made.

She fell into step with him. "Hotel," she said. "To get you out of sight."

"A hotel would be good," Ari said, "But there's no hurry."

She frowned at him. "You could be recognized."

He shrugged. "Recognized by who? Think about it. My name is Conti Goba now. I'm a national visiting from my distant farm, and I'm walking the streets of the capital city with a beautiful American girl. Who will stop me?"

"The police?"

"That's their prerogative, yes," he said. "But so what if they do? The police in Oûros understand that our most important import is tourism. They ask—and ask frequently—for ID, but if you have any documentation at all, you get no more than a cursory glance. I can already recite the details of my papers." He tapped his shirt pocket. "And Conti, he is not one to cause trouble. So you see? You have made me very safe indeed."

"But Stefan will be searching for you."

"Stefan Mihal thinks he knows me and what I am doing, yet he lets me leave that island. It's not as if that boat captain had been given orders to ensure I didn't escape—if he had, I'd still be up in that guest compound, poked and prodded by doctors. No. Mihal wanted me to be freed, once he had me long enough to ensure I was no danger to anyone, especially myself."

"Oo-kay..." Fran had no idea where Ari was going with this, but she could see how he'd drawn these conclusions. It wasn't as if they'd snuck off the island. They'd merely asked, and it'd been allowed. Ari's reasoning that it had been a deliberate allowance was on the money, but she suspected that his understanding diverged sharply from hers after that point. "But why?"

Ari shook his head, remaining far too cheerful. "That is the question, isn't it? And a good one at that." He spread his hands. "But such questions will be answered in time. For now, I am Conti Goba, son of Maria and Josef of Makila and without a care in the world. Within that framework, I could be anyone I wanted to be, take on any personality. It is very freeing, no?"

A pang struck deep in Fran's heart and she searched Ari's face, instantly worried. Did he guess the truth about her? Could he possibly know? "It could be..." she said, her tone cautious.

"It is," he insisted. "When I came up out of that water after my crash, the seas eerily calm after what had clearly been a terrible storm, I knew two things. One, I was alive. Two, I was Ryker Stavros, the luckiest pilot to ever ditch into the sea. Things went downhill from there, but I was someone. I had a purpose, a past, a place in this world. It was my job to remember them, and that proved impossible." He spread his hands. "But Conti, he has no such obligations. He could be anyone. And so I have decided I am going to fashion him exactly the way I want."

Fran grimaced. Ari's optimism was probably the healthiest attitude he could take, but she'd encountered her share of troubles falsifying her own identification. The fact remained that the men in the tavern had offloaded Conti's papers pretty easily. For all that she'd hoped they'd do exactly that, it made her nervous. "Unless good Conti is in jail. Or dead. Or wanted for murder."

"You worry too much," Ari said, apparently unwilling to be brought down by her pessimism. Fran wondered at that. Was he truly that good natured, or had nothing bad ever happened to the royal prince?

Even as she thought the words, she rejected them. Ari had been held prisoner for a year, forced to live in what amounted to little more than a kennel, and made to work in a country where he had no rights. He'd doubtless been beaten, abused, drugged— probably starved at some level, and certainly threatened with it. Regardless of his lifestyle before the accident, this was a man who'd endured serious hardship.

Then again, perhaps this was also a man who recognized hardship when it was presented to him—and when it wasn't.

His next words confirmed that line of thinking. "I think first we must find something to eat. Someplace off the beaten track. We have money and I have papers, and it is a glorious day in the city." He took her hand. "Remember, I'm walking with a gorgeous American girl, too. What could be better?"

She let him draw her down the street, away from the seedy bar. No one appeared to be following them, but how long would that last? "We should get new clothes."

"After lunch," Ari agreed. But he didn't slow down, and his long strides ate up the pavement until they were out of the marina district and into a more pleasant area of the city. This wasn't quite the tourist area, but it was right on the fringes, and small shops began to line the cobblestoned streets. The first one that looked like a café drew Ari's attention, and a moment later Fran found herself inside a cool, shadowy hideaway.

"Ah! This is perfect." Ari turned brightly toward the older woman who stepped out of the back room and began speaking to her in Oûrois. Though there were plenty of chairs and tables in the small space—most of them empty—the woman raised a hand and beckoned them to follow her.

"What's this?"

"Something to make that last hint of worry disappear from your eyes," Ari said.

He led her past a kitchen down a short hallway flanked on either side with restrooms, and then outside again. Immediately, Fran understood. "A courtyard!"

"You see? Conti Goba takes care of his woman," Ari grinned. He turned to the old woman and relayed more information to her. The woman nodded several times, then bustled away.

Ari chose a table and drew out a chair, seating Fran with a flourish. Rather than sitting as well, he held up a hand. "I'll be right back," he said.

Instantly, she tensed. He was giving her the slip, she reasoned immediately. He was seating her in this interior courtyard and then escaping. She should let him go—he wasn't a prisoner—but how could she face the queen if she did that?

Her panic must have telegraphed itself to Ari. "No, no!" he

said, shaking his head. "You worry too much. I will be back, sweet Francesca. Conti Goba would no more leave you alone than he would stop breathing."

With a short bow, he pivoted on his heel, leaving Fran staring after him. "What in the world?" she muttered after the café door settled behind him. Ari's gentlemanly affection had to be some kind of elaborate act.

Then again, who truly was Ari Andris? The articles she'd read on him had all been uniform in their compliments, but she'd taken that to be political propaganda. Yes, he was tall and strong. Yes, he was a credit to his family and his country. But all the accolades of sensitivity, humor, shrewdness, and politesse... that she'd assumed was exaggeration.

Yet here he was, without a meaningful memory to his name, acting with more grace and princely chivalry than, well...anyone she'd ever known.

Before she could puzzle out more, Ari was back, bearing a tray of glasses and a large carafe of water. "The good mother, she has guests in the front room of her café, so splitting her time is a hardship. I told her I could as easily carry water to us as she could, and this way we could wait for her convenience."

He sat the glasses on the table, then poured them both drinks. Fran did her level best not to stare as he handed her a glass. "You should drink more water than you do, Francesca," he murmured, watching her as she downed the water. "It's a very different climate here than America. More tropical."

"It's certainly that," Fran said with a grimace. She watched as Ari settled into his own chair, his long legs sprawling out in comfortable relaxation. "How did you know this place would have a courtyard? Have you been here before?"

"Not at all," he shook his head. "I suspect this part of town is a place I never explored, which is a shame. That woman in there —she works hard, but she is happy. Her kitchen is filled with pots and pans, much laughter and love, here in this tiny little restaurant tucked into a street I've never seen. It's not right that I do not know it."

Fran lifted her brows. "You can't expect to have seen everything in the city, though. It's a big place."

"Not that big," Ari countered. "And I have lived here all my life. I know it in my bones. Yet here this lovely woman lives and works and feeds her neighbors, and I didn't know she existed—didn't know that this street existed. What else have I been missing, I wonder? What life might I choose to live, once my memories return to me?"

Fourteen

R yker knew Francesca wasn't taking his words as an idle question, and he liked her more for it. As if it would be possible for him to like her any more than he already did. Her gentle manner, her soothing touch, her beautiful expressive eyes were already weaving a spell around him he didn't want to break.

Before she could speak, however, he posed the same question to her. "What about you?" he asked. "Here I know nothing of your life, but that's only fair, as we don't know anything about mine. What life do you wish to live, Francesca Simmons?"

As he spoke, he tracked the progression of Francesca's emotions from tension to immediate relief. This was a woman who didn't want to talk about her past—not to him. He suspected not to anyone. But there would be time for that. There were so many other things he wanted to learn about her. A person's path was important, but their heart—that's what mattered, he thought. Your feet might get you to a place, but your heart is what got you through it.

Francesca didn't respond right away. He leaned back in his chair, completely at ease. She watched him, and eventually a smile played at the edges of her lips. "Are you interrogating me, Mr. Goba?"

"In the most insistent and demanding of ways." He nodded. "You must tell me everything or I will subject you to hours of intrusive questions."

"I see." She reached for the carafe, then halted as he smoothly lifted it and poured more water into her glass. "You don't have to serve me, you know," she protested.

"I don't, no. But if it doesn't bother you?" He raised a brow at her and she shook her head, which made him grin in genuine pleasure. "Then you must know I enjoy doing it. Everyone works hard in this world, but not everyone is taken care of. I get the impression you focus more on caring for others than others do for you."

She blinked at him. "I don't need anyone to care for me."

"Oh, but there you are wrong." Ryker spread his hands. "We each need someone to care for us, even if we can manage quite well on our own. We are strong because we need to be strong. I am, you are. Our sweet nana inside is, cooking her wonderful meals. But our hearts are never so full as when they beat in time with another's. It's what hearts were made for, yes? It's what makes them complete."

Her eyes widened. "You can't seriously talk like this all the time. You sound like..." she broke off and blushed again, hard. "You sound like a poet."

He laughed, but he couldn't deny his rush of excitement at the expression on Francesca's face. He'd surprised her, and in surprising her he'd peeled away another layer of her wariness, revealing another facet of the woman underneath. He got the feeling there was more—so much more to Francesca than he could imagine, and even now he felt the press of time.

He leaned forward. "So answer my original question. How

would you live your life if you could choose any path? What would you do?"

She tilted her head. "I've chosen a path I love," she confessed, and he found himself believing her. "I help people become more whole, more their true selves. That's really the goal of my work, I think."

"The work you did with the soldiers?"

"Well—that was more to help them give a voice to what they'd experienced," she said, and her gaze shifted away from him as she went to a place in her own memories. Not all of them happy memories, he suspected. "I couldn't heal them. I'm not a doctor. I couldn't tell them it would be okay, that they'd get better. Some of them will, some of them won't. The things they saw..." she shook her head. "I never realized how sheltered I was in my own world, even with its challenges, until I saw a glimpse of their truths, their experiences."

"And you gave them words to express that truth?"

"Words, sometimes," she said with a soft smile. "Or I simply gave them a safe place to share it. To let the ugly or hurtful or terrible thing into the sunlight, where they could see it outside of themselves, and realize it was part of their experience, yes, but not who they were, not really. That they had endured it, but they no longer needed to carry it if they didn't want to."

Ryker felt his throat tighten at the naked emotion on Francesca's face. It was an emotion she probably didn't reveal to those she was helping, but her grief was almost transparent, her empathy for these strangers so strong that he could feel their remembered pain as if it was shimmering between them now. "That's a gift," he murmured.

She blinked at him, and her wariness was back. "It's a blessing, really. Except I'm the one being blessed. I researched all the different careers out there, what I could do, what I wanted to do. When I first realized I was able to go to school to learn how to help people in this way—that was unbelievable to me." She smiled, only it was a smile she would give a stranger, one intended to deflect, not to invite in. "I was very lucky."

"You were," Ryker said easily, taking no offense at her caution. There was nothing in Francesca's revelations that merited such concern as far as he could see—but he hadn't walked in her shoes, hadn't carried her burdens. Eventually, he would understand her, but he could pursue that end as cautiously as she pursued everything. "And you will be finishing your studies soon?"

"I will," she said, her relief at being on more solid conversational ground obvious. "I have to present my final thesis, defend it, as they say, but the preliminary work I've already submitted has been well received. I should have my masters and could start work counseling as early as next year."

"Ah," he said, sitting back. "So you would like to become a counselor, then. For soldiers?"

"No—not exclusively." Francesca shook her head quickly. "I don't pretend to know everything it takes to understand the needs of military personnel. They give so much more than people believe they do...I've seen the barest amount. I'd have to do far more intense work in that field before I would consider myself an expert. But for the public, yes. I think that would be very rewarding. To help them get connected with who they really are, live their best life. That sort of thing."

He nodded. "You'd be very good at it."

"Maybe," she said, then she flashed him an uncharacteristically confiding glance. "But first I'd travel."

"Like you're traveling now, you and your friends?"

"Well...we're not traveling as much as we expected." She laughed. "We've stayed in Oûros longer than any of us thought we would, with Nicki's, ah, recovery."

"Fair enough." He poured more water into her glass, pleased

that she let him do so. "And where would you travel once you leave our shores?"

"Paris," she said definitively. Then she quirked a look at him. "It was supposed to be the highlight of our itinerary. Have you ever been?" She blinked at what he knew must be the clouding of his expression, so she hastened to take back the question. "I'm sorry—I didn't mean—"

"You worry too much." He shook his head. "In truth, I don't know. But the not knowing gives me no pain." It didn't, either. He'd probably been to Paris, he thought. If so, he was sure he'd remember the details of that visit when it was necessary to do so. But so far, there was nothing related to the City of Lights that caused him distress. And he could imagine streets, buildings, churches, monuments. So that, at least, was progress.

When their food arrived, both he and Francesca seemed to realize how hungry they were at the same time. The lunch lasted through another carafe of water and a bottle of wine, the conversation between them light and easy once more. He told her information about the city—not specific memories, he still couldn't grasp those—but facts that came to him so readily it was as if he'd read them off a placard somewhere. He tried to recall if he'd done exactly that, perhaps on the day-long boat ride to Asteri Island or while he was there.

He hadn't, though. And the reason was—there'd been no information available either on the yacht or the island. No magazines, no tourist brochures, no newspapers.

"What's wrong?" Francesca asked, and he realized she was watching him again, her brows drawn together. "What are you thinking?"

"I—it's nothing," he said. "But the island had no WiFi, no electronics—at least not in my guest house. Nothing on the ship, either. I haven't seen a newspaper or website or television..." he laughed. "In over a year. An entire world is going on around me, and I don't know the first thing about it. I would have thought…" he shook his head. "I would have thought they would have wanted me to catch up. They didn't, and I didn't ask. Which seems odd, don't you think?"

"Not odd. You are recovering, healing. Your mind wanted to take things slowly, is all." She regarded him a little nervously. "I suspect the doctors didn't want you to be overwhelmed, either. Which is also reasonable, right?"

Something in her tone seemed off, but he knew no good could come of pursuing this path. Later, maybe when she was asleep, he would find a newspaper or a bar with a working television. Anything he learned would be worthwhile.

Nevertheless, a small, contrary part of him was willing to put off the inevitable end to his ignorance for a few hours longer. He didn't want to see Francesca worried, he wanted to see her relaxed. If that meant avoiding the news for a few hours more, it was a sacrifice he was more than willing to make.

Instead, he could focus on her.

"Come on," he said. "Let's find a place to hide for a while."

As he'd suspected it would, her entire face eased, her tension flowing away in a wave of relief. "I'd like that," she nodded as they stood. "There's got to be someplace near here that will work—not too fancy, but safe. Private. Not too close to the marina."

"That sounds exactly perfect," he said, and reached for her.

When she put her hand in his, it felt like coming home.

Fifteen

Fran kept her fingers entwined with Ari's the whole way up the three flights of stairs from the tiny front lobby of the hotel. She'd been in far worse accommodations, to be sure. And given that Ari had lived in a cage for the past year, she figured no matter what the room above held, he'd not complain.

More importantly, the hotel fit her need for keeping Ari out of sight until nightfall. Little more than a half mile from where they'd hidden away in the Oûrois café, the hotel was on a quiet back street off the tourist district but in a very respectable part of town—and the street was a curved one that didn't dump into a courtyard. There would be no long sightlines for watchers to observe them.

There was also a back entrance.

They'd stopped and bought clothing and bathroom supplies —as well as more food and wine—at a series of small shops along the way, though neither of them was hungry at this point. To all the world they looked like a couple out for a lazy afternoon walk, she thought. She didn't think Ari took such walks very often. He exclaimed too much over too many details, and never with a wince of pain. He was discovering his city as an outsider would, and his delight knew no bounds. Everything was beautiful and charming or majestic and impressive, and she got the feeling that she could pick up a dusty stone and he'd declare it his kin. He so clearly belonged here—in this city, this country. Surely it was only a matter of time before his mind breached the fences that were keeping him from all his memories.

Ari chuckled as he fit the long key into the door. "I don't think the desk man believed we were simply exhausted from a day at the beach."

"Good. We won't stand out then," Fran said, still focused on the logistics of getting one of the most famous men in the city out of sight. When the door opened inward on the room, however, she pulled up short.

"What's wrong?" Ari asked, stepping in beside her.

"Nothing—nothing." She stared, startled to the point of not saying anything more. The room was...well, it was something out of a fairy tale. And she'd stopped believing in fairy tales a long time ago.

It was simple, yes—a swept wooden floor with a bright red rug, an iron bed with bleached white covers, gray walls with white trim. The bathroom was down the hallway, but there was a small table with a carafe of water and two glasses beside the main window which was tall and standing open, looking out over the street.

"Hardly roughing it," Ari observed wryly, and Fran laughed, pivoting around the tiny space.

"It's perfect," she said, beaming up at him. "Exactly right. We can stay here for hours and no one will see."

"Good," Ari said. He held up the bag containing their food. "Hungry?"

"Not even remotely."

"Then wine it is." She followed him to the table as with quick, efficient movements he laid everything out. The water cups were immediately transformed into wine glasses, and he poured two generous servings, then offered a glass to Fran.

She accepted it, suddenly a little shy, as he held up his glass. "Thank you, Francesca," he said, and there was that tone in his voice again that kept making her nervous.

"For what?"

"For this room, for this day. For you."

It was exactly the kind of thing he'd been saying since he'd become Conti Goba, and she didn't know how much of his sweet gentility was truly Ari and how much was an act. Then again, he wasn't the only one acting here. She wasn't the elegantly calm Francesca Simmons, either, but the ballsy, desperate Frannie Lambert, dashing along fast enough to keep ahead of everyone else. She needed to keep her center and not forget who she really was.

"Well, thank you," she said. "You would have been fine coming to the city all on your own, though. Other than nearly dying on the open sea, anyway. For that, you definitely needed me along." She tried to infuse her voice with a teasing lilt, but she could hear the tremor behind it. *Keep your center*, she reminded herself. But the way Ari was looking at her now, her center was dissolving into a warm puddle of need.

That...couldn't be good.

Apparently oblivious to her distress, Ari fished in his pocket and pulled out the cloth packet of his identity card. They'd agreed not to study it closely until they had time to view it behind closed doors, and as he produced it Francesca exhaled in relief, glad for the distraction.

"Yes," she said. "Let's see what sort of man you are, Conti Goba."

Ari set his glass on the table and unfolded the cloth, letting it fall away. He opened up the small booklet, nudging it toward her. "Those men, they chose well," he said. "I'm quite a fine fellow of thirty years—which I can pass for with this beard—born and currently living in Makila. That's, what, about fifty miles inland," he mused, rattling off the information as if it wasn't important.

Fran stared at him, unwilling to stop the flow of his thoughts, though inside she cheered. His random geography lesson was yet another indicator that his world was beginning to flow in around him, taking on form and function.

"Father Josef, mother Maria...what do you think?"

He held up the picture beside his face, and Fran had to laugh.

"It's—close," she managed, staring at the small black-and-white photo of a swarthy-faced man who could have passed for Ari, yes...after a bar fight and a weekend in jail. "You'll need to grow your hair longer to really pull it off."

He grimaced. "I shouldn't have cut it after I left Turkey. I could have been this man's cousin. Which reminds me..." he threw the identity folder down on the table and focused on her.

"First, to Conti," Fran said hurriedly, lifting her glass. "May his life prove as interesting as his picture." She winked at him. "He looks like quite a troublemaker."

Ari picked up his glass again and touched it to hers, but his eyes had gone from curious to sensual in the space of a moment, and her own worry morphed back to desire with startling speed.

"You will have to watch out for Conti," he said. "He has a weakness for cheap wine and fine American women."

"I've heard that about him," Fran said as she tipped the glass to her lips. Cheap or not, the sweet red liquid went down easily, and Ari joined her, tossing back his drink as well. Then he leaned forward intently as she lowered her glass.

She knew what was coming, welcomed it. Anything to get Ari to focus on something other than asking questions. Questions might cause her to have to spin some tales she'd have to keep track of, but there was nothing make-believe about the way Ari made her feel. And surely she could have that for a little while longer.

Ari seemed to be thinking the same thing.

"It's a vice poor Conti can't control," he said. Then he shifted the last inch to close the space between them and pressed his lips to hers.

Fran didn't know how her glass found the table or how Ari moved so quickly, but a moment later she was being lifted up, Ari pressing her against the wall as her hands cradled his face. The roughness of his beard scraped her palms, adding to the sensory overload swamping her. He reached down and cupped his own hands around her backside and lifted her up against the wall, and she encircled his hips with her legs, savoring his strength as he braced her weight.

"Francesca," he murmured roughly as his mouth left hers, trailing kisses up the side of her face and along her ear. He repeated her name over and over again, like a benediction, and she groaned as his teeth grazed her earlobe on his way to her neck. She knotted her hands in his shirt and pulled the fabric tight, bringing him up short as he drew away from her face and stared at her.

His gaze was so filled with longing it took her breath away, and Fran had no doubt he wanted this, wanted her. She also couldn't deny how much she wanted him. He wasn't her patient, he wasn't her charge. The doctors were clear that he was healthy. But could she—should she continue down this path with him? Shouldn't she be the responsible one?

"A—ahhh," she caught herself, hiccupping over the name she almost called him. And then the moment of her resistance was lost as Ari arced his body backward, and she felt every inch of his arousal as it pressed against the most intimate part of her.

Ari, of course, surprised her again.

"You are worried about me, aren't you?" he asked, one hand flat against her back, bracing her against him as he shifted away from the wall. He easily strode the few steps it took to reach the bed and stood there, staring down at her. "I can see it in your eyes. So much caution, so much fear. But in this, you don't need to worry. I'm not sick, Francesca."

Before she could reply, he leaned down, easing her lightly to the bed and stretching himself over her, his left hip sliding to the side as his right leg bent, trapping her in the frame of his body. He dropped a light kiss on her shoulder, where her shifting tank bared her skin, and she shivered at the pent up energy she could feel even at such a brief touch.

"But your memory—" she tried again, only to have Ari roll over her, his body pinning her to the soft mattress, his hands braced to either side of her head.

"My memory will return when it's ready to return," he said. "Until it does, making new memories will have to suffice. Like this one."

Sixteen

Ryker bent over Francesca's beautiful face, staring at her. If he never remembered another moment of his former life, it would be a tradeoff worth having because she was in his arms, in his bed. There would be time later for rational thought. For now, he wanted to think with nothing more than his body and his heart.

For now, they could live solely in the present.

He met her gaze as her lips slowly teased into a smile. "If you're sure?" she asked, and the soft tremor in her voice turned him inside out.

"I'll stop and rest if I get tired," he said. He leaned forward then and brushed his lips down her forehead, across the tip of her nose, and then lightly, so lightly against her perfect mouth. "So far, I think I'll manage."

Her lips pursed together to stifle a giggle, but Ryker kept going. He found the pulse jumping at the base of her neck. He kissed that too, reveling in the way it kicked up its pace, then traced a line of kisses down the collar of Francesca's delicate tank top. She was right. Their clothing was too well-made for the likes of two shiftless twenty-somethings out for a day in the capital city, but no one had looked twice at them. Everyone had seen what they'd expected to see.

Now Ryker wanted to see more.

Francesca's tank was the type that buttoned down the front. Moving himself over to one side, Ryker reached for it, batting away her hands when she realized what he wanted.

"It's been a long time since I've had the pleasure of undressing a woman," he said roughly. Francesca's hands stilled, her large eyes fixed on him as he worked the long line of pearlized buttons free. He spread the fabric wide and took in her smooth skin beneath. Her breasts, snugly wrapped in a bra the same color as the shirt, rose and fell beneath his gaze, and her stomach trembled when he drifted his hand across it. He traced his fingers up to the front clasp of her bra and smiled wryly at her.

"This is almost too easy."

"I didn't want to overtax you," she said, and he laughed again, amazed at the unfettered joy that being with her brought him. Then he sprang the clasp on her bra and smoothed that material away as well, the need in him spiking high at the sight of her full, stiff-peaked breasts. But slowly, so slowly that it was almost a torture to him, he drew his fingers up and over the swell of one of those breasts, zeroing in on the tip as it pebbled beneath his fingers. Francesca's breath caught as he grazed the tight nipple once, then twice.

"You must tell me what you like," he murmured as he leaned into her again, his mouth following where his fingers led. He tasted the soft heat of her skin while her heart clamored beneath his lips, his own mouth going dry as he kissed her right breast, his hand closing of its own volition around her left.

"That," she managed in a strangled cry as his lips closed around her nipple. "That," as he suckled harder, her back arching off the bed. The intensity of her reaction galvanized him, and he slid his hand down her belly, his fingers catching on the waistband of her pants. He slipped the button easily as she hissed a soft breath between her teeth. Then he felt the slide of the silk beneath his fingers, and it was all he could do not to rip the clothes from her body.

"R-Ryker," Francesca managed, and the soft desire in her voice wound him up further. He leaned back so he could see more of her. Her gaze remained fixed on his face as he smoothed his hand over her belly, edging his fingers down again, unable to stay away from how her body flowed in such smooth and perfect curves.

"I want to see all of you," he murmured. When she didn't say no, he glanced up to meet her eyes.

It was there again—the caution lurking below the need he could see reflected back at him, a need surely as strong as his own. "All of you," he repeated, like a mantra, and she nodded once, then a second time, her lips creasing into a nervous smile.

She didn't need to tell him again. Ryker hooked his thumbs into either side of her pants, slicking them over her hips and all the way down. He didn't trust himself to focus on anything except removing her clothes until the very last moment. As he pulled the clothes free of her feet, she slid back on the bed, toward the headboard, working off her bra and tank and throwing them aside. Then, suddenly, she was adorned by nothing but her long dark hair, spilling over her shoulders, half covering her breasts. She wasn't self-conscious, he realized. Not about her body—nor should she be. She was perfectly formed, broad shoulders, a gently curving hourglass torso, rounded hips and long legs that even now bent as she sat higher on the bed.

The next words out of her mouth, though, had him blinking in confusion. "I don't think I like the way you do things in Oûros."

"What?" He tore his gaze away from her body, and she gestured to him.

"You've spent your time taking my clothes off, but what about giving me something to look at?"

The color was higher in her cheeks, so she wasn't as brazen as her words made her out to be, but Ryker laughed. "I can see how that isn't very fair," he rumbled, "but I would ask for a special dispensation to kiss you first."

Her smile was sweet, but a little confused. "You haven't done that already?" she teased.

"Not like this."

Francesca breathed out a hum of surprise as he crawled back on the bed. One of his hands slid up her ankle to hold her in place when she would have brought her legs together. He angled between her legs and kissed the inside of her calf. Her entire leg jumped with the touch, and he chuckled, her nervousness adding to the intense pleasure of exploring her in such a new and unfamiliar way.

"You are so beautiful," he murmured, moving up her leg to the inside of her knee, stretching her wider as he noted her fists knotting up the sheets. She was affected as much as he was, he realized, though there was no way a body this exquisite could have been denied the touch of a man as long as he'd been barred from touching a woman. Still, when he reached her thigh, it quivered. Francesca's laugh was shaky as his mouth edged yet higher, his breath warming her skin a moment before he replaced its touch with his lips.

"Ryker," she managed, but her voice caught as he reached his destination, and he leaned the final inch, drawing his tongue along the most intimate part of her. Whatever she said next was lost in a sigh as her body seemed to become boneless beneath his touch, and he reached up until his fingers connected with hers.

Instead of knotting the sheets any longer, she gripped his

hand, and that encouragement was all he needed. He drew his mouth along her quivering sex and explored each fold and peak, mapping the intimate territory so that he might return again and again.

Which he fully planned to.

When his tongue brushed over the most sensitive nub, Francesca drew in a sharp breath, going rigid beneath him. "Okay, my turn," she pleaded, her free hand coming up to brace itself against his shoulder. "I'm pretty sure you're breaking some sort of international treaty here and I demand equal time."

"You'll get it," he said, but he didn't shift position, and as he spoke her body arched beneath him again, his words a rumble against her as she quivered. "But not before I do—this."

Seventeen

Fran couldn't quell the roar of need thundering through her body, a train that had no intention of stopping. The touch of Ari's mouth drove her impossibly close to climax. Then he'd shift again, moving ever so slightly off the most sensitive bundle of nerves, so that she was let hanging from a cliff by her fingernails, not quite able to let go.

Worse, she was pretty sure he was doing it on purpose, winding her up so tight just to let her unravel again, stretching out her release.

"You're killing me," she moaned. Without consciously realizing she was doing it, she drew her hands together and buried them in his thick hair, tightening her hold enough to stop him when he tried to shift off a third time. His laughter reverberated against her and she quivered, a sensual tuning fork struck at precisely the right place. He didn't say anything—he didn't need to say anything. With a sigh that she felt all the way to her toes, he tilted forward a final time and slid his tongue in exactly—the right—way—

She shattered.

Fran was never one to do things by halves, but the fact

she didn't scream loud enough to peel the paint off the walls was perhaps her greatest feat of self-restraint. Loosening her hold on Ari's head, she flailed for a pillow, jackknifing her body away from him as she buried her face in the soft coolness of the freshly laundered pillowcase and gasping as her body was racked with convulsions. No sooner had she retreated, however, then the man who'd blown up her world reached for her, wrapping her in his arms and muttering nonsense in a foreign language while she tried to remember what the hell her name was, let alone his.

"Shh—shhh," he murmured as she clung to the pillow and he clung to her. He'd removed his shirt and trousers, she realized vaguely, the warmth of his legs and arms now surrounding her, the strength of his broad chest against her back. It was so right, so perfect that she could feel the tears welling in her eyes, and she fought them back ruthlessly as she snapped back to awareness of who she was, where she was, and who she was with.

Fran turned in Ari's arms and gazed up at him, his gaze intent as he stared down at her, searching her face. "Good?" he asked when she didn't say anything.

She smiled. "Very good." She untangled her hand from the pillow and flattened it against his chest, pushing him back. He allowed her to roll him over to his back, but his hands stayed gripped on her, and she sprawled over his body as he stretched out across the rumpled sheets.

Her eyes snapped to his as she realized he'd done more than remove his trousers. "I thought I was going to get equal time," she grumbled, coming up to her knees on either side of his hips. The movement ground her against his shaft and his gaze flared hotter as he stared up at her.

"I'd thought this would be more efficient," he said tightly.

"It seems that way," she smiled and widened her legs slightly, seating her more firmly against him.

Ari clothed looked like a slightly shaggy, heavily tanned version of the man she'd seen in countless royal photos. Roguishly handsome, quick to grin, with sparkling eyes to offset the almost painful beauty of his features. In those photos his cheekbones and chin had been sculpted, his lips perfectly formed, his gaze piercing in what she supposed was a princely way.

But the man lying beneath her now, staring at her with such intense need, was about as far away from princely as she could imagine. The face hadn't changed much except for an ineffable age that seemed to settle on him, the result of a year's worth of harsh living that she suspected wouldn't go away. But his body was traced with fading bruising and a constellation of small scars—some thick, some thin.

Her breath caught as he shifted beneath her, the sensual heat of him a needed counterpoint to her discovery of the trials he'd undergone. "You've been so hurt."

"I haven't," he growled, his hands tightening on her. "Banged up in the crash, and the work at the construction site was hard. I wasn't mistreated. If it's me you're concerned about, don't be. If there's something else..."

His gaze held hers and she saw the question in them. It was all she could do not to laugh out loud. "You're not seriously about to question whether or not I want you to make love to me," she murmured, and the relief in his gaze was immediate and sharp. He opened his hand, where she realized he'd been clutching a foil wrapped condom, and she lifted her brows.

"When exactly did you pick this up?"

He grinned as she ripped open the package and scooted back along his legs, but his gaze left her face and dropped to her hands. "It was part of the identity kit I bought," he joked. "In Oûros we believe in safety first."

"Do you?" She finished sheathing him and slid forward again, kneeling as she walked her hands along the bed until her face was level with his. "I have to say," she murmured, "I like your country more and more the longer I'm here."

Ari's next words were lost in a hiss as she fit herself over his shaft, pausing a moment to let her body get used to the sensual intrusion. Twin desires warred within her—one to let her eyes drift shut and simply enjoy the moment, the second to open them wide, drinking in the sight of Ari's face, his body, his taut expression as she slid over him inch by careful inch, the pulse of their bodies finding their own perfect synchronicity.

"You—feel incredible," he murmured and there was a year's worth of wonder in his words—a year and probably more. The depth of his pain went beyond missing the simple pleasure of a woman. It extended to the deeper, more damaging loneliness of being without a friend or countryman or even the solace of his memories.

Fran leaned forward and pressed her lips against his. He kissed her back almost tentatively at first, his hands coming up to cradle her face as she slid further over him, taking him fully into her body. They were one unit, one being, and the rightness of it shook her to her core. She didn't trust herself to speak or even to look at Ari anymore, so she sighed and deepened the kiss.

He didn't seem to mind. One of Ari's hands slid around her head, the other down the length of her back as they moved together, both of them memorizing the other, fixing this moment in their minds.

She exhaled deeply and drew herself upright again, finally trusting herself to open her eyes. Ari lay bathed in sunlight, his face arrested with pleasure, his hands now on her hips. His gaze roamed over her body, but she was pretty sure her view was better.

She smoothed her hands over his chest, her fingers taking in the raised surface of a myriad of scars, her mind refusing to process everything she was seeing. When she met his eyes again, for a moment she saw challenge there, a challenge and maybe a little fear. Then Ari pulled her down to him, his arms wrapped around her body and her breasts compressed against his chest. In a smooth, athletic move, he reversed their positions, and once again she was stretched out on the bed and he was on top, staring down at her with glee.

"Don't think you've got the upper hand because you're on top," Fran sniffed, her assertion clearly so ludicrous Ari laughed out loud. "I can be very tough if I need to be."

"I'll keep that mind," he rumbled. Then with a sigh he bent over her and took her mouth with his.

Eighteen

R yker wasn't sure what heaven might feel like, but he was pretty sure he was experiencing it now. Francesca was everything he was certain he'd always loved most in women—confident, strong, and driven to achieve. Right now she was about to drive him to distraction, but he could manage it—would manage it.

She had no idea how much he needed this right now. Needed her.

Beneath him, Francesca sighed again and stretched out over the plush mattress, a bed he now appreciated so much he would happily take it with him from hotel to hotel if it meant more moments like this. She shifted again, and the pressure on his shaft ratcheted up, scattering his thoughts then hyper-focusing them into one blinding need.

"You're so beautiful," he murmured, and she smiled in a way he suspected meant she was used to hearing such platitudes. But he couldn't take the time to explain why his declaration was different. She wouldn't believe him—not here.

And there would be time for talking later.

Leveraging his weight to one hand, he reached out with the

otherand cupped her breast as her eyelids fluttered open again. As she watched him, he squeezed, his fingers parting to allow the tight tip of her nipple to peek through. She hummed with a purely feminine pleasure. That hum, and the slight curve of her lips, knocked him up to another level. He had no illusions that he was going to last this first time.

He also had no doubts that there would be many future opportunities to make up for his lapse.

He rocked into Francesca, gritting his teeth as her legs fell open, allowing him to fill her more thoroughly. He bent and covered her mouth with his again, smiling as her lips opened against the pressure of his mouth. She was baring all to him, he thought. Or, perhaps not all, but all she could.

Her hands lifted and settled on either side of his back, guiding him thrust for thrust. As he lifted himself again, moving to his knees, her fingers fell away. She bent her knees, opening wider. The resulting shift of her body slid him nearer to her center, and he was surrounded by her damp heat, the pressure of her slick and tight around him almost too much to bear.

He would have been able to bear it—would have been able to continue indefinitely—were it not for the expression on Francesca's face.

Her eyes weren't closed, exactly, but they'd narrowed to near slits, her lids drooping sensually as she stared at him, her mouth slightly open and her breath coming out in pants as he slid into her then out again, each time pressing harder, deeper. Her face was a study, not in relaxation, but a soul-deep expression of satisfaction. When he murmured a sigh, her gaze flicked up and he was taken with its intensity for all her apparent languor. In that moment, she was perfect—not solely for him, but for this place, this country, this world. The one thing he knew that was right and true in his life, when everything else was in shambles.

Francesca chose that moment to smile, and her bright and sudden joy was all that it took to send Ryker crashing over the edge. He stiffened and her hands tightened on his arms, her eyes now flaring wide as she understood what was happening, wanted it to happen. As ready for it as he was, his climax came swift and strong, so powerful that he clamped his hands on her hips and held her as his eyesight dimmed then flashed white.

When he shook his head it cleared again, and there was Francesca beneath him—beautiful, serene Francesca, watching him knowingly.

"Beautiful," he murmured again.

He leaned down to kiss her then rolled away, ridding himself of the condom then grabbing a fistful of towels from the stand by the door. Suddenly, the weight of the day's events over-took him, and he stumbled his way back to Francesca, restored by her quiet laughter as he climbed into bed with her once more.

"We should stay indoors, I'm thinking," he said as he moved up beside her.

If he was afraid that she would be self-conscious, he needn't have worried. Francesca rested on her bent elbow, as relaxed as he'd ever seen her. She nodded. "A lot depends on where you want to go, but no matter what, nighttime is better. Stefan and his men will have likely moved out of the city by then, or they'll restrict themselves to wherever they think you might be. That can't be too many places, especially in a city as small as this one."

He lifted his brows at her. "Now that so much time has passed without me doing any harm to anyone, do you truly think they'll be searching for me so diligently as that?" he asked, testing her. "Why would they care? Stefan assured me I had not committed any crime, and if I should stumble across someone who knows me or my family, what is the harm in that?"

Francesca's response was stilted. "They want to ensure your safety is all. That you return to your family healthy and whole."

He shook his head. She knew Stefan would be searching for him. If he hadn't committed a crime, there was but one explanation. "That's not reason enough." He sighed. "I know the truth."

Francesca went still, and he shook his head. "I'm not an idiot, Francesca. I was flying an expensive craft and wearing expensive gear when I crashed. I was being very well paid to do what I did, and someone likely feels guilty for what I have suffered."

Her brows went up. "Guilty?"

"It's the only explanation that makes sense," he said. "Whoever put me into that plane on a regular basis is now trying to ensure I return to my family healthy and whole, as you say. To put me up on the island of the royal family, give me the level of care they have, watch over my every step—they are a very rich group indeed. And I am grateful. But their guilt is misplaced." He grimaced. "And that doesn't change the fact that I have a family out there—perhaps in this very city, perhaps all the way to Mikala, with my friend Conti Goba. If my benefactors are not willing to contact them, that is certainly their choice. But it is my choice to attempt to find them. To piece back together this life I've been unable to live for so long."

He leaned forward and touched his forehead to hers. "You watch me with such concern, but this is the right thing for me, Francesca. I don't have my memories, no. But I have my back, I have my hands. I have my mind, what's left of it. I was able to row a boat and steer a larger craft as if I'd been doing it my entire life. I suspect I'll be able to pilot an airplane as well. Or run fishing lines. Or do whatever it is I did before the storm dumped me into the sea. I know things about this city, this country—just not about my own family. All I have to do now is find the trailing edge of that life and follow it back to my family."

"But every time you think of them, or remember something about them, you experience pain," Francesca said, frowning. "Don't you think that's a warning? Not about your family, necessarily, but—I mean, shouldn't you have a professional with you when you go searching for these answers?"

"I do have someone with me," he said. "I have you."

The flash of wariness was back, skittering over her features before she once again composed herself. "I'm not a professional anything," she said. "Not yet, and certainly not with you."

He lifted himself on one elbow. This was a good enough time as any to learn a bit more about her. "I don't know about that. You seem to have some skill with knowing where to acquire false papers in the capital city of my homeland—which is some trick, considering you're American."

"I wondered when you'd get around to asking about that."

To his surprise, Francesca didn't balk at the line of questioning. Instead, she lay back on the pillow, her gaze on him light, her manner deceptively easy.

"Where I grew up, the neighborhood bar was a favorite hangout for college kids—and kids who wanted to be college age," she said. "There was a thriving market there for fake IDs, and the locals had gotten pretty good at it. Then, when I went away to college, one of the neighborhoods near the campus had the same sort of bar on the same scrubby street. I went inside, and it might as well have been an identical collection of guys in the back, setting up shop."

He lifted his brows, and she shrugged. "I've traveled a little with school, not always in the nicest of towns, and it's sort of become a thing for me. I find the shabbiest little bars near a thriving tourist or student district, especially if there's a port or a marina or a border crossing—anywhere people can get through that doesn't require public credentials. Chances are, you'll find a bar like the one you went into today."

"It sounds like you should travel in safer circles," Ryker said. Francesca laughed, as he'd hoped she would. She slanted her gaze away from him, relaxing yet another notch. It didn't take much convincing for her to shift in his arms, her back to his chest, and drift in the soft sunlight.

As she settled into a drowsy slumber, Ryker kept his gaze on the window, focusing on keeping his body loose, his breathing even. He lowered his face to her hair, kissing her softly, but he knew the truth.

Francesca was lying to him.

He didn't know why, or about what, specifically, but he suspected it was to protect him, not her, and that made no sense. There were too many things that made no sense, but that was going to change, he decided.

Starting tonight.

Nineteen

F ran's nerves ratcheted higher with each block they passed. Ari had insisted on taking a taxi to the municipal airstrip where small engine planes were kept, including the planes of the royal family. He didn't say that's why he wanted to go, but it didn't matter.

She should be happy, she knew. He was clearly remembering more. He knew he was a pilot, and he knew he had taken off from this airstrip. Whether that was simple deductive reasoning or legitimate memory, she didn't know, but Ari was getting closer to a breakthrough.

She could only hope it didn't come with a breakdown.

Ari had agreed to a clothing change, but his new attire was no less distinctive—loose cut work pants and a work shirt. He'd even acquired a belt of tools that now lay next to him in the back of a cab. He looked the part of a mechanic, and he sat forward, tense and alert, with each turn the cabbie made to get them closer to the airstrip.

"What if they don't let you in?" she asked.

"They will, I feel certain of that," he said, patting the tools. "Workers come in and out all the time."

"But workers for planes that people actually own. People you don't know." She shot him a glance. "Right?"

He shrugged. "Right." Still, his expression was intent as the cabbie slowed, cutting off their conversation. Ari paid for their fare with cash, and then he was out the door, holding it for Fran as she stepped into the warm evening sky.

The airstrip was a smaller affair than she expected, and to her shock—it wasn't fenced off, not in any meaningful way. "Don't you people believe in security?"

"It takes a special kind of criminal to steal a plane, and all flight manifests are logged," Ari said automatically. "Cars require clearance. Foot traffic usually goes through the main building, but not always."

Fran frowned at him. "You're remembering this?"

"Not specifically, no. It's simple knowledge." Ari fixed his attention fixed on the squat metal building at the head of the field. "In the evening, though, there's a simple watch. One man, generally the same man who's been here all day."

Ari's wince told her that remembering did cause at least some pain, but he pushed on. "He'll be tired now, probably bored, but a distraction would alarm him. No one but an asshole sends his mechanic out to tune up an airplane in the evening unless they're getting ready to leave at an odd hour."

Fran scanned the building. A parking gate blocked its driveway, with low fencing stretching out in either direction. No one in a vehicle could enter the drive without keying themselves through the long bar. She glanced at Ari as he strapped on his tool belt, and she had to admit, he did appear to be a man who knew his way around airplanes. But they were on the outside of the airstrip, looking in. And there remained the man in the security building.

"Okay, how do you plan to get in?"

"There are some men out there," Ari said, gesturing to the

field. She could see two or three small golf-cart-style vehicles—but not their drivers. "It's not a matter so much of getting in among the planes as looking like you've been there for some time."

"But..." Fran shook her head, still confused. "If you go trotting across the field—the security guard will see you."

"He would, ordinarily," he nodded. He pivoted to her then, and the expression on his face was one she recognized all too well—and not from the halls of the royal family.

"Oh no," she said, lifting her hands. "You can't expect me to serve as your cover. I don't speak Oûrois! I can't even credibly ask for the bathroom."

"I don't need more than a few minutes," Ari said. "You see that plane over there—the larger one?"

She squinted in the direction he was pointing. "Yes," she said warily.

"The insignia on the back—it's the same as was on the royal family's yacht. I don't know Stefan Mihal's role with the family, but I suspect it's prominent if they gave him the run of their pet island."

Fran stifled a groan. "And that's good, why?"

"If I get stopped, I'll tell them Stefan Mihal sent me, and they can call him themselves." Ari grinned.

"Won't they check your ID?"

He shrugged. "If they do, I'll tell them to contact Stefan Mihal. They'll have no choice but to do so. Fortunately, it's dinnertime and I'm sure like any good aristocrat, Stefan has obligations. It's possible he's still on the royal island."

Fran rather doubted that. Once they'd decamped to the city, she suspected the island had been deserted within a few short hours. By now, everyone would be back in the capital city, searching for them.

She glanced around the remote airstrip. There hadn't been a

limo sitting idle in the parking lot, so maybe they hadn't guessed Ari would be here. But they would, eventually. "What is it you think you're going to find?" she asked. "The plane you flew— even if it took off from here, it's gone. And if you're out in the field, you won't be able to check flight records, even if they do keep those onsite from so long ago."

He shook his head. "It's not the plane I'm looking for, it's…" he sighed. "When I remember something, truly remember it, it's not simply enough for me to conjure up an image in my mind, an image I think or hope might have happened. The pain doesn't come unless I'm physically experiencing the place where the memory happened, or actually seeing something that sparks the troublesome memory. That's what I'm hoping for here."

Fran didn't like the sound of that. "You're hoping you see something that triggers pain?"

He nodded, as if he wasn't consigning himself to a grueling test. "I'm counting on it. I was a pilot, and I have very high-level keepers who came to fetch me once they figured out I survived the crash. This airport isn't for commercial flights, but private ones. If I'm right, it's the last place I was in Oûros before ending up in the sea. It's possible that walking these steps will be the bridge I need to remember more about what happened that night…or at least to explain why I can't recall more about my family or my work."

He sighed. "There's a block I'm throwing up, and I don't know why." He jerked a thumb to the airstrip. "The answers might be there."

"But what if you collapse out there?" Fran asked, searching his face. He didn't seem distressed—though he should be, this close to such potentially impactful revelations.

He shook his head. "I won't," he said. "I've got to see this for myself, but I don't feel the pressure I expected. I feel excitement. Anticipation. It's different."

"I don't have a second phone for you or any way to contact you if something goes wrong, though." Fran bit her lip. "If you could just wait until we pick up a burner phone..."

"Nothing's going to go wrong." Ari turned to her, and Fran's heart kicked hard at the look in his eyes. Since she'd met him, he'd regarded her with need, affection, camaraderie, and even simple laughter. But the expression on his face now was different. It was one of hope.

"I'll be careful, Francesca," he said. "I know I can't keep asking for your help, but this one thing is critical. If you could distract the security guard until I have a chance to walk among the planes, in the last place I know for certain I was before my accident... I think it could change everything."

She sighed, then squinted at the squat building. "Okay. I'll help you—or at least I'll try. What is it you want me to do?"

Twenty

R yker watched Francesca all the way until she disappeared into the building. Then, he immediately moved to the structure's far side, taking the corner at an ambling walk.

Francesca's role was simple. She was to tell whomever asked that she'd taken a taxi to the municipal airport by mistake, not the international one. She'd gotten out and trotted up the drive before realizing her error. If the guard would be so kind as to call her a new taxi, she would be so grateful...and if he could talk to her a little about what he did, that would be even better. She adored Oûros and all its people, and this little airstrip was so cute, and...

In the end, she'd agreed it was a reasonable plan.

Ryker knew it was more than reasonable. Francesca's beauty would bowl over the grouchiest of security guards, and her sweet manner and quiet speech would make her seem every inch the lady, despite her casual clothes. By the time the taxi pulled up, he'd be back on the street as well, ready to hop in a taxi and speed back to the center of the city.

Now that he was alone and walking through the airstrip

though, he wasn't so sure. There were maybe about a half-dozen planes parked here, each in its own clearly marked section. The big plane with the royal crest stood at the far edge of the field, but there was plenty to look at while he walked.

To look at and churn through.

He hadn't been entirely honest with Francesca—in fact he hadn't been honest at all. The pain rioting through his mind right now was enough to make his eyes water, and it got worse the closer he stalked to the royal plane. There were purple flowers growing wild at the edge of the airstrip, definitely more of the borage blooms, as familiar to him as the back of his hand. He knew that, without question, he'd made this same walk hundreds—even thousands of times before. Sometimes alone, sometimes with others. Laughing, talking, joking—always joking. His heart had been light in this place, too light almost. It didn't seem like he'd come here to work, as he'd thought.

But who came to an airstrip for pleasure?

He gritted his teeth, nearly stumbling as another flash of pain seared through him. He passed a man on his right who climbed out of the cockpit of his craft. Not a mechanic but a pilot, Ryker could see at a glance. The man glanced up and offered a half wave before checking the motion, his expression confused.

Then Ryker was past him and the man grunted something he couldn't hear, and turned back to his plane.

There was no additional pain in his recognition of that man, if in fact he even knew him. He wasn't the problem here.

So what was?

Ryker blew out a long breath as he reached the royal plane. He stared hard at the insignia on its tail, its loops and swirls tugging at his memory. He'd been almost sure he was a pilot for the royal family, but now that he was here, even that certainty was wavering. His sight was beginning to flag with the intensity of his headache, but no one had challenged him as he crossed the field. He glanced back to the squat security station, and his blood ran cold.

Another plane stood there that he hadn't seen at first, smaller than the royal craft. It was every bit as luxurious as the royal plane, though. Sleek and light, it was painted bright white with a similar insignia on its tail to that of the Oûros royal family. Similar, but not quite the same.

"Who do you belong to?" he muttered, as he staggered onward, certain that he needed to reach the royal plane. This second plane wasn't the goal, wasn't the problem. It couldn't be. His answers were tied up with the royal insignia—answers that were so close to the surface of his mind, so close. If he could just...get...closer.

Ryker finally made it to the plane on wobbly legs, his hand reaching out to stabilize himself against the wheel well.

The moment he touched the smooth metal of the plane, however, lightning seemed to crack in his mind—and he went down amidst a cacophony of screams.

Twenty-One

Waiting for the taxi, Fran stared out the window as the security guard rattled on about the illustrious history of Oûros, then drifted her attention to the wall beside it. And blinked.

"Who's that?" She blurted, pointing.

The man turned, then snorted as he followed her line of sight. "Minister of Tourism, Count Silas Saleri. He keeps his plane here. He also slaps his picture on everything he can to promote Oûros. You've probably seen him on posters around the city. You can't turn around without seeing the man, but I suppose we need him to keep the tourists flowing to our beautiful country. Who would know about us otherwise? And there is so much to see here."

"Minister of...Tourism," Fran echoed, a little shakily. She'd seen this man before—knew him. And not in a good way. But how? Had he been at a party at the palace? Someone she'd seen on the street? A billboard or poster, like the security guard said?

A word slipped through her mind, jagged and awful. *Monster.* "He's friends with the royal family?"

"More than friends—related. Cousin of the queen, distantly.

They say his daughter was intended to marry Prince Aristotle, before—"

"*What?*" Fran barely managed to keep herself from squeaking as she stared back at the security guard, and flapped her hand to try to recover. "That's so sad," she finally managed.

"Truly sad," the security guard agreed dolefully. Then he brightened. "But his brother, Prince Kristos, he's strong. Dedicated. He'll make our proud country shine like never before. He'll..." The man droned on, allowing Fran the opportunity to glance out the window again...just in time to see Ari drop to his knees.

Ari sprawled over the wheel of the farthest plane, the aircraft with the mark of the royal family, and her heart practically exploded to three times its normal size. She was about to blow her cover sky high when Ari staggered upright again, wheeling away from the plane. She counted three long moments until he was past the view of the window, then refocused fully on the guard. Now the man was expounding on the importance of air flight to Oûros's economy, still diligently practicing his English on her. According to the large digital clock on the wall, she waited another two full minutes until she broke in.

"You've taught me so much in such a short time," she gushed, mentally projecting how long it would take Ari to get from the plane to the road, assuming he was running straight— and didn't encounter a fence without a gate he could exit through easily. "I'm sorry to have interrupted you, and even sorrier that I couldn't see that the airport wasn't the right one. I'm sure my taxi is near—I'll go out to meet it."

He beamed at her. "It's no problem at all, Miss. You will catch your flight?"

"I'm sure I will. That shouldn't be a problem," she said breezily. Ari had to be nearly clear, even staggering. "I'm meeting friends and they have my bags. I just couldn't pass up the opportunity to shop a bit more."

"Ah, yes," the attendant said, his grin knowing. "I have three daughters. Shopping, it is very important."

She thanked him again profusely, and said she'd return if the taxi didn't arrive, but it took another full minute to convince the man that she really and truly did need some fresh air.

By the time she got out of the building, Ari was nowhere to be found. Fran started up the road, walking fast, and within about a minute a taxi crested a small rise ahead of her. She flagged it down and practically leaped into the back seat, speaking fast.

"You speak English? Yes? Did you see a man on the road, probably staggering, maybe looking drunk? Holding his head like this?"

The cabbie's eyes widened as she demonstrated, and he nodded several times. "He hurt you?" he asked, instantly outraged.

"No! No, he's my friend. He's very sick, not drunk. I have to help him get back to our hotel. Where did you see him—?"

The taxi driver frowned at her. "I thought you had to go to the airport?"

Anger snapped hard in Fran's gut, but she flashed the man her most desperate smile. "I couldn't very well tell the security guard that I'd lost my boyfriend, could I? But—could you help me? Please?"

Maybe she sounded as frantic as she felt, because the taxi driver shrugged and wheeled the car around, heading back up the road. By the time they surged over the small hill again, Fran was almost in the front seat herself, leaning forward.

"There! That man, there. Oh my God, that's him."

"You sure he's not drunk?" the driver said skeptically, but he slowed the car.

"He's not—his head, he gets terrible migraines. Headaches." She resisted the urge to pound her own head with her hand. Instead, she pulled out a thick wad of euros. "I have enough money to get us back to the city—our hotel—and a big tip for you if you'll wait while I get him in the car? You don't have to help. I know he seems out of it."

"Bah! Of course I will help." The man's mood shifted, either because of the money or because the entire country of Oûros really was full of chivalrous men. He cruised slowly to where Ari sat hunched over. Fran was out of the car almost before it stopped, but she caught herself immediately. Taking a deep breath, she forced herself to move slowly, carefully toward Ari.

"Ryker?" she asked. Ari merely groaned, shaking his head in confusion.

"Honey, we need to go now," she continued. "I have a taxi for us, and we can get you something for your headache."

Ari blurted a string of words in Oûrois, and the taxi driver stiffened. "He says the bastard tried to kill him."

"He did! Well." Fran's smile grew a little strained. "I think he's in a great deal of pain."

The man snorted. She tried again. "Honey, can you hear me? It's Francesca. Could we—I'm coming up to you now to help you. I'm here to help."

She took the final step and, swallowing, laid a hand on Ari's shoulder, her entire body poised for flight. To her shock and relief, he didn't lash out, but peered up at her, his entire face haggard. "Help?" he rasped in English, and she didn't hesitate. There was no recognition in his eyes, but no fight either.

"Help—yes." She slid his arm over her shoulder and looked at the driver. "Can you try to explain? Normally, his English is very good."

The man hastened up to her and drew Ari's other arm around his neck as well, and together the two of them muscled him toward the cab. He was bigger than she remembered, but that was what dead weight would do to a body. She'd dragged more than a few drunks across the floor of Bert's Bar & Grill, so she knew from experience.

When they were almost to the taxi, Ari finally found his feet. He half-stumbled the rest of the way into the back seat as Fran held the door open as far as it would go. As soon as she slammed it behind him, she raced around to the other side. "I swear, if he gets sick or does any damage to your vehicle, I'll pay you three times the fare. I am so grateful—"

"Enough, enough!" the man was half-laughing now as he slid behind the wheel, though Ari lolled back crazily in his seat and sagged against the far window. "I'll get you where you need to go. He is lucky enough to have you by his side, eh?"

Whether Ari heard the man's words or simply was responding to her nearness, he reached out and grabbed one of Francesca's hands. His own hand was on fire. She brought it to her face, laying the back of it along her cheek as she braced his forearm against her. She gave the cabbie the address of their small hotel, and as the night drew down, they bounced back through the streets of the city, Ari continuing to mutter in Oûrois.

What was she going to do if he had somehow forgotten how to speak English? She had her phone, sure, but that took forever. And she'd left her phrase book back at the royal palace.

The palace. Fran closed her eyes, willing the nightmare to end. Here she was supposed to be helping Ari, protecting him in some small way or, at the very least, doing no harm as he struggled through his recovery. And she'd pushed him all the way to a collapse! She should have known the airfield was a bad idea, no matter how much he'd lobbied for it. She should have known he would go too far, have some sort of psychic break. She'd been thinking too much as a layperson and not as a soon-to-be coun-selor, and she should have known better!

They rode in relative silence the rest of the way to the hotel. By the time they reached their tiny street, Ari appeared to be asleep.

The cabbie regarded her dubiously as she counted out the bills. "Are you sure you'll be okay?" he asked, and Ari stirred.

"I'll be fine," Fran said with a confidence she didn't feel. She popped the back door, flooding the taxi with light. "Thank you —truly. For all you've done. And for simply being there when I needed you." She forced herself to stay cheerful. "You don't know how much that means to me in a foreign country."

The cabbie was no longer focusing on her, and she glanced over at Ari, who was now fully awake, his eyes clear and lucid, his face unnaturally pale beneath the cab's dome. The driver's face was screwed up in confusion, and dread pooled in her gut.

"You know," he said, sliding his glance back to her. "He looks very familiar, now that I can see his face."

Ari's rich voice filled the back of the taxi. "I have that kind of face," he said in perfect English, and Fran almost sagged in relief. Then he pushed open his own door and stepped into the night.

<h1 style="text-align:center">Twenty-Two</h1>

R yker stretched his neck as he held the door for Francesca, allowing her a few more moments to soothe away the cabbie's questions. He couldn't remember how he got in the taxi, let alone all the way home, but he felt like he'd run a marathon.

Francesca joined him on the sidewalk and pushed the taxi door closed, then they both stood in silence for a long moment as the taxi pulled away. He sensed her concern, and he cursed himself for his clumsiness. He didn't know what he'd done to upset her, but he suspected it had something to do with the unremembered taxi ride.

"Should we go upstairs?" she asked cautiously, and he considered that, then glanced down the street. The night life was starting to stir in the city, and he could not bear to be cooped up. Not when he'd already missed so much, and not when so much anxiety tightened his gut, refusing to let him be.

"Would you wait for me there?" he asked, pointing at a corner café with tables, some of which were already filled. "I'd like to change clothes to match you, but I don't want to have you—"

"No," Francesca said, her vehemence startling him. "I left

you alone once tonight. I'm not doing it again. If you want to change I understand that," she gestured to his tool belt, now sagging from his waist. "But I won't leave you."

Her tone was fierce, and Ryker found he didn't want to argue with her. He couldn't ask her what he'd done, not yet, but he had no desire to cause her any more pain.

Instead he nodded. "Then if you would escort me upstairs and wait while I change?" he asked, offering his arm.

She took it, but her manner was too fraught for his liking, and they didn't speak as they mounted the stairs to their room and stepped inside the bedchamber. The shower was down the hallway, and he grabbed both clothes and supplies before Francesca could come up with a reason for him not to bathe. At least she didn't insist on standing with him in a public shower, for all that sounded enticing.

As water sluiced over him, Ryker took stock of his mind again, as he'd tried to do since coming back to his senses first at the side of the airstrip, then in the cab. There was a chunk of time he could not account for, from the moment he'd left Francesca and rounded the metal security building to the moment he'd awakened at the side of the road. Intellectually, he knew he'd gone to the airport to walk the strip and see the planes. He'd dressed as a mechanic to fit in, though he'd known he'd have no planes there.

And yet, he did have a plane there. He'd flown it.

A piece of memory slid into place, weighing down everything beneath it, like a house of cards about to fall. The plane—his plane—it had also born the Oûros royal seal on it. Further, the airstrip was surrounded by borage blossoms. So something had happened there—at the airstrip, at his plane. Something bad.

So. He'd been a pilot for the royal family, flying one of their planes, and something terrible had happened right before he'd taken off in said plane. He could not picture anyone in the family, but perhaps if he saw their photos, met them—perhaps then he would gain some clarity.

It shouldn't be that difficult to find images of what had to be the most famous family in the country. Yet another reason to go out tonight with Francesca.

Francesca. He stepped out of the shower and picked up his razor, soaping his skin and drawing the blade over his beard with quick, sure strokes. He'd lived for too long as a ragged prisoner. Now felt like it was time to be someone else. Perhaps the someone he really was? That he didn't know. But certainly someone who shaved.

By the time he re-entered the room, it was full dark, but Francesca sat at the window without even a lit candle to see by. She jumped a little as he opened the door.

"Oh!" she said. "I—I didn't want anyone to know we were here. In case there were watchers."

His heart twisted a little, and he held out his hand to her. "If there are watchers," he said, "let them watch."

She peered at him then. "You've shaved," she said, sounding dismayed for a half-second before her face brightened. "It looks good! You look good."

He studied her. "It'll take a few days for my skin to darken, but eh...it was time. You prefer me bearded?"

"No, but—you said you were clean shaven before your accident," she said, her voice once more cautious. "If you were trying to hide..."

"Perhaps I no longer have any appetite for hiding."

She laughed, but it was a sad sound as she stood and crossed to him. "You're hungry?"

"Ravenous. And I need the fresh air while you tell me what we experienced over the past hour. Let's go."

They exited the room, but Francesca said nothing more, not

even after they stepped outside and into the balmy evening. Ryker's shirt was loose, his sleeves rolled up, but the quality of the cloth was fine and he felt better than he expected to. Silently, Francesca tucked her hand in his and they walked, not stopping at the corner café but continuing deeper into the city. They didn't speak for a long while, and he let the silence wrap around them, unwilling to break the spell quite yet.

It was Francesca who finally spoke first.

"What happened at the airstrip?" she asked, glancing up at him. In the mix of streetlights and shadows, it was impossible to clearly see her face. "Do you remember?"

"I do now," he said grimly. "I remember sending you inside, then rounding the building and setting out among the planes. Then I remember...mostly pain, actually." His brows went up as that new detail crystalized in his mind.

"The pain you get when a memory is triggered."

"Stronger than that, even. This was clear and present, and it strengthened as I got closer to the royal family's airplane."

Beside him, Francesca squeezed his hand. "We can take this slow," she said. "Your hand is shaking."

"Then it's good you're here to hold it," Ryker said, tightening his hold on her fingers. But he didn't want to go slow. He wanted to understand. "I reached the plane and—I turned. I saw it."

He stopped abruptly in the middle of the sidewalk, and Francesca stopped with him, her attention riveted to his face. "I'm here, Ryker," she said with quiet urgency. "Let's step back, off the sidewalk, let's stop here."

She pulled him out of the mix of people and he let her drag him to another side street, where a collection of benches sat along the traffic circle-style intersection. He sank gratefully onto the closest bench, but it wasn't the bench, the street, or the sidewalk he saw in his memory.

It was another plane.

"There was someone else there that night," he said, his words low and urgent. "The night I flew out into the storm. I was angry, careless. Didn't perform all the checks—because there was someone there who upset me."

Francesca had lifted her other hand to his, holding it tight. Vaguely he realized her hands remained cool on him while he felt like his were on fire. Her thumbs moved rhythmically over his knuckles and back. "Do you know who it was?" she asked, her tone almost casual. As if the answer didn't matter, as if he could tell her or not, it was all the same to her.

He relaxed another notch as he focused on the rhythm of her soft hands moving over his. "I don't," he said. "I did then. I should now. But I don't."

"You will or you won't, and it'll be okay, no matter what," Francesca said simply, and her words were like the lull of the tide, washing over him and drawing him out. A sense of languor spread through him, and he sighed, settling more deeply into himself.

"I don't remember what happened after that. I...woke up in the street. Then again in the taxi. You were there." He squeezed her hands. "It seems you're always there for me."

"You fell," she said, as if she was discussing the weather. "You dropped to your knees by the royal plane, then got up and moved away as fast as you could, though I don't think you could see well. Somehow you got off the airfield. You were at the side of the road when I drove up in the taxi. The driver helped get you in the car."

"He knew me," Ryker said, and he sensed the tension in Francesca, though she continued smoothly.

"He may have, or you may have reminded him of someone he once knew," she said carefully. Then her tone became teasing. "Either way, he wouldn't recognize you now. Your skin beneath your beard probably hasn't seen the sun in a year."

"Oh." He straightened self-consciously. "I didn't think about that. Is it bad?"

She looked up at him and sighed, then shook her head. "It's not bad, no," she said. "In fact, you're now probably the most handsome man in Oûros, bar none."

Twenty-Three

"You say that like it's a bad thing."

Ari rumbled the words, and Fran held on to her teasing tone, as it seemed to comfort him. "Well, it's been nice having you all to myself. Now that you no longer look like a beach bum, I might have to start fighting off the other women."

He laughed and stirred on the bench, and she sat away from him, then stood as he did. His left hand remained locked on hers, and she let him tug her back to the sidewalk. Some sort of festival was going on near the center of town, and Ari gravitated toward it.

She didn't much notice the difference in his skin tone between his cheekbones and his chin, especially in the evening light, and she suspected that a few days in the bright Oûros sun would blur those lines further. But there was no longer any denying the similarity between Ryker Stavros/Conti Goba and the missing-presumed-dead Aristotle Andris.

Despite her serving as a distracting cover, she knew she shouldn't allow him to walk around the city, but she didn't see how she could keep him from doing so without explaining why. Even now his brain was valiantly trying to link up the disparate bits of data it had—he was a pilot, he recognized the royal seal, he'd had a near collapse at the municipal airfield walking among his treasured planes.

What had he meant by his muttered phrase at the side of the road, though? "The bastard tried to kill me." He hadn't spoken those words again, and she wondered if it would return to being buried in his psyche. Clearly, however, there'd been someone at the airfield who had caused him distress, someone that he'd been able to recall vividly tonight. One of the other mechanics? A pilot? She didn't want to push him to find out. She felt that he was right on the edge of discovery...but now that discovery was becoming more perilous by the minute.

"You're keeping all your thoughts to yourself." Ari's words tugged her back to the moment, and she offered him a rueful shrug.

"I spend a lot of time alone," she said. "I get used to thinking more than talking."

"The hallmark of a good counselor, I suspect? As long as you listen too."

She laughed, forcing herself to unwind another notch. "We try to listen most of all," she admitted. "So many recoveries are already right there, in the minds and hearts of the patients, that listening is all that's required to tease them out."

"And who listens to you, Francesca?" Ari's voice was light, flirtatious, but his question struck a deep pang of wariness inside her. "Who do you go to when you are done with all that thinking? I can't imagine Nicki slows down enough very often for conversation."

Fran chuckled. "Not if she can help it."

"And your other friends?" Ari stopped as if he'd realized something new. "Your other friends—they're staying at the palace now, yes? You are all guests of the royal family."

"Yes," she allowed, praying that he didn't ask why.

"Then we should go there," he announced, so fervently that Fran would've laughed if her head weren't spinning. "I'm convinced there's a link between me and the palace, one I need to understand if I'm ever going to regain my memories. If you are returning to your friends, surely the royal family would agree to see me." He scoffed. "They footed the bill for my private rehab on Asteri Island. I can't imagine they wouldn't want a thank you for that."

"We should go see them," Fran agreed—how could she not? And it had to be better than letting Ari run around loose in the city. At least if he was inside the royal palace, they could keep him away from prying eyes. That mattered now more than ever since he'd decided to shave. "Tonight?"

He sighed lustily, considering. "Not tonight," he decided. "Tonight is for laughter and music and the beautiful American woman who has stood by my side, no matter what."

Fran shot him a glance. "Staying with you hasn't been a problem."

"And yet, I refuse to let you downplay it." Ari's voice was growing boisterous, and a few tourists turned their way, lifting their glasses. Fran quickly shifted into the shadows, tugging Ari with her.

As they moved deeper into the city the music grew louder, a mix of international house music and tunes that almost sounded like country reels. As the city's center opened up into a series of mini town squares, she spied food carts and drink stands, open doors on bars and cafes alike, and everywhere, tourists.

Not solely tourists, either. Fran was no expert on native Oûrois features, but there were enough Mediterranean, dark-eyed revelers of every age in the mix that she was sure the celebration wasn't merely for vacationers. The decibel level rose to dangerous heights as conversation vied with the crashing music, but it all served to form a cocoon of sights and sounds around Ari, who'd pulled her yet closer the nearer they got to the center of the celebrations.

She stepped up on tip toe. "Do you know what they're celebrating?"

He shrugged. "In Oûros, you do not need a reason, only a few like-minded friends. Celebrations like these are why so many people come to our—"

He drew in a sharp breath and Francesca's hand immediately went to his temple, her body pressing in close against his in case he should need her to brace himself.

"It's fine—it's fine," he said, breathing in a measured cadence as she watched him with a critical eye. "A memory that was important—might become more important. But nothing I could pin down." He sighed, shaking his head. "Perhaps there was a similar celebration the day I took off. Something like this."

Fran pursed her lips, considering that possibility. "I don't think so. It was raining, right? Unless there'd been some sort of holiday in progress, I'd think that'd put an end to any serious revelry."

"Fair enough. But if the storm wasn't expected until later..." he shrugged. "I don't know. But it would be interesting to compare the timetable of the crash with what came before it, to see if anything matches up."

Francesca grimaced. With the added ripple of Ari believing foul play was involved in his crash, or at least being angry with someone related to the night of that event, she couldn't let him continue not knowing who he was. But how did you tell someone they were a dead prince?

They walked along for another block, and Ari stopped, buying them both drinks with Fran's euros. He crinkled a grin at her as he handed her the plastic cup. "It seems like we should toast to something," he said. "Every time I lift a glass it feels like a celebration."

She eyed the clear liquid in the cup and swirled it around.

"This is tsipouro, isn't it?" she asked. "So I know what to tell the nice police officer when we fall down in the gutter?"

He laughed. "It's not so bad." He lifted the cup higher. "Here's to many reasons for celebration," he suggested, and Fran clicked her cup to his, trying to follow suit as Ari tossed his drink back. She drank as well but more slowly, allowing the fiery burst of flavor to take its time as it hit her stomach and nervous system.

Then they were off once more, weaving through the crowd hand in hand, standing close together as music played and laughter flowed around them. Another street vendor yielded a sticky pastry, and Fran suddenly felt like she was a kid again at the county fair, wandering past the rides on her way to her father's beer truck. There were no funnel cakes or frozen lemonades on the city streets of Oûros's capital, but the mood was the same.

"Ari?"

The voice was startled and feminine, and Ari paid no attention to it. Of all the names he was focusing on tonight, that wasn't one of them. But Fran's entire body jolted, every sense on high alert. She swung around in a careless arc and grabbed both of Ari's hands, tugging him toward her as she scanned the crowd.

Sure enough, there was a woman standing not ten feet away, her own cup forgotten in her hand as she stared. She was beautiful, and she looked rich, her thick, dark hair cascading over her shoulders, her tunic and pants an expensive drape of cream fabric, and her beaded high-heeled sandals like something out of a fashion magazine. She shook her head, stepping forward, and Fran did the one thing she could think of.

She dropped Ari's hands as he blinked down at her, then pressed in close, her hands flat on his powerful pecs, her face straining up toward his.

"Kiss me," she implored.

Twenty-Four

R yker stared down at the impossibly beautiful Francesca, her lips traced with sugar but her eyes full of passion for him, and thought he was quite possibly the luckiest bastard who'd ever been born.

"If I must." He grinned and did her one better, picking her up and swinging her around, tucking her tight to his body as he bent toward her. When their mouths touched another surge of desire shot through him, quick and hot, and he found he didn't want to let Francesca go.

They broke apart, and she leaned up against him, apparently as content to stand with him as he with her. He looked up and around. They'd stumbled into a small gallery-like city park off the main square of the festival. There were others here, mostly couples, walking and talking under sparkling pin lights. Ryker bent down for another kiss, embracing Francesca in the shadows, then she whispered against him.

"Is there somewhere quieter we could go?" she murmured. He tensed with anticipation, his body responding immediately to her feminine entreaty. The beach was too far, their hotel was too far, and he didn't know the city well enough to find another park like this, but less crowded.

"No one's bothering us here," he said.

She leaned back in his arms, wrinkling her nose. "But anyone could come by."

"Then we should let them," he said. "I am Conti Goba, squiring around the prettiest girl at the festival."

She snorted. "Not the prettiest."

"There you are wrong." Still, he turned. She fell into step with him, the two of them wandering further down the shadowy pathway through the trees. This gallery felt familiar to him, but his simple pleasure at being with Francesca outweighed any pain that might want to ring in his ears. Her hand was warm in his, her body close, and every statue, bench and tree beckoned to him as a welcome shelter.

A commotion at the festival end of the park sounded again, someone shouting, and Fran tugged him deeper into the shadows. "I think there's a fountain here," she said urgently. "Oh! It's beautiful."

He pulled his attention from the other end of the street to the wide concrete apron that abutted the cobblestones, and let his gaze travel up. It was an ornately carved fountain featuring Poseidon with his sea nymphs bursting up around him in a spray of water. From their outstretched hands, streams of water fell, and Fran leaned forward, trying to catch some of the spray with her fingers. "I don't have a coin or I'd toss it in for luck."

He lifted his brows as she glanced back at him. "And what would you wish for?"

"If I could have anything?" Her face seemed suddenly wistful, and Ryker quieted as she gazed at him. "It's not fair of me, and it's not possible, but I wish this night wouldn't end." She glanced back to the sparkling fountain, and the park beyond, lit with yet more fairy lights. "That's selfish, I know."

"Selfish," he murmured. He reached for her and she let him take her hand and pull her deeper into the city park. It was quieter here, though the place didn't have an abandoned feeling. More like it was holding its breath, waiting for the sun to rise.

When she didn't say anything more, he squeezed her fingers. "Selfish how?"

"I've had you to myself all day—for a couple of days, really—but you've got things to do. Like finding your friends. Your family."

He snorted. "A family I can't remember." Nevertheless, something about this park felt familiar, as the whole city felt familiar, calling to him with a siren song of his own history. It seemed so much closer to the surface here, but he didn't want his past, not right now. He wanted his present, this moment, with Francesca.

"You will though." She shook her head, as if she could hear the melancholy in her voice. "And you should. You have an entire life waiting for you just around the corner."

Despite her words striking a definite chord within him, Ryker didn't want to hear this. He tightened his grip on her hand and she glanced up at him as he slowed to a stop. "You can't say goodbye to me yet, Francesca," he murmured. "You've barely said hello."

Her smile was so gentle it seemed to hold the grace of angels. But what he felt for this woman wasn't angelic.

"I'm not saying goodbye," Francesca said. But a new sense of wrongness settled over him, and he stared down at her.

"Then why do you hesitate?" he said. "Do you not want me to kiss you—like this?" he leaned down and brushed his lips against hers, and her breath caught. "Or would you prefer it like this?"

He lifted her against him then, and there was no way she could miss the hardening of his body as he fit it against hers. Her soft groan deep in her throat egged him on, and he plundered her mouth, kissing her lips, her jaw, then back to her mouth again, slipping his tongue past her parted lips to taste her, explore her. He wanted to be inside her, and the lone thing stopping him was the fact that they weren't alone in the park, not perfectly alone. Not the alone he would need for what he wanted to do with this woman, the two of them entwined together so tightly that it would be impossible to tell where one ended and the other began.

Francesca slid down his body as he pulled away, but he didn't let her go. He liked the way she stared at him, her eyes wide and confused by what had happened between them, as if it wasn't something she could predict in her carefully ordered life.

He didn't want her careful or ordered, however. He wanted her to be his—whoever he was. Wherever he belonged, she belonged too.

"Where should we go?" he rumbled, and before she could answer, he lifted a finger to her lips. "Not tonight. Not in the city. But where should you and I go—together? If you could picture any place in the world, where would you like to visit—specifically with me?"

"Ha, well that's easy enough." Her face transformed in the shadows, seeming to be lit from within. He knew what her answer would be before she said it: *Paris.*

She still surprised him, though.

"I know it sounds ridiculous, but—when I was a little girl—my dad had this cheap little statue of the Eiffel Tower. It was the funniest-looking thing, and then I found out some people in Paris built it for a fair. I mean, it was a World's Fair. But still, essentially it was an overgrown fair. Anyway, then they kept it because it became a national symbol, and I thought that was the most incredible thing. That people could build something as a novelty that would become a symbol of love and travel the world over. It made me think that no matter who we are, or how we start out, we can become something different—something meaningful." She glanced away, a blush crawling up her cheeks.

"So I wanted to go to Paris. That's a big reason why I took this trip with my friends. And I love my friends, don't get me wrong. But one of the stops on our itinerary was Paris. We were supposed to be there for three whole days, and Lauren promised me that she'd book us into a hotel that had a view of the Eiffel Tower. That we could visit and go to the top, no matter how long the lines were." She shook her head, glancing down the long park toward the brighter lights at the far end. "I still have that silly little Eiffel Tower somewhere. It's one of the few things I kept. I couldn't throw it away."

Ryker sensed her restlessness, so he let her tug out of his embrace. He followed as she pulled him along the walkway, away from the celebration and toward the bold lights in the distance. "Will you go to Paris, then?"

She laughed. "Honestly, I don't know. Maybe not this trip after all, but one day. I've heard it's beautiful, though I'm sure it has the same problems any big city has." She sent him a sideways glance. "Can you remember now, if you've been?"

Ryker lifted his gaze up past the treetops as they walked, taking in the starlit sky. "I can," he said. "I don't know when or how, but I'm certain that I've been there, and that those memories aren't bad ones either. They're simply waiting for the right time to come out." He squeezed her hand. "I feel good about them. I think Paris was a good place for me. That I was happy there."

"I think you probably were, too," she said softly.

They walked to the end of the park, and when they finally cleared the last of the trees, Ryker saw why there had been so many lights. A building soared above the city streets, walled and gated but lit brightly enough to seem like full day. And to either side of the gates was the symbol he'd come to know so well in his short time back among his own people. The royal seal.

His heart started hammering in his chest for no reason, and he regarded Francesca with a frown. "Why have you brought me here?" he asked. "I thought we agreed—not tonight."

"Because it's time that you saw it," she said, pointing to the royal palace. "This...well, this is your home."

Twenty-Five

Ari stared at the castle walls, lit up like a birthday cake. "What are you talking about?" he rumbled. "It's the royal palace."

She nodded, but inside Fran was roiling. Was this the right thing? Was it time?

There was no way to know. But there also was no denying that Ari had already been recognized twice today. First by the taxi driver, though he hadn't realized exactly who he was seeing, and second by the beautiful woman at the festival.

The beautiful woman... Fran pressed her lips together. Was she the woman rumored to be the prince's fiancée? Or just a friend of the family, one of the endless swirl of beautiful, elegant noblewomen she'd watched swirling around the dance floor at the Visitors' Palace? It didn't matter, really. It didn't.

More importantly, Ari was regaining memories at a rapid rate. It was only a matter of time before they all came crashing down on him.

Whether Fran wanted it to happen or not, time was running short, and if she didn't want Ari to be blindsided by what she was about to hand him into, she owed him some explanation.

Coward. This wasn't solely about Ari, if she was being honest with herself. This was about avoiding any more of his questions—questions which made her yearn to spill all the stupid, inconsequential stories of her past, stories she'd never been able to tell. Couldn't tell.

Wouldn't tell.

So, the most effective redirect she'd managed to date to escape revealing her own secrets? Telling Ari about his.

"It's as I thought," he said, his words startling her out of her self-castigation. "I work for the royal family. I knew it had to be something like that."

She grimaced. "Well...that's not exactly it."

Fran continued before she lost her nerve. "Twelve months ago, Prince Aristotle Andris left the royal palace on the eve of a terrible storm over the Aegean," she said, holding on tightly to Ari's hand as it began to shake. He never took his eyes off the castle, though, and he didn't turn away. She plunged on. "He took off in his two-seater plane from the municipal airfield south of the city, and never came home. Pieces of his plane were found, but no body. After months of searching, he was officially declared dead."

"Dead?" The shock and growing panic in Ari's face seared Francesca, and in her heart she knew she'd done the right thing in telling him. He would have time to process the information... and his mother would never have to see that look of profound loss on his face, the bewildered betrayal.

"But how could they do that without a body? Didn't the royal family object?" he asked. His other hand flailed, and she reached for it, locking them both in hers. He stared at her in wild confusion.

"You were missing—and no one could believe you were gone. That you wouldn't come back. Your parents threw every resource into the search, but nothing came of it. The entire country sank into mourning, and as the weeks dragged into months, your parents could see the grief was damaging the spirit of Oûros," she said. "The people were broken with your loss and couldn't heal without moving on in some way. Your younger brother—"

Ari jolted and glared at her, his eyes widening in disbelief. "I have a brother?"

She nodded, not trusting herself to speak for a moment given the hope and wonder in his face, the realization that he did have a family. Then she cleared her throat and carried on, despite the strangled pressure in her throat. "Kristos. He also refused to believe you were dead. Your best friend, too. Your parents. None of them could accept it, but the country needed to recover, needed to have a reason to hope again. They—the people wouldn't let you go, otherwise."

"It's a proud country," Ari murmured, and there were tears glistening in his eyes as he gazed back at the palace walls. "Proud and fierce and passionate in its grief. For any of its lost sons."

"And you were their prince. Their future king," Fran said, though Ari shook his head. "But your brother resisted until... well, it was less than a month ago that he finally agreed to be the crown prince. A job he's quite sure he'll hate."

"My job," Ari said. He turned back to her, incredulous. "You're saying that's my job?"

"You're the eldest son."

"But Ryker Stavros..." he said the words almost plaintively, and Fran nodded at him. He didn't need to be told 'no' right now, he needed to be drawn to the 'yes.'

"Ryker Stavros was a name you'd chosen for yourself when you were young, when you and your brother would imagine you were warriors and pilots, off on grand adventures."

"Pilots." Ari barked a laugh, then a new realization seemed

to strike him. He pulled his hands free from hers, stepping back. "You knew...all of this. You knew who I was. And you didn't tell me. You let me believe I was—" he glared at her. "We made *love!*"

Guilt smashed into Fran like a fist, and she could feel the blood draining out of her face.

This is why you don't fall for your patients, she told herself. *This is why you don't get too close!* Even if he wasn't a patient, she'd violated Ari's trust...

Wait a minute. Fran scowled. Ari wasn't an idiot, and he wasn't her fucking patient.

Just that fast, her anger spiked equally hot.

"Don't give me that," she snapped back, her Midwestern twang loud in her ears. "You knew I had some idea of who you are. Stefan knew your family, and Nicki was my friend. You saw us talking—you knew. You're right, I should never have—we should never have..." she flapped her hands as he scowled at her. "But we did. We did and—*shit.*"

Ari blinked, but he wasn't Fran's only problem right now. She'd known standing in front of the royal freaking palace was like dangling candy in front of a baby, and she'd been right. Two men came striding out of the front gates, backed by a trio of big, burly types that had to be members of the ONSF. Ari was about to be collected, whether he was ready to be or not.

"Look—you don't owe me anything," she said hurriedly to Ari. "But I'd appreciate it if you didn't let the honor guard bearing down on you know about the sex, okay? That's probably not going to sit too well with them."

"The honor..." Ari pivoted, staring. "The captain and Stefan."

"The captain's name is Dimitri, and you should cut him some slack," she said, her words low and tight—but there remained so much Ari didn't remember, and so much that he needed to. "Out of everyone, he never *ever* gave up on you. He blames himself for you leaving that night."

"He what?" His anger redirected to shock, Ari gaped at her as the men arrived, exactly as she wanted to happen. She stepped back as Stefan strode right up to the prince, his gaze swinging from Ari to Fran.

"He knows," Dimitri said, also drawing up short. The three of them squared off like adversaries, the tension tight enough to crackle. "She told him."

"Of course, I told him." Fran's irritated outburst was perhaps a bit louder than she intended, but it also served. At least her voice was back to its cool Northeastern sophistication. "It took you long enough to get out here. I was about to start hanging ornaments on his family tree. He knows." She riveted her gaze on Ari. "He knows."

"Knowing isn't the same as remembering," Stefan said, and she could have kicked him in the shin.

To her surprise, though, Ari laughed. "I knew that I'd met you before," he said, holding out his hand. "Stefan Mihal. Thank you for rescuing me. And for doing what you could to make my way back easier."

Stefan took Ari's hand without hesitation. "Sir," he said.

Ari turned to Dimitri, who stared at him with a belligerence that Fran knew was the only thing holding the gruff captain back from sudden, unwanted tears. Ari reached out and put his hand on Dimitri's shoulder. "I do not remember you, Dimitri. I want to. I will. I do feel that I know you, though. And that I can trust you with my life."

Fran clamped her lips together, fighting the sob that had no place in this meeting. But Ari gestured to her as he gave Dimitri a wry grin, including her in the discussion when all she wanted to do was run away. "Francesca tells me you wouldn't give up searching for me, even after a year. Have you always been so stubborn?"

"Always," Dimitri said tightly, and he nodded with military precision to Ari and Stefan, then rounded on his men, biting out commands in Oûrois. The men fanned around them, including Fran in their cage.

Fran stuttered out a protest. "I'm good, really. I should go back for our—"

"We'll send a car," Stefan said. "The queen will want to see you, Miss Simmons, immediately. She's most grateful that you both have come home."

As they trooped back into the royal palace, Fran wasn't sure that sentiment would last the night.

<h1 style="text-align:center">Twenty-Six</h1>

R yker...Ari...whoever the hell he was, he knew he should have been leveled with a crashing headache at the prospect of stepping foot in the royal palace. But too many emotions were churning through him at once to settle on any one thing.

The shock at discovering who he really was. The unruly reaction to the knowledge that here were two men who'd dedicated a year to searching for him...and he didn't truly remember either of them. His pent-up outrage and betrayal at Francesca—*Francesca!* Who likely had been bullied into serving as his babysitter, who clearly had secrets of her own she was desperate to hide, and who now walked behind them like she was hoping to slip away when no one was looking.

Well, that wasn't going to happen. He reached for her hand, dragging her up beside him as they crossed under the gate. She'd been by his side for his every step in Oûros. She wasn't giving up that job yet.

And if he was being truly honest with himself, he didn't want her to give it up yet. In the shortest of times, he'd become used to her being there, whether watching him with absolute serenity or snapping at him with a few choice curse words. He liked both sides of Francesca, and he suspected he would like any other side she chose to reveal to him. He could afford to wait.

What couldn't wait, however, was apparently a royal audience.

Ryker tried to process all he was seeing as they walked along the hallways of the royal palace. Everything in the home was stunning—hardwood and marble floors, artwork lining the walls, gilded fittings, but it didn't have the pretentious feel that it should. He didn't know why—perhaps because he'd grown up here, gotten used to all of the luxury.

Either way, there was still no pain, for which he was exceedingly grateful. He knew there would be more eventually, but he would take what breaks he could get.

"Sir," Stefan said, and Ryker realized they'd stopped. The ambassador was assessing him critically. "Can you recall anything about this place yet? Anything at all?"

"Not yet," Ryker said.

Stefan nodded. "Then you're in luck. The royal family will be at their most cautious. Don't take their reticence for a lack of relief, though. They simply don't want to break you."

"Break me?"

But Stefan was already through the door, and Dimitri gestured him in, the look on the captain's face inscrutable. As if he'd lashed down his emotions tight enough to withstand a hurricane.

"Break me?" Ryker asked again, this time of Dimitri. The captain's chiseled face remained tense for a moment longer, then quirked into a smile.

"The queen...you'll understand when you see her," he said. "She's been grieving your loss for an entire year, and she's afraid that if she makes the wrong move, she'll somehow worsen your condition."

Ryker frowned. "But that makes no sense."

Dimitri lifted one shoulder. "She's a mother before she is queen sometimes. And she's been through a lot."

Then another man he didn't recognize was at the door, a staffer, looking out to see if anything was wrong. Ryker took a deep breath, and entered the receiving room.

It was like walking into a frozen wonderland.

Before him, arrayed in careful precision, were people who he assumed were his family. An older couple and a man maybe two years his junior, all of them dressed casually but in a manner that implied great care was taken. Were these clothes they thought he would recognize? He didn't.

The silence in the room was deafening, and Dimitri stepped to his left while Francesca tightened her hold on his right arm.

Stefan spoke first. "Ryker's probably the best name to use, so we'll start there," he said crisply. "Ryker Stavros, you already know your real name is Aristotle Andris. I'd like to introduce your family to you."

His hand pinning Francesca to his side, Ryker stepped forward. She gently disentangled herself from him when he reached his family unit, but she didn't retreat.

The first person in line was his mother, or he assumed it was his mother. She was lovely in the way he instinctively assumed most older noblewomen in Oûros were. Her dark hair and eyes spoke of a life well-lived, while her skin was still that of a much younger woman. She smiled at him as her eyes filled with barely banked tears, her gaze searching his face.

"You don't remember anything, do you, sweetheart?" she murmured.

The sound of her voice made Ryker stiffen and his hand went to his head as his mother gasped.

"Ari—" this was a male voice, and the next man stepped up quickly, steadying him as the pain leveled through his brain. He brought his head up, gripping the forearms of the older man, and suddenly—he knew. His *father*—this was his father, King Jasen. This was his father, and he was Ari Andris and a flood of memories nearly took him to his knees, a lifetime of laughter and shouts and tears and studies and dinners and travel and—

"No!" he gasped, wheeling away, only to collapse into a third man, whose eyes were unabashedly full of tears, tears that were now running down his face. Unlike his parents who were trying so hard to do what was right, what was safe, Kristos practically bowled Ari over with a hug, Ari's arms instinctively going around his younger brother as Kristos burst into rough, racking sobs.

"I've missed you so much—so much," Kristos gritted out, and it wasn't the sound of a grown man, but of a little brother left alone to face the world without preparation. His sobs came from a place of isolation so deep and profound that Ari felt his own wellspring of recognition growing.

"Kristos," he managed. "Kristos—"

His brother jerked his head back and searched his face. "You remember me? Or did they tell you." He whirled on Francesca. "Did you tell him ? You had to have told him."

"Kristos," Ari said again—and he knew without question his name was Ari, knew these people. His brother shifted and Ari realized the pain was no longer quite so strong. "I remember you. All of you, but not everything about you." He turned, his brother loosening his hold and took in his mother and father, both of them holding each other since they could not hold him.

"Mamá," he said, holding out a hand, and the queen gave a short, strangled cry. It was Jasen who helped her take the faltering step toward Ari, and she bypassed his hand and lifted her fingers to his face, laying them along his cheekbone.

"I missed you so much, Ari," she said, echoing Kristos's words. "For so long I begged the gods to return you safely. Then, when that didn't work, I prayed that you were healthy, or not in pain or—at least somewhere safe. I couldn't—I couldn't imagine you hurt, or trapped, or—"

Ari wrapped his arms around her, but lifted his gaze to his father's. King Jasen nodded. His mother had been told the truth —but perhaps not the whole truth. Ari hoped not, or she'd never let him out of her sight again.

The sound of a deep, sonorous chime echoed through the palace, and the queen stepped back, her back going straight as she lifted her hands to her face, whisking away the tears.

"Who would call at this hour?" she demanded, and Ari saw Stefan signal to two of the guards, while Dimitri considered him and Fran with lifted brows.

"There *is* a lot of activity going on in the city tonight," Dimitri said sardonically. "I don't suppose you two were out and about?"

Ari frowned, then rubbed his chin. "A bit," he said, slanting a glance at Francesca. She'd folded one arm across her waist, effectively creating the impression of a shield. "Francesca wanted me in the shadows, but, well...there was a festival."

Stefan groaned and his mother whirled on him, her brows going up, once more the woman he realized he was used to seeing. "You were seen, I would imagine," she said. "Of course, you were seen. We'll have to arrange a press conference, a briefing." She pointed to her assistant and rattled off several requests in Oûrois, and the woman left the room at a run.

Beside her, Jasen shook his head, and Ari got to see him fully for the first time. His father had aged, he realized with sudden clarity. This year he was gone had been hard on Ari, certainly. But how much harder on those he'd left behind?

No matter that he couldn't remember so much, he couldn't

leave them hanging, now that he was back. What was it Francesca had said—Fake it 'til you make it? Now it was his chance to do exactly that.

A commotion in the hallway drew everyone's attention, and a stunning dark-haired woman burst through the doorway.

"Ari!" she exclaimed, her voice filled with excitement, joy, and relief.

Then she ran for him.

Twenty-Seven

"**E**deena!" The queen's voice came out as a whipcrack, but it didn't seem to have any impact on the gorgeous woman who ran pell-mell through the receiving room until she launched herself into Ari's arms. Fran took several steps back from Ari and would have backed all the way out of the room if she hadn't slammed into Dimitri's chest.

"Chicken," muttered the captain. Fran glared at him, if only to avoid the bear-hugging scene in the middle of the floor.

"Who is she?" Fran hissed back. In all the time she'd been with Ari, she hadn't thought once to ask if he had a girlfriend, let alone one he was supposed to get married to. But that had to be who this woman was. "Shouldn't someone have mentioned he had a fiancée?"

"Not a fiancée," Dimitri said, lifting himself on his toes and rocking back as Ari and Edeena finally broke apart. They began chattering in non-stop Oûrois, and Dimitri continued. "Edeena Saleri and Ari dated briefly when they were in their early teens, but they grew up as distant cousins, though there's no true blood tie—only by marriage."

"Oh" Fran eyed Edeena and Ari dubiously. "You're sure they're not, ah..."

"Close? No," Dimitri said, though he grinned as he watched Ari. "With any luck, she's not asking him anything about their former lives together. The woman has a mind like a steel trap, and Ari is still springing quite a few leaks."

As if the queen suddenly came to the same conclusion, she strode forward, interrupting the reunion. "You caught us out, Edeena," she said smoothly, speaking in English—a fact which wasn't lost on Edeena. She was even lovelier up close than how Fran remembered her at the festival. "We'd hoped to keep Ari's healthy return a secret until tomorrow."

"Ha! Then you shouldn't have let him sneak out into the city." Edeena also spoke in English, and she grinned around the room until she spotted Fran. "*You*," she fairly shouted, and the sudden command in her voice was unnerving. You could always tell a first born. "You were with him weren't you?"

She swung her gaze back to Ari, and her expression didn't waver. "Tell me she's not your nurse. If you've fallen in love with your nurse, I'm going to tell every last tabloid from here to Hungary, and you're never going to hear the end of it."

Despite herself, Fran couldn't help but like the woman, but Ari answered smoothly. "Not my nurse," he said. "My injuries were profound, yes, but I was all but healed before my benefactors realized my identity and reached out to my parents a few weeks ago. By the time I arrived in Oûros, I was declared a full recovery."

"Benefactors," Edeena echoed skeptically. "There's a story there."

"Not one of any merit," Stefan put in mildly, but there was no denying the steel lacing his tone. "Tomorrow's papers will say the same thing, but there's no reason you shouldn't know it now. Last June, flying in heavy storms, the prince was blown distinctly off course and crash-landed near an island off the coast of Turkey. He was rescued and tended to without the villagers knowing who he was, and he remained in their care for several months, recovering slowly. Shortly after he was officially declared dead, a fisherman who'd seen the coverage recognized him, and set about the process of notifying the royal family. He has been under a doctor's care for the past several days, and is now ready to resume his life with the royal family." Stefan gestured to Ari. "As you can see, he's quite healthy...if a little sunburned."

"Healthy and fit," announced Kristos suddenly. He turned to his father. "Healthy enough to take on all his roles. Even the one he foisted off on me."

"Now, Kristos," Jasen raised his hands, but Dimitri snorted.

"I wondered how long it would take Kristos to realize he wouldn't have to remain crown prince," he said dryly.

"The Late Lamented Prince Returns," Edeena agreed, a grin playing around her lips. She put her hands on her hips. "It's a good headline. It'll stand up under cross-examination of the press, and most of Ari's adoring fans," she winked at Ari, who seemed to watch her with far too much affection for a friend, in Fran's book. "But you're going to need more help keeping the matchmakers off your back. With Kristos falling for an American and you kissing yet another American girl, there's going to be an outcry. Especially from my dad."

"Your...father."

Fran's eyes sharpened as all the color drained out of Ari's face, his entire body going rigid. Fortunately, the king spoke next, drawing all eyes to him.

"One of the most cherished features of Oûros is the freedom we grant our people—in life and in love," he said. "That said, there is no need to rush the process. We have time to observe the old traditions."

Ari stared woodenly at his father, devoid of all expression, but the queen clasped her hands together, her face suddenly radiant.

"A ball! You mean a ball. Not an Accession Ball. It's far too soon for that, but something special, don't you think? A celebration."

Fran lifted her brows and the men in the room groaned, while Ari clearly tried to keep up. At least his face looked better, his expression clearing. Whatever had startled him, he as rapidly recovering. This was her cue to exit stage right before Edeena refocused the attention on her.

She slipped behind Dimitri, glaring at him sternly to counter his mocking glance—and faded back to the door. Then she slipped out.

The halls of the royal palace seemed almost strange to her, and she'd only been gone a couple of days. She had no idea where the other girls were—probably in their rooms—but she couldn't quite bring herself to meet up with them yet. So much had happened in such a short time. She needed time to regroup, re-center herself. Time to remember who she was, and the role she needed to play.

Fran walked down one long hallway, then another, then noticed a soft light filtering out from a room at the far end of the corridor. This part of the palace seemed abandoned, and she reached the room quickly, slipping inside as she glanced back over her shoulder. There was no one following her, she realized with relief. The royal family—probably all of Oûros—would be focusing on Ari for the foreseeable future. Exactly as it should be.

She scanned the room and realized she shouldn't be surprised to find this place with the lights still lit. It was the royal gallery, home to generations of Oûrois kings and queens. The most prominent portraits were of Catherine and Jasen, of course, but there were also several of the princes. Fran smiled as she saw a pint-sized Kristos, gazing up at his older brother with all the adoration a four-year-old could muster. And Aristotle, for his part, looked strong and fierce, his lips pressed together in a heart-breaking attempt to appear mature, and his gaze intent, as if the fate of all Oûros rested on his pudgy shoulders.

He'd been groomed to lead this country since he'd been very small, Fran knew. He'd return to that role, despite his current confusion. He'd already begun to piece things together, and what he didn't know, he'd be told—as often as needed. Most of all, he would be loved and supported, carefully shielded from harm until he was strong enough to fight his own battles once more.

Everyone deserved that, from a prince to a scrubby little girl.

A large wing-backed chair stood facing a couch in a formal conversational set, but it was the thick knit wrap draped over it that drew Fran most. Her dad had dozens of these shawls, the only things he'd kept from his own grandmother, and she'd treasured them. It'd been the hardest thing to leave behind when she'd finally walked out the door of Bert's Bar and Grill for the last time. But unlike the Eiffel Tower, she hadn't taken a single strand of the crocheted wraps.

Dreams you could keep when creating a new life, but too many memories weighed you down.

<h1 style="text-align:center">Twenty-Eight</h1>

Ari felt like a weight was pressing down on his shoulders. Gazing around the crowded room, he struggled to maintain his composure as his homecoming transitioned from an intensely emotional personal welcome to a state event. Most of this was Edeena's fault, but he couldn't bring himself to yell at her for it. They weren't children anymore.

Still, he grimaced as the familiar pain streaked through his brain, leaving fog in its wake. That pain had spiked when Edeena had entered the room, so strong that Ari's eyes watered. And then when she'd mentioned her father, it was like a punch to his gut. What was he not remembering? Had he felt more for Edeena than for the other members of his family? Surely not.

He studied her now, her head bent with the queen as they discussed something about a ball. He vaguely remembered state events, but they remained deliberately hazy, as did most of the recollections he'd had since breaching this room. He suspected his memory would return in fits and starts, but he couldn't help thinking he was missing something significant. Something that would matter both to him and his family.

"How much of your life before do you truly remember?"

Ari didn't turn his head. His father had moved over to him as Kristos, Stefan and a new man—who Ari recognized as Cyril Gerou, the royal family's chief advisor—discussed the elements of the state address he would need to make. But Jasen was staying out of the fray for the moment, using the opportunity to ask his quiet question.

"I remember that I had a life," Ari said, honestly. "I'm certain that I am this person you all tell me I am. I remember bits and pieces—mostly from when I was very young, less from more recent years. I remembered Cyril without being introduced, and that I could trust him, but I can't say I feel comfortable meeting anyone else of any standing."

"You knew Edeena too?"

That was trickier. He frowned. "I knew that I was supposed to know her, and that there was some tension around the memory. Then when she came at me all smiles, the tension was tempered with relief. But I don't know why I think these things."

He shifted his weight and realized with a glance that Francesca was no longer in the room. How long had she been gone? And why hadn't he noticed her absence before?

"Edeena is...a friend. She's always been a friend to you, since you were children." Jasen said. He grimaced. "Her father is a difficult man."

Ari stiffened. "I can't remember him, not directly. But I sense that we were...very much at odds." That's all he would betray, for now. He couldn't accuse the man of anything until he remembered more.

Jasen snorted. "I'm not surprised. In the way of many fathers, he tried to push the romance between you and Edeena, unwilling to believe that you would not immediately fall for her. And, I suspect, she would have gladly entered into an engagement with you had there been genuine attraction there, if simply to escape her father's eternal sour mood." He sighed. "As well as escape the curse, of course."

Ari blinked. "There's a curse? On Edeena?"

"The kind of curse only the gods could create," the king replied sourly, though it was clear his attention had been diverted. "Something to ask your mother about. A moment."

He strode across the room and Ari watched him, feeling suddenly helpless in the gears of the machinery he'd unwittingly set in motion. Another man stepped into the breach left by his father. This man, at least, he was beginning to remember in more detail.

"You seriously don't know half of what's going on here, do you?" Dimitri asked.

Ari shook his head. "It becomes clearer with each new interruption, but in a word, no." He glanced at Dimitri. "Where did Francesca go?"

"Probably not back to her guest room. I think she's a little overwhelmed by the planning brigade." He nodded to the queen and Edeena. "She wisely suspected she'd get pulled into ballgown duty."

"She has friends here though, right? Nicki Clark I've met. But there are two others..." he frowned, the names all running together in his head.

"Emmaline Andrews—soon to be Emmaline Andris, you should know." Dimitri nodded to Kristos. "That's the woman Edeena was referring to. She showed up the same morning Kristos was finally going to accept his princely duties as your replacement."

"Finally..." Ari frowned. "But I was declared dead months ago."

"And your brother did his level best to make believe that was not so." Dimitri shrugged. "He wanted to stay in the military, not to be a prince. And now—assuming you really are fit for returning to that duty, and that you want to—he can return to the ONSF."

"That'll make you happy, I suspect." Ari's eyes widened as Dimitri glanced sharply at him. "There, you see?" Ari said triumphantly. "*That* was a memory."

"It could have been a supposition."

"No, a memory. You serve with Kristos in the ONSF, and you're proud of him. You'll be glad to have him back." Ari frowned. "But that's just one girl. There was a fourth, right?"

Now it was Dimitri's turn to grimace. "Lauren Grant," he said.

"Lauren…" Ari hesitated. "That sounds familiar."

"Grant family hoteliers. She's the eldest daughter, rich as Midas with a temper to match."

Now Ari focused more fully on Dimitri. "You normally don't speak so critically of our guests." He lifted his brows. "See? Another memory."

"I normally don't," Dimitri said, and his voice was so dark that Ari instantly knew.

"You're sleeping with her. This Lauren Grant." He peered at the man he could believe was his best friend as every new minute passed. "Worse than that. You've fallen in love."

"She's a menace," Dimitri muttered, then he met Ari's gaze with a challenging glance of his own. "You're one to talk. I leave you alone for one day—one! With a pretty American, and by nightfall you have her fleeing from the room to get away from you." He grinned as Ari's gaze darted to the door. "Don't think of leaving yet, either. You need to get Edeena out the door and your mother off to bed before you try to hunt down your Francesca."

"She could be with her friends by then."

"Negative," Dimitri shook his head. "These Americans, they tend to hold their problems close to the vest. Not one of them is good at sharing their troubles." He gestured to where Cyril and the others were arguing. "You go deal with them, and I'll find your little American. With any luck, it'll be before Edeena does."

"She's not my—" but Ari broke off as Dimitri laughed. The captain turned away quickly, but not before Ari could see the sheen of brightness in his eyes. He watched the man retreat through the door, raking through the newly awakened memories he had of Dimitri Korba. There were plenty of them, ranging all the way up to long, hot days training in the sun last summer.

Training...

A new memory assaulted him—about Dimitri. Stefan. A dozen—no, a *hundred* men and women who worked in and around the castle, serving the Crown as representatives of their patron gods. *Gods!* He staggered a little, the whole of it flooding back. These mortals were demigods, gifted with improved minds and bodies by virtue of their long ago blood tie to the gods, and all of them—for at least some period of time—served Oûros.

More memories poured in like the tide. The gates of Olympus, the Temple of Winds, his family's role as gatekeepers. It was all he could do not to bury his head in his hands and shout with the chaos of it.

There were no new memories about the crash, though.

For whatever reason, as Francesca had said, Dimitri hadn't been with him that night. It felt odd, thinking that. He got the feeling the man...demigod...never missed an opportunity to take off on an adventure with him.

The demigod. No wonder Dimitri had been so pissed that he'd flown off without him. Well, he was glad of it. It was one thing that Ari had gone down on that plane. If he'd dragged anyone else with him—even, *especially,* a demigod of Zeus—he wouldn't have been able to forgive himself.

Ari squared his shoulders, striding over to join Cyril, Jasen, and Stefan before his mother and Edeena realized he remained in the room. Bad enough that he would have to navigate the tangled web of politics as he worked his way back into the family business. To have to endure the details of planning a royal ball would be enough to send him back into the streets.

But soon enough, he knew, the questions would settle and the talking would cease. And then he would be free to find Francesca.

He may not have all his memories, but he knew the layout of the palace like the back of his hand.

Including all its secrets.

<h1 style="text-align:center">Twenty-Nine</h1>

F ran stirred groggily in her chair, trying to remember where she was. Her first sight was an entire wall of portraits, lit by one softly glowing lamp far down the room.

Then her gaze dropped. She jumped, instinctively pulling her blanket further around her. "Hey," she said.

"Hey." Aristotle Andris sat across from her at one edge of the long couch, still perfectly unmussed in his white shirt and soft trousers. He might have been sitting there for a moment or for hours, she had no way of telling.

But what was certain was that this was Aristotle Andris sitting here. Not Ryker Stavros, not Conti Goba. Regardless of what else he'd learned in the receiving room, meeting his parents and his beautiful childhood friend, he'd claimed his identity. He knew who he was.

For a fleeting second, Fran wondered what that would be like.

Ari gestured to the tray on the low table between them. "I didn't know if you'd be hungry. You've got to be thirsty, though. You've been asleep for a few hours."

"Hours?" Fran straightened, allowing the blanket to fall

away as she reached for the water. She was thirsty, and she appreciated being able to occupy her hands while her mind raced. "Where are the others—what time is it? And what are you still doing awake?"

Ari shrugged, but his gaze followed her every move. The water poured into the glass, the glass traveling to her lips. It would have been unnerving from anyone else, but Fran knew that drill. She studied others like it was her job, too.

She suspected Ari's memories hadn't all returned.

"I refused to let anyone else move you, and for a long while my parents stayed with me here, though we were at some distance." He gestured down the room where a similar collection of chairs and couches stood beneath another constellation of paintings. "It was my turn to ask them questions." His expression tightened. "So many things have happened in the past year. It seems like I've been gone a lot longer."

"And how are you doing?" She set the glass down again and leaned forward, her elbows on her knees. Ari seemed remarkably refreshed for someone who'd been through yet another trauma in the past few hours, while she felt as tired as a worn-out shoe.

She was pretty sure Edeena Saleri never felt like a worn-out shoe.

Ari seemed to consider the question seriously, measuring his response. That was different too, though more subtly so. Ryker had been less reserved, more rash in his replies. How else would the new Ari, the real Ari, differ from the man she'd only just begun to know?

"I'm not as frustrated as I would have expected," Ari said. "The role comes more naturally than I feared it would when I first understood who I was supposed to be. I don't remember all the details—most of the details, if you want the honest truth— but I remember the people. I remember their influence in my life. My parents, my brother, Dimitri, even Stefan and Cyril. I understand who I can trust, which is pretty much everyone I've met now. I understand that there are those out there I won't be able to trust, but I don't yet know why." He shrugged. "And I feel stronger, in a strange sense."

That made her lift her brows. Ari was such a vital force, she couldn't imagine him ever feeling weak. Before she could ask what he meant, he continued.

"Up to now—the life I led and the way I led it—came with an acceptance that, of course, this was the way it was going to be. But now it's more than simple acceptance. Now I'm choosing to be this person. I'm deliberately making these decisions. It's a different approach." His lips twisted. "One my parents aren't entirely sure what to do with, I suspect."

Fran lifted her hands to her hair, relieved it remained caught up in its series of clips. She had lost her own sense of deliberate action since returning to the palace, and she needed to reclaim it, too. "Your mother doesn't know everything about the work camp."

Ari shook his head. "Not everything, but most of it." He gestured dismissively. "Eventually, I'll tell her the truth. It's not information she can't handle. There's simply no value in her knowing it now. She would want to do something with it—tell someone, demand answers or justifications. And that's not practical."

That sounded so unlike Ryker that Fran felt the smallest twinge of remorse. She pulled off her blanket completely, folding it up as Ari watched. "There wouldn't—" she hesitated, then firmed her resolve. Francesca Simmons didn't hesitate. She was calm, cool, and above all, serene. She asked for what she wanted because by asking, she likely got it. And right now, Fran wanted more than anything to be alone in a space with four walls and a closed door, recovering her equilibrium. "Is there a guest room where I could spend the night without waking Nicki or the others?" she asked. "I can't imagine they know I'm here yet."

He nodded. "Of course." He stood with her, his gaze raking over her body, as if making sure she wasn't leaving anything behind. "The others have no idea you're here, and they're together. Dimitri and Kristos won't betray your presence until you're ready—or at least until dawn when Lauren and Emmaline wake up demanding answers."

"Ha! Well, then I have what, a few hours?"

"At least." Ari stepped around the table and gestured her to precede him, then shifted slightly and held out his hand instead. After the smallest of hesitations, Fran took it, blinking away the flash of quick tears that sprang to the backs of her eyes at the touch of his fingers on hers. Now, suddenly, this man was a stranger to her—as if she was the one who'd lost her memories, not the other way around.

"There's a room nearby that looks over the city, all the way down to the ocean," he murmured. "Will that suit?"

She twisted her lips. "As long as we're not right on *top* of the ocean, it'd be perfect."

They stepped out into the hallway and Fran noted it was also softly lit—and abandoned. No guards stood at the ready. Dimitri and Stefan weren't lurking at the far end of the corridor. "They've given you the run of the place?" she asked. "That seems...trusting."

Ari laughed, stepping onto a staircase at the second corner. "I suspect their largesse doesn't extend beyond the palace's exterior doors." But his manner was easy, as if living under a microscope was no hardship. Then again, after his past year, he might be grateful for that level of security. He squeezed her hand, the gesture once again striking her as more Ryker than Ari, and she found herself wondering at the distinction.

The explanation probably wasn't all that deep, she decided. She knew Ryker—she didn't know Ari. And now one had been replaced with the other.

She'd done what she needed to do. The prince was back in the arms of his family. She could move on with her life...would move on. Tomorrow. First thing.

"It worries me when you're too quiet," Ari murmured as he climbed another flight of stairs. "I always suspect you're thinking too much."

The teasing note in his voice drew a smile to her face despite herself. "No one has ever accused me of that."

"In that, I suspect you're wrong. Here we are."

The stairway emptied out to a hallway as well-appointed as the ones a few floors down, the long corridor carpeted with a rich golden rug, and the walls lined with mirrors and artwork, even in such an out-of-the-way corner of the palace. Ari stopped before a door outfitted with an unusual keypad—a slender black screen instead of the standard hole for a metal key or a numerical pin. With a rueful chuckle, he pressed three fingers to the pad, and the lock snicked open.

"They told me it would still work," he said, his voice wistful. "I made that keypad when I was a teenager in a fit of rebellion and ordered all the keys to the room destroyed. I always knew my parents had some way of overriding it, but they didn't take it down." He shook his head. "They should have, after a year."

He pushed the door open and the size of the room instantly struck Fran—it was small. Probably the smallest guest chamber she'd seen in the castle, the size of her own room back home in her Georgetown apartment. But the far wall consisted almost entirely of glass, with a view that swept down the city and out to the distant sea.

"When the sun rises, it's like the entire world lights up," Ari said, staring out the window.

"It's beautiful now." Fran couldn't help but stare, too. In an instant, she knew this wasn't simply a random guest room, but Ari's own bedroom, set off from the rest of the royal apartments, a tiny cramped space by comparison, but one that was uniquely him. This is where he'd brought her, and she understood the significance of that, too. They'd have their final idyll together, whatever she wanted to make of it.

She found she wanted to make a great deal.

Thirty

Ari tensed as Francesca moved away from him, toward the enormous window that dominated the room. It'd been a risk to come here. He'd told his parents he would see to it Francesca didn't spend the night in the gallery, and they hadn't asked him where he would deposit her. By that time in the evening, he'd proven his understanding of the royal palace layout had survived in his memories, regardless of anything else.

And the room was exactly as he'd left it, he realized. Apparently, his parents had programmed an override code, as he'd often wondered. Someone had come in to dust, anyway. But he suspected that his clothes remained in the drawers and closet, his watches still in their tray on the dresser. He expected—hoped—that everything inside the dressers remained intact as well. The only thing that seemed different was the stack of journals on the table by the bed. There was a new bin beside the table, a year's worth of magazines neatly lined up.

But right now, all he was interested in reading was Francesca's mood...and he couldn't. As usual, she played her cards close, putting on the face that people expected to see. He didn't want a mask., though He wanted the woman beneath.

She turned and lifted a hand to him. "Show me?" she asked, and though he didn't quite understand her question, he readily moved down to join her at the window. When he reached her, he paused a moment, taking in her profile. Francesca was beautiful, lit by the distant glow of the city, the murky blue of the far off sea giving an otherworld cast to her skin.

"How long have you used this as your bedroom?" she asked as he settled in behind her. She shifted back, her shoulders to his chest, and he understood the meaning of that small gesture, her willingness to touch him—to be touched by him. His heart shifted in his chest and his arms naturally went around her, the feel of Francesca in his arms as right as the crashing of the far-off waves.

"Since I was ten," he said, brushing his lips over her hair. "I found the room while exploring the palace. Back then it was used as a dusty, forgotten study, somewhere for my grandfather to tuck himself away, reading his endless books. When he passed, I declared it my own sanctuary." He chuckled, recalling the work that went into the room. "I took down the shelves and replaced them with cabinets to store my equipment out of sight. Then I removed all the curtains. My mother was horrified, but— they let me do it. I think they were glad for anything that kept me quiet for long hours at a time."

"It's perfect," she murmured, her voice a soft murmur in the near darkness.

"It is," he agreed. Far more so because she was there.

As if she could read his mind, Francesca looked up at him, her body wrapped in his embrace. "Thank you for bringing me here," she whispered. And when she lifted herself up on her toes, it was the most natural thing in the world for him to meet her halfway. Their lips touched, and suddenly it was as if there was not enough time in the world, not enough oxygen for them both to breathe. His arms tightened, and he felt her knot her fingers in his shirt, her intensity flaring as hot as his. He wanted her—and she wanted him back, the relief of that revelation almost making his knees buckle...

Almost.

Instead, Ari growled and turned Francesca back toward the bed, happier than he had any right to be that the room was so small, the furniture so scant that there was nothing blocking their progress. They tumbled to the bed in a rush of urgency, and he wasn't sure who was moving faster to remove the other's clothes. But Francesca laughed, her eyes bright with excitement, her warmth radiating out despite the coolness of that room, and he wanted to capture that warmth, to hold it against his heart against any pain and darkness that might come his way.

There would be no darkness anymore, not as long as Francesca was in his arms. He rolled over to reach for the nightstand drawer, but she took advantage of him stretching out on his back and moved sinuously on top of him, her legs straddling his hips. Batting away his hands, she reached over to the stand, her precarious position wobbling to the point where, to be a gentleman, he needed to plant his hands on either side of her hips.

It was a hardship, his life.

He drank in the sight of her as she opened the drawer and rooted inside—the long extension of her arms, the flowing curves of her waist, belly, hips and breasts. He'd seen her naked in the sunlight but this—with the glow of the moon setting her alight, her hair once more spilling out of its pins to tumble halfway down her back—this was the Francesca that would fuel a thousand fevered dreams. This was how he would always remember her...and he, more than most, knew the power of memory.

She giggled, finally sitting upright and triumphantly holding up a glinting foil-wrapped package. "You make a habit out of bringing girls back to the palace?"

"No, but I had to keep protection somewhere."

"Uh-huh. I can't believe your parents left your room this intact." She surveyed the package critically. "Assuming this isn't ten years old." Her mock-serious gaze transferred to his face. "Because that would be bad."

"It's definitely not ten years old," he assured her, but he kept his tone light, easy. There was no reason to betray the first thought he'd had in his head at her teasing words, but the truth of that thought burned through him, removing all others that came before or after it.

It would not be bad to have a reason to keep Francesca by his side for a lifetime. It wouldn't.

Even that realization fled his mind a moment later when Francesca's fingers drifted up his shaft, galvanizing his attention. "I think, first," she murmured. "There's something else I'd like to try."

He lifted himself on his elbows, staring as she slid down his legs and dropped between his thighs. She bent forward and kissed her way along his upper leg, not unlike what he'd done to her earlier that day, except he had nowhere near the level of restraint she did. It had been so long since he'd been kissed so intimately that tiny explosions of anticipation and panic were skyrocketing through his brain—getting louder and more intense as she reached the straining length of his shaft.

"Francesca," he gritted out, but she chuckled, the tremor of her mouth against the soft skin of his sac twisting him inside out. She drew her tongue up the length of him once, twice, teasing him with her mouth as she sighed out a gentle breath over his hyper-sensitized skin.

"I think...one thing more," she said. Then she closed her mouth over him. Ari collapsed back, the sensations ripping through him a thousand times stronger than anything he could remember happening before, and he felt the climax build inside him as if he was seventeen not twenty-seven—not a full-grown man who could hold himself in check, for God's sake. She plunged down over him again and drew all the way out, and his back fairly arched off the bed. At some point he began cursing—but in Oûrois, his language skills deteriorating as Francesca finally took mercy on him. If mercy could be what you called it. She sheathed him and then, finally, with a slowness that nearly made him pass out with need, settled her beautiful body over him and slid home.

Ari's eyes flashed open. He hadn't realized he'd had them closed. He blinked to see Francesca smiling down at him, her hair now fully down around her shoulders. When had that happened?

"Better?" she murmured, as she moved against him once, twice.

"Better," he growled. But he clasped his hands to her hips, not to guide her but to hold her in place as he rolled her to the side, then onto her back.

She widened her eyes, then sighed as he pushed deep inside her. "Oh..." she sighed. He settled his mouth over hers, kissing her lips, her cheeks, then a soft, coursing line to where he could whisper in her ear.

"Though this is better still, ," he said, and he filled her further, reveling in the way she tightened around him, slick and hot. "I want to be able to touch you, to kiss you." He pulled back and stared at her, knowing he could gaze into those eyes a million more times and never tire of the passion he saw in their depths, the passion and rightness and truth. "I want to watch you while I make love to you, and learn every possible way to make you happy."

Her eyes darkened at the intensity in his voice, which sent another surge of desire racing through him. Good. She should know he was serious. Francesca had become more than the woman who had rescued him from the sea of his own lost memories, the companion who'd supported him when he needed her most. At this point, she was his anchor and his rock, his beating heart. He didn't fully know where she'd come from, but he knew where she belonged.

With him.

"Is that a royal command?" she said as if he'd spoken this last thought out loud, her voice ever so slightly teasing.

He braced his hands on the bed, and leaned toward her again, knowing that nothing would ever feel so right as this.

"You better believe it," he whispered.

Thirty-One

Fran awoke in a rush, her sense of equilibrium once more shattered, her confusion paramount for a harrowing split second.

Then a warm arm shifted along her side, dropping to her belly to pull her close. Ari. Or Ryker. Or it could be Conti for all she cared.

"Morning," he murmured as she reached up to push back her hair. She and Ari were tangled together in a flurry of sheets, the pillows half-tumbled off the bed. But they might as well be in a theater, as strongly as her attention was drawn to the enormous screen in front of them. Not a screen, of course. A window.

"You've got to be kidding me," she breathed, slipping out of Ari's grasp and sitting upright.

The sky over the distant Aegean Sea was startling in its beauty. Rich, rolling pink clouds skidded through a gradually lightening sky, and the sun rising to the left, out of sight, sent beams of glittering wonder across the glassy sea. She grabbed up a sheet and wrapped it around herself as she moved toward the window, trying to see everywhere at once. From this vantage point the city itself looked like a fairytale construct: vehicles scooting down narrow alleyways, chimneys puffing out smoke from the bakeries lining the streets, even a few townspeople up and about—on their way to work, to the beach, or simply out for an early morning stroll.

She didn't move as the bed creaked, Ari's feet hitting the floor with a thud that was oddly reassuring, given the fantasy world in front of her. Without him in the room with her, she would have been unmoored. "It's like this every morning?" she asked.

"Most mornings." His voice was gruff, gravelly, and she realized—she wasn't used to waking up with him. Her entire understanding of the man was summed up in a few days of intense experiences, not a true foundation of who and what he was. The thought made her unduly melancholy, and she was glad he wasn't looking at her as he came up to the window. "The sea changes more than you think it should, morning to morning. The city, it changes all the time. Buildings go up and come down, festivals and parades pop up in one part only to move seemingly overnight to another. It's a never-ending stream of change." She could hear the happiness in his voice. "I don't need to watch TV to get a fix on the pulse of the city. I simply need to watch. The world around us, it's not so easy. But here, it's different."

"It certainly is." Francesca leaned against him, surprised that with him so near, she felt less anxious, not more. Ordinarily, she could never let anyone get too close, but Ari was different. He had lost his past and was focused on recovering it. He had no reason to care about hers.

His next words confirmed that. "You'll want to go to your friends this morning, before the press conference—and before my mother gets her hooks into you. She'll want every detail of the last few days you can spare, and it's probably better that she knows none of them." He squeezed her shoulders. "And you'll be glad to know that we found Conti Goba."

"Oh?" she glanced up to search his face. "Please tell me he's not dead."

He smiled, and she saw the soft burr of beard coming in again along his jawline. "No. Nothing so alarming. But your comment about how those identities get fashioned, the ones that can be sold so easily and for such little money, it got me thinking. It had to have been stolen. Conti could have been injured or in jail."

She nodded. "It's a risk, but in a city where flashing credentials is done so frequently..."

"You have to have something to flash. But he's in the hospital, as it happens." He waved off her flare of alarm. "His wife is having a baby. They didn't trust the local hospital in Makila. In the rush to get her to the hospital, Conti dropped his pack and everything went flying. When he realized he had his passport, his wife's passport, birth certificates—they live in the country and didn't know what would be required—he thought he had it all. It was only later that he realized what he was missing." He shrugged. "But since he had the rest, he wasn't worried. He simply assumed it was lost. Dimitri texted me early this morning that it had been returned to him, with no one the wiser."

"Good," Fran nodded. "With any luck, you'll never need false papers again."

"True." He winked at her. "Though if I do, I'll know where to go to find them."

He meant the seedy bar in the marina district, she knew he did, but his words still set her on edge. She lifted her hand, masking a feigned yawn. "I should go."

"I have fresh clothes for you—and the shower is that way," he said, pointing through a door she hadn't seen last night. "Not as fancy as at the hotel, with accommodations down the hall."

She grinned, her good mood returning. "Not everywhere can be so nice." She tilted her head and hoped her words didn't betray her relief at having time to herself. "You're leaving?"

"I've been summoned to a breakfast briefing, and the press conference is at ten. I'll be tied up with appearances for the rest of my natural life I suspect." Still, he didn't seem unhappy about it. The perspective of a year in captivity could change a lot of things, Fran suspected.

"When you're ready, you can take the stairs to the first or second level and ask anyone to direct you back to the guest apartments. Or the pool." He shook his head. "Dimitri seemed to think that's where your friends would be. It's apparently become their second home."

"Thank you," she said. Once again, leaning toward him to kiss him seemed the most natural thing in the world to her, for all that she knew their magical idyll was already over.

Perhaps Ari knew it too. With the same affability that he'd displayed regarding his upcoming appearances, he left her with a brief kiss and a warm smile, as if there was nothing unusual about the crown prince of Oûros leaving a strange American woman alone in his room.

Then again, who was she to know how things usually rolled in Oûros? For all she knew, Ari could have had a different woman in his room every week. Somehow, though...she didn't think so.

It was another half hour before she made her way down to the first floor, where a staff member insisted on guiding her to the pool. The young man practiced his English the whole way, beaming with every smile Fran gave him, so that by the time she reached the pool area, she too was feeling more upbeat.

And ready for the combined screams of Lauren, Nicki, and Emmaline.

"Oh my *God*! She lives!" Nicki saw her first from her

vantage point in the pool, and she hauled herself up out of the water as Emmaline and Lauren pivoted in their chairs. Then they too were scrambling up, everyone talking at once.

"When did you get back? Last night?" Emmaline asked. "What's he like—Ari, that is. Is he better? Does he remember everything?"

"Dimitri said he was better, nearly back to full speed, but Dimitri lies all the time," declared Lauren with a knowing grimace. "He thinks I don't know it, but I keep telling him I've been around far less scrupulous men than he realizes." She laughed. "Of course, that doesn't make him feel any better."

"Stefan thinks he's remembering more too," Nicki put in, "But he's also cautious. They'll imply he's completely up to speed. If anyone challenges Ari, I think they'll lower the boom and tell the reporters to back off. Fortunately, he's not been involved in the setting of any real policies at this point. His own Accession Ball was still in process when he had the accident, so he hadn't started any official duties."

"Kristos lives in the hope that he can return to the military, but I think he's willing to stay crown prince for a while, so long as Ari is back." Emmaline said. "But how are you doing, Fran? Dimitri said you helped more than they could have ever imagined?"

"I—" Fran blinked as all three of the women focused on her, and she knew it was time for her close-up. She understood her part, and she understood her audience. This endlessly sympathetic trio of women had been there since she'd first begun believing that she could be the person she'd fashioned for herself, the woman who could one day graduate with a good job, good friends, and the incredible experience of helping people all around the world.

They were here, they genuinely loved her, and all she had to do was smile.

Instead, she burst into tears.

"Fran!" Nicki reached her first, enveloping her in a sturdy hug, but Emmaline and Lauren were right behind her. Emmaline joined the hug while Lauren dragged her to a chair under an umbrella.

"Sit," Lauren ordered, as the others let her go only long enough to pull up chairs beside her. "Talk."

"I'm fine, really, I'm fine. I don't know why I'm reacting like this. There's nothing wrong. How could there be anything wrong?"

"Uh, maybe because you just helped nurse the crown prince of a mythological kingdom back to health without even having finished your graduate degree yet?" Nikki asked dryly.

Emmaline chimed in, her soft hands tight on Fran's, damping down the worst of their shaking. "And because you went off on an adventure with him, making your way through the streets of his city and allowing him to see it with new eyes? Oh, and *then* you helped him reconnect with the family he loves so much?"

"And maybe you fell in love a little bit along the way?" Lauren reached out and wiped Fran's tears away, the gesture so gentle it was all Fran could do to stem a new tide of waterworks. "I mean, that'll do it every time."

"I can't fall in love with him, I'm a monster," Fran hiccupped, not realizing what she was saying until it was too late and the words were out there, ugly and hulking.

"What? What are you talking about? No!" The girls erupted in a chorus of disavowal and disbelief, and though Fran immediately jerked back into the role she was playing, the role she needed to continue playing. It didn't change the fact that her secret was out now, in the open. She had given it energy and spoken its name aloud. *Monster*. She was a monster.

No other name or term could describe her so well she

thought, and it wasn't even for all the expected reasons. Sure she was a thief and a grifter, a liar and a cheat. A hustler and a con artist, but those were simply things she had become, skills she had learned to survive when she had no one else to depend on. But monster...that felt right. That felt true.

That felt horrifying.

The buzzing outrage of her friends penetrated her haze a second later, and she knew she needed to take immediate evasive action to stem the tide. She lifted her hands to either side of her face, laughing only a little hysterically, at least to her ears. "I'm sorry—I'm sorry!" she laughed, shaking her head quickly as they finally subsided. "That came out totally wrong. I didn't mean that I'm, like, a monster-monster, but guys, I feel so bad. There was—I mean—Ari saw a woman tonight. Someone he knows, or at least who knows him. And I...oh, god, I'm the *worst.*"

That shut them up, as she knew it would. Three sets of eyes now riveted on her, Nikki looking intrigued, Emmaline with her hands clasped to her chest, and Lauren with a sly smile on her face.

"Oh yeah?" Lauren asked. "Do you know who this mystery woman is?"

"I didn't then, but she recognized him for sure. And I didn't want to let him go. I should have, right? It would have been so natural and easy to figure out a way for them to meet, but I...I just couldn't. I distracted him, pulled him away from her. I know that's horrible and selfish. I have no claim on him, I have no right to keep him from the people that he loves, but—"

"Wait, didn't you march him up to the palace last night and hand him over to his family?" Emmaline asked. When Fran blinked at her in surprise, she waved her off. "Oh, please. I've been tagging along with the queen for long enough that I know how to find things out. They kept all the details out of what happened after you showed up, but I knew that you arrived with the prince the moment I woke up this morning. You're a freaking hero, Fran, not a monster."

"I mean, I guess that depends on how you distracted him," Lauren said, waggling her brows. Then she grinned with genuine delight. "You kissed him, right? You totally kissed him in front of the gods, the world, and everyone. I'm surprised Eros didn't show up and declare a national holiday."

"Give it time," Nikki groaned. "These people have more holidays on their calendar than anywhere I've ever been in the world. And I've been some places."

"Well, I'm glad you did kiss him," Emmaline announced. She met Fran's eyes with a steady gaze, her smile genuine. Happiness radiated out from her like the warmth of the sun. "He would be the luckiest man alive to fall in love with you, Fran. And we'd be right there cheering you on, every step of the way."

"Stop—" Fran protested, as the others piled on. "You'll make me cry again. Just tell me everything I've missed over the past few days."

But as the girls laughed and chattered, she heard the hissing accusation ripple through the air, and knew it to be the truth.

Monster.

Thirty-Two

"You're going to do splendidly, dear. You always do."

Ari looked down at his mother, marveling anew how small she seemed to him. Had he thought that before, in the weeks and months leading up to the fateful airplane flight that had taken him so far away from these people? He honestly didn't know. He seemed to be remembering much more, but the process wasn't a conscious one. It wasn't as if he could suddenly recall every detail of his past life, but more that he realized he wasn't missing the major details. After a lifetime of living less than deliberately, he didn't have a firm sense of what he'd forgotten versus what he'd never truly remembered in the first place.

"The message is simple enough," he agreed, rewarded by his mother's quick smile. She wanted more than anything for him to be well, to be healthy. She didn't want to let the press corps loose on him, though by conducting this meeting now, before the regional feeds could get a person in place, they were heading off most of the media circus before it began. All Ari had to do was show up and look the part. Fake it 'til you make it, Francesca had said. Truer words were never spoken.

His parents and Dimitri entered the press room first. The questions started almost the moment they hit the door.

Fortunately, the plan was simple. An announcement, a series of questions, then Ari would make an appearance like a magician stepping out from behind the curtain. They'd already agreed that he'd continue answering questions until the reporters had exhausted all the ones of relevance, and they'd gone over a list fifty items long of increasingly more ridiculous queries. Ari was prepared for anything—but most of all, he realized, he didn't mind. The questions lobbed by the reporters looking for an angle to titillate their viewers weren't intended to harm him personally, or to harm his family. There was no danger here.

The tiniest shiver of apprehension skated up his spine. That didn't mean that there wasn't any danger, anywhere, of course. But not here. Not in this scripted, highly public space, where what mattered most was his performance—not what truths he could tell. Later, however, there would be time to ensure that every threat was run down...even, especially, those he could not quite remember.

"Are you ready, sir?" Stefan came up beside him at the door, ready to enter the small auditorium used for intimate gatherings of the press or special video presentations for honored guests. Ari couldn't remember the last time he'd been in here. Still, he'd attended dozens of such briefings before as the silent son, solely to help the family put on a united front.

"Does he always call me sir?" Ari asked Kristos, and his brother grimaced.

"Whenever he thinks other people are listening. You refused to let him call you, 'Your Highness,' so he gets by as best he can."

His brother was dressed in his military honor uniform, the braids and decoration making Ari feel particularly unimpressive. But his path hadn't been through the military beyond his two years of compulsory service. His path had been through these doors in front of him, addressing the media on behalf of the royal family.

It felt right, he realized, whether he had all his memories or not. It felt like what he should most be doing.

"They're ready," Stefan said, his hand at his ear where a mic sat permanently affixed to his brain, from what Ari could tell. Kristos led the way, and Ari followed, with Stefan at his back.

He entered the room and to his surprise, the press corps was standing. He didn't think they normally did that, but he smiled as a hundred different cameras flashed and video cameras rolled in the back. His father stood beside the podium, and Kristos stopped before it, allowing Ari to pass in front of him. Three men of the royal family stood arrayed for more photos, while Stefan stood back by the door. Beyond his father, his mother sat, and Dimitri stood at the other door.

He was surrounded by the people who loved him most, Ari realized, and pride and gratitude swelled in his chest, threatening to choke him.

He looked out into the crowd. "Before I answer any questions, I wanted to take a moment." He glanced at his father who had nothing but approval and encouragement written across his face. Ari could probably start quacking like a duck and the king wouldn't blink. "And my apologies for going off-script with the first words out of my mouth."

He turned back as the press corps rumbled a laugh. "I'm standing here today more grateful to be back in my own country than I can express. Not because I was treated badly, and not because I fell ill. I recovered as fast as could reasonably be expected with my injuries, and was returned as soon as my benefactors realized who I was—as I'm sure my parents have told you."

Several reporters looked eager to ask him for more details on that score, and he pushed on. "But to be so far away from my country, to not be able to return, makes a man appreciate what he has. Appreciate the hardworking men and women who make up our communities, appreciate the compassion we show our neighbors, our dedication to good schools, strong military, and a thriving business environment. I'm lucky to be alive, many would say. And I'd be one of them." More laughter. "But I'm luckier still to be able to represent Oûros once more. To walk these streets and see these people, and know that I've come home."

He gestured to the crowd. "Any questions?"

The press corps surged forward, pelting him with a barrage. How long had he been unaware of his surroundings? Where had he been flying that night—and why fly at all into a storm? What had gone wrong with his plane? Where had he crashed, specifically? What injuries had he sustained? What was his timeline for returning to duty? What were the doctors' reports on him?

He handled all of them with an ease he hadn't expected, grateful that his short-term memory at least remained rigorously intact. It surprised him how simple it was to recall the information he needed, to say it in exactly the right way. He'd been briefed well, but it was more than that. It was a realization growing within him, almost too big to fully grasp.

A new question refocused him. "There were some reports that you were seen in the city streets with an unknown woman last night. Care to comment on that?"

Beside him, King Jasen tensed and Ari could almost feel the concern radiating from his mother as the queen beamed at him. Francesca had been seen, and as much as he wanted to claim her, this was not the time. The briefing was being held in

Oûrois, but no matter what the language, he knew any attention he paid Francesca now would only cause her harm.

He had to do things carefully, and he had to do them well. It wasn't solely his future at stake here.

"I don't think it would come as any surprise that I would find a beautiful woman to squire me around," he said with a deliberately rakish grin. "Though before you ask, we're not married." The laughter sounded in the room again, the moment successfully handled. "And the street festivals of our capital city were one of the things I missed the most. I couldn't resist walking the streets and hearing the music, for all that, once again, it wasn't on script. If any of you were out last night, I think you'll agree that our city shone with celebration. It was truly the moment that I felt like I was home."

His mother had stood during his little speech and the reporters turned to her expectantly. "With Ari's return, I am in the very happy position of being able to announce the return to our original plans all the way from last summer, as well," she said, beaming with such delight that everyone straightened. "The question of Accession will be handled in due time, but with all that we have to celebrate, we will begin making plans for a new national holiday in Oûros, in tandem with our business and tourism department to ensure it brings the greatest value to our fair country."

She gazed at Ari with unaffected tears in her eyes, though her smile never faltered. "We'll call it National Homecoming Day."

<h1 style="text-align:center">Thirty-Three</h1>

Fran staggered under the weight of yet another dress that Lauren pulled off the rack, rocking back a step.

"Don't drop anything!" Lauren ordered. "I swear to God, if I'd known being a queen meant you had immediate access to clothes from the country's top designers, I would've rethought my career choices."

"You think Dimitri wouldn't move heaven and earth to get you clothing if that's what you really wanted?" Nicki teased. "He'd install your own line of seamstresses by nightfall."

An earlier version of Lauren would have shot back a witty comeback, but as Fran watched, this Lauren simply smiled, her eyes fixed on a faraway point as her fingers flicked past hanger after hanger of gowns. "Yeah, you're probably right," she said, and Fran's heart shimmied again, threatening a repeat of the waterworks from earlier this morning.

That had been easy enough to explain away. She was tired, overwrought, and had just helped navigate a prince back to solid ground when no one truly had known how Ari would react to her. She'd managed to get through that unscathed, and while local media mentioned a mysterious woman at the festival last night, they'd also reported that Ari had brushed off the insinuation that she'd been anything other than casual arm candy. Which was exactly what he should have insinuated...

And yet.

"Are you really sure the queen wants us all dolled up again?" Nicki asked plaintively. "I mean, don't get me wrong, I will rock these stilettos, but it seems like we were kind of a nuisance the last time around."

"You're definitely not a nuisance, and this ball isn't like that one," Emmaline said. Fran wheeled around with the last of Lauren's picks to see Emmaline cross to the bed. They'd all gathered in Emmaline's room because it was the biggest suite—large enough to hold the trunk sale's worth of ball gowns the queen had sent up for them. But Emmaline didn't need a new fancy dress. She'd been delivered a dozen of them during the first week of her engagement to Kristos, and she didn't even have the ring yet.

The ring. Fran's brows went up. Would Kristos propose officially at this upcoming ball—with a royal diamond? She dropped the gowns on the bed, a flurry of satin and tulle, and focused on Emmaline, keeping her voice casual. "How is it different?" she asked, picking up a cool green confection.

"You can't go with that one. You did green last time." Lauren took the offending garment out of Fran's hands and trooped back to the rack as Emmaline selected another gown and held it out to Nicki.

"This one is more a celebration, not for any specific reasons," Emmaline said. "There will be family and friends invited, a few local notables, but the point isn't the Accession or the age-old question of who the prince will marry. It's a Homecoming Ball, the way the queen describes it. She's test-running the idea in advance of a larger function tied to the official state holiday she wants to be declared."

"Right," Nicki said, holding a dress up to her athletic form. "I'd totally look like a coconut cupcake in this." She handed the dress back to Emmaline, then continued. "So why are we having to dress up like 'Toddlers in Tiaras' if it's not an official state visit or a matchmaking gig?"

Lauren's laugh was both feminine and derisive, in the way no one but Lauren could pull off. "Maybe because the queen isn't simply test-driving the holiday, she's test-driving potential brides for Ari?" she asked. "If *we're* supposed to get this fancy, you know that she's inviting other women. It would be totally weird otherwise. And of those other women, how much you want to bet we'll see a return showing of the crew from Kristos's pre-engagement bash?"

"But I'm sure Edeena Saleri is coming to this new event, and I didn't meet her before," Fran said, as casually as possible. "I would have remembered her, I'm pretty sure."

"Oh, the family was represented, but not by Edeena," Emmaline said. "Just the father."

"Really?" Fran tilted her head, trying to remember. "Do you remember his name?"

Emmaline raised her gaze to the ceiling. "I don't know. Silas, I think. Yes. Silas Saleri."

"Silas Saleri." Fran jolted. The man she'd seen in the promotional poster at the municipal airport...the man who'd made her afraid, though she didn't know why.

Monster. The word skated through her mind—but who was the monster in this scenario, her? Him? Why couldn't she place the man? Had Silas been among the older guard of men scowling at Kristos at the Accession Ball? They all blended together after a while.

"This one!" Lauren announced, pulling a gown out of the pile and thrusting it at Fran. "You have to try this on."

Fran took it dutifully enough, but she frowned at Lauren.

"It's green," she said. "I thought you said you didn't want me to wear green again."

"It's not green—it's *cream*, with a sage green bustle and gorgeous emerald embroidery. And it's going to be perfect on you. We'll need to put your hair up—even though guys generally like hair down. With that kind of neckline, you're totally going to want to keep your hair off your shoulders. Try it on."

Fran shrugged, and Nicki moved to her side to help her undo the fastenings of the gown. "I thought this wasn't supposed to be a meat market."

"Everything's a meat market," Lauren said, refocusing on the racks. "And that gown would cost ten thousand dollars retail. Someone ought to wear it, and it might as well be you." She frowned over her shoulder at Nicki. "Nicki, stop fussing. You've got to try this gown on."

"Yo, my meat's totally off the market now," Nicki objected, while Lauren shook out a new dress, markedly different from the belle-of-the-ball gowns she'd been pawing through before. "I hate these kinds of events, anyway."

Lauren held out the sheathe of black, shimmery fabric. "All the more reason for you to wear this. Stefan's entire face is going to melt. He'll hustle you out of that ballroom so quickly your head's going to spin."

"Ohhhh," Nicki said. She pulled the gown from Lauren's grasp and held it up to the mirror as Fran worked her head through the neckline of her gown with Emmaline's help. Nicki grinned and Emmaline laughed, giving Nicki an enthusiastic thumbs up.

"I have to be in the room when he sees you in that," Lauren said triumphantly. "Dimitri will have his hands full keeping all the marriage-minded misses from tripping over Ari, so I need something to bring me joy."

"That dress will definitely do it," Fran agreed.

Nicki grinned, kicking out a leg to follow the line of an impossibly high slit in the deep black gown. At the last ball Nicki had worn a toga dress, which as Fran recalled Stefan had taken slight exception to as well. But this gown put that one to shame. Flowing, sleek, and perfectly proportioned for Nicki's compact but lithe figure, the material practically shimmered as Nicki swung around to face them all again.

Then she stared.

"Oh my God, Fran," she breathed.

"What?" Fran's hands went instantly to her hair, knocked askew by her efforts to get into the dress. "What's wrong?"

A knock at Emmaline's door immediately distracted them, and Lauren pivoted sharply as a voice called from the corridor. "Girls? It's Catherine. May I come in?"

"Of course!" Emmaline called out before Fran could ward her off. She was too far away from the mirror to see what had startled Nicki so, but a moment later the queen burst into the suite and took them all in with a sweeping glance.

She froze when she saw Fran, her face arrested.

"What?" Fran cried, looking down at herself. "What's wrong with me?"

"Nothing at all, my dear," the queen said, walking around her. Her eyes were lit with speculation as she surveyed Fran from top to toe. "Nothing at all. This will do very nicely."

She slanted a glance toward Lauren. "You picked this out, didn't you?" she charged, and Lauren laid a modest hand on her chest as Fran lifted her skirts and finally positioned herself in front of the mirror.

"Oh," she managed, blinking fast.

She of all people knew the truth in the statement "The clothes make the man." She'd gone through several identities, and her outward appearance had as much, if not more to do with her success than the paper trail she'd created both before she arrived and after she left.

But nothing could have prepared her for this gown.

It wasn't like Emmaline's fairytale pink confection from the ball a few weeks ago. That gown had done everything to showcase Emmaline's ethereal beauty and incandescent joy. This dress was every bit as big but it was...elegant. Sophisticated. It slid along Fran's body as if it had been tailored specifically to her, but somehow made her seem taller, almost regal.

It wasn't a gown for a princess. It was a gown for a queen.

And it was a queen who walked up next to Fran now, the two of them standing shoulder to shoulder in the mirror's reflection. "You are absolutely stunning, Francesca," Catherine said, her arm snaking around Fran to give her a hug. "In that dress, I believe you could do anything."

Thirty-Four

Ari stomped down the hallway, his head buzzing with too many meetings, too many file folders, too many screens of information. His memory was dropping in new facts and realizations by the hour, and what it wasn't willing to provide, Cyril was ready as backup.

But none of it was providing him with the information he most sorely needed.

Something had happened in the run-up to his flight from the municipal airport. According to Dimitri, Ari had been toying with new gadgets for days, talking about taking a flight to test his new instrument panels. So he hadn't been fleeing headlong into the skies that night—not that it would have made any sense, anyway. Dimitri hadn't even known he was going to attempt a flight.

According to Cyril, there had been no threats to the royal family recorded in the days prior to or immediately after his disappearance—no activity at all, in fact, other than a building excitement about the prince's planned Accession activities. The night of his flight, he'd attended a state function with his parents and had rubbed elbows with all the usual government officials, captains of industry, and members of Oûros's noble families.

Though the Andris line had sat atop the throne for centuries, Oûros had started as a collection of tiny city-states, each boasting a landowner with the title of "Count." With the consolidation of power under a central king, the original monarch saw the value of allowing the tiny fiefdoms to retain their noble titles, regardless of whether their estates were governed by the larger whole. The result was a country full of noblemen and women, each with varying degrees of royal blood in their veins.

Ari's allotment of royal blood was about to boil over, however, if he didn't soon figure out who he'd been—

"Aristotle." The voice cut across his thoughts so abruptly he halted, gaping at his mother.

"I—I'm sorry," he said, blinking quickly as he re-set his expression. "My thoughts were a million miles away."

"Walk with me?"

Ari was instantly on his guard, but he tidied the papers he'd been glaring at while walking into the folder and tucked them under his arm. His mother usually didn't make a habit of strolling through the south wing of the palace, so her presence here was suspect. This was the main area for the business of the kingdom, and she usually left that to her husband...and to Ari, he realized, the certainty of that memory merely serving to heighten his concern.

Still, he nodded to her, gesturing her down the hall. "The gardens aren't too hot at this hour," he suggested.

"My thoughts exactly." She beamed at him and he sensed more danger here. His mother was up to something. He suddenly felt the weight of all those still-lost memories piling on his shoulders. Was there something he should have known, should have done already? He couldn't imagine what.

They stepped out into the coolness of the early evening, and some of Ari's tension rolled off him. He remembered this place, and now each new memory that returned to him was no longer accompanied by pain. But this garden had been one of his favorite retreats once he'd started frequenting the government section of the palace. It was rarely used and could always be counted on to be quiet.

His mother remained silent until they rounded the first corner of the manicured space. Then she began almost casually, ensuring Ari was ready for anything from a breakfast menu discussion to war time alliances.

What she said, however, still managed to take him by surprise.

"What do you know of Francesca Simmons—truly know of her?" she asked.

He blinked down at her. "Know? Not much beyond Stefan's report." His mother didn't need to know that he'd pored over that report among all the stacks of documentation he'd been delivered that day. They had done fairly complete workups on the four girls after Kristos had taken a fancy to Emmaline. "Psychology graduate student at George Washington, completing her coursework within the next year. No prior arrests, no tax evasion charges, family in upstate Michigan. Her father remarried after her biological mother died, and she has two step-siblings from her step-mother's previous marriage."

"I noticed that," the queen said since, of course, she would have been given access to the girls' files as well. "There's not a great deal of information about her family beyond what's in the file, however. No mention of grandparents, no social media profiles, nothing." She sighed. "And believe me, I looked."

"Why?" Ari tried to keep his tone light, but he could feel his irritation expand. His mother was allowed to be protective of him, sure. But from what he'd been able to pry out of Dimitri, she was the one who'd most wanted Francesca thrown in his path. Now she was worried about whether or not Francesca's grandma had a Facebook page?

"She's just so—polished, I guess is the right word. Seasoned. She's different from the other three girls, who are all lovely, don't get me wrong. But they don't have the sense of presence that Francesca does. Like she's seen more in the space of her young life than any person should—and yet it's shaped her in the best possible way."

"Well, she did decide to go into psychology," Ari said. "Maybe experiencing some of the trials in her own life gave her the idea that she could help others get through their troubles, too. That would tend to encourage you to grow up fast."

"True." His mother still seemed unconvinced, and she slanted him a questioning glance. "Why did you ask her to go with you when you left the island and struck out for the capital city?"

"Why?" Ari hadn't remembered his mother's cross-examination being so oblique. Had it always been that way, or was this a new development in the past year? When she kept her serenely expectant gaze pinned on him, however, he took a stab at a response.

"I—well, because she was easy to be around, and she'd been there with me when I had...an episode, for lack of a better term. I remembered something that caused me distress, and she—well, she held my hands. She didn't say anything, really. She simply was there. Steadying me, supporting me, I suppose, until I was ready to go on. I appreciated that about her. Both that she stayed, and that she didn't try to do anything but be there. It was all I really needed, and I think she knew that, somehow." He shrugged. "Again, she's had some training in this area, which you knew before you sent her my way."

His mother didn't take offense to the accusation, but she

also didn't seem convinced either. "And when you landed with her, where did you go, exactly? We know about where you lodged, but...well there's a story we can't fully refute from a taxi driver who insists he saw you. Yet the tale he tells is of a ragged, raving worker with a young American tourist—strangely enough, a tourist he'd picked up at the municipal airport." She studied him. "Why did you go there?"

For a split second, Ari thought about lying. But he couldn't afford to. Not until he understood if there had been any threat to the family, real or imagined.

"I wanted to see the airfield where my plane had been that night. To see if it jogged any memories." He shrugged. "It didn't." None that he could understand, anyway.

"And this delirium the taxi driver mentioned?"

Ari grimaced. "The attempt threw me a little. I recovered, but I'm sure I wasn't the most pleasant of fares."

"But Francesca was there."

"Yes," he said, studying her. "She was there. Why?"

"It makes me happy to know it, dear," his mother said, patting his arm. "We all should have someone with us when we most need them, don't you think?"

A deferent cough had them both looking up, and Ari was surprised to see Cyril standing there at the edge of the garden. "Your Highness. If I may borrow Prince Ari?"

"You may borrow him and this lovely evening," she said with a smile. She made her goodbyes and moved off, leaving the two men gazing after her.

"Cyril—" Ari began, but the advisor lifted a hand.

"Not here," he murmured. "Your mother has bugged this garden within an inch of its life. Follow me."

They walked a short distance to one of the reinforced cabinet rooms set aside for official business, which could not be breached by electronic surveillance of any kind. They weren't the first to arrive. Stefan and King Jasen were there, along with Dimitri. Opposite them, across the conference table, three rugged, weathered Oûrois operatives, two women and a man, stood in a tight formation. Their gazes shifted to Ari the moment he walked into the room, but they said nothing.

"Forgive me," Ari began without preamble. "You look like ONSF, but I can't place you."

The nearest woman's lips twitched. "You wouldn't, Your Highness." Her voice was low, no-nonsense. "We served well before your time."

"Marta and Delia Aetos, as well as Grigori Bouras, are all demigods of Poseidon," Stefan confirmed, and Ari's gaze sharpened. "Mercenary fighters, no longer affiliated with the Crown, but still friends of Oûros."

"I see." And he could, too. All three wore their hair cropped close to their skulls, and looked to be in impressive shape. While tall and slender, the trio were built like Olympic swimmers—broad backs, long arms, their torsos slightly longer than average, and their hips and legs muscled without being heavy. "What brings you to the capital city?"

"Repayment of a favor," Grigori said with a quick flash of even teeth, startlingly white against his tanned face.

Dimitri snorted as the two demigods shared a grin. "Our paths crossed earlier this month. He and I had the opportunity to work together. Not every day that the descendants of Zeus and Poseidon get that chance."

"Since then, Grigori and his team have proven to be a valuable resource," Stefan continued. "They have gathered some Intel that we think might shed light on some of your experiences in Turkey."

Ari studied the man. Again, like most demigods, he was slightly larger than life, but not in the heavily built way of

Dimitri or the lean grace of Stefan. "Any clarity that I can have about that would be very welcome."

At Stefan's nod, Grigori reached into his bag and pulled out an electronic tablet. He powered it on, tapped it a few times and crossed the room to hand it to Ari. "Your Highness," he murmured, meeting Ari's eyes. "We're glad you have returned to your family. Poseidon's nymphs worked tirelessly to find any scrap of information, sending out the call world-wide to ignite any of their line. But what we found was…unexpected. The need for the royal family to serve as gatekeepers for the seas as well as the land is clearly at hand."

Ari took the device, glanced down, and froze. A basilisk straight out of Greek mythology stared back at him, looking very much alive. Its rooster beak stretched wide in a squawk of fury that seemed to convulse its red-scaled body, and its thick, spiked lizard tail thrashed.

"By the gods," he muttered, gripping the tablet hard. Memories crowded in, dark and feral. Memories that only grew sharper as he flipped through the rest of the pictures. There were more basilisks in cages, some of them carcasses; what looked like miniature versions of Nemean lions with their glossy golden coats and razor-sharp, unbreakable claws; and the eye-watering monstrosity of a miniature chimera in what looked to be a four-foot-square kennel. The utterly impossible combination of a lion's head and legs, a goat's head screaming out of the creature's back, and a tail that terminated in a snake's hissing head was the stuff of nightmares. His nightmares, in particular.

He looked up to find the attention of the entire room riveted on him as he handed the tablet back to Grigori. "Those creatures, or creatures that looked damned close to them, were imprisoned with me in that hellhole. Where did you get these images?"

Grigori returned the tablet to his pack. "The last couple I

paid for, working my contacts off the coast of Libya. The first I took myself in southern Turkey. It's only been a few weeks since Stefan cleared the cache they held in Alaçati, but that raid sent most of the importers underground. The trafficking of these creatures is a dangerous business."

Ari made a face. "There's a market for them? People *pay*?"

"Hundreds of thousands of euros." Grigori nodded. "Unfortunately, the creatures have a disturbing tendency to die, so getting them delivered and keeping them viable long enough to receive payment is tricky. A few of the species, namely the ones you see here, and particularly the Nemean lions' hybrid breed, are attracting interest. There are orders three years out for any cubs that stay alive long enough to ship and can survive at least a few months."

"Orders from whom?" Ari curled his lip. "And where are they getting these creatures? How are they getting out of Olympus?"

His father fielded that one. "The borders enclosing Olympus are not escape-proof, Ari. You know that."

"For *nymphs*, yes. The occasional minor god looking to party." Ari waved an irritated hand. "But these? How? They don't have the brains to breach our defenses."

"They could with help...especially if that help came from the minions of Typhon who can survive the ocean's deepest depths," Stefan said. "Poseidon's control has loosened on his domain."

"Not loosened," Grigori objected, lifting a hand. "Refocused. There's a great deal happening across the seas that requires his attention right now. Pollution, the destruction of native species that keep the oceans healthy, the disruption of ancient habitats. It's gotten worse over the past several years, and it never occurred to us that there might be a reason for that escalation beyond the simple negligence of mankind. That's been damaging enough...but what's happening now is far worse."

Ari's brows lifted. "You think Typhon is behind the poisoning of the seas?"

"It would explain some things," Stefan put in. "Of all the gods, Typhon has done the most to maintain his cult into the current century. He tends to target captains of business, as well as the heads of multinational companies with a global footprint and a need for overseas travel by ship. It would not be a difficult thing for him to harry Poseidon and his agents enough to hide the transport of his own dedicated creatures out of Olympus, especially if he did so quietly and in small deliveries."

"But to what end?" protested King Jasen. "Since when does Typhon need to market hybrid mythological creatures?"

"Typhon is a monster," Ari said slowly, seeing it come together in his mind. "He's also a god. What better way to regain the attention, fear, and veneration of mortals for gods than to remind them that monsters truly exist?"

Stefan nodded. "As gods go, he's gaining traction. We saw that with the Smithson debacle last month. And while Grigori is right, and most of these creatures die before they reach their human preserves, we've unearthed enough conspiracy theories and Internet stories devoted to them that Typhon's plan is already working. Imagine the damage if he starts whispering in the ears of more major gods, offering them passage out into the wide world? What if one of them gets an urge to explore what lies beyond Poseidon's domain?"

"That can't happen," Ari looked hard at Grigori. "Do you have his ear?"

Grigori only shrugged. "Poseidon also seeks a stronger tie to the earthly plane. He, like all the gods, laments what has been done to the world by mortals—particularly to the oceans. He's pissed, flat out. If he thought the occasional god turning up on some tourist beach would help turn the tide, if you will, on the devastation of his domain…" he grimaced. "Could you blame him?"

"That's not a viable possibility." Ari leveled a glare at his father. "Did you know this was going on?"

"We knew something was going on." King Jasen said grimly. "We knew Typhon had increased his fan base, certainly. We didn't know about the creatures."

He turned to Grigori. "But the conditions Ari was kept in were squalid. Poorly funded. Why would *that* be where he sends such precious creatures?"

Ari scowled, remembering the screams of the animals, the bloodied caretakers who hadn't been careful enough with their charges. "I can guess that one," he said, before Grigori could reply. "Typhon is a god, but he has limits to what he can do. He hasn't yet found somebody with the vision to farm these animals correctly. What he can find are assholes with the funds to force their lowest level thugs to try to keep the creatures alive long enough to turn a profit. But somebody will have that vision. Maybe already has. We just haven't found it yet."

"That's what I'm afraid of too." Stefan said. "And make no mistake, if a rash of Greek monsters is suddenly discovered by any viable news agency, the resulting story will trace back to us." His lips twisted. "That will make for a new advertising angle for the Ministry of Tourism, to be sure."

Ari winced. "Speaking of, who else knows of this? It can't be common knowledge."

"Nobody outside this room," Jasen confirmed. "And until we know more, know enough to throttle this export at the source, it's got to stay that way."

Ari refocused on Grigori. "We need to know more, and to watch more closely. What do you need to help us do that? Whatever it is, we have it."

The mercenary smiled a little wolfishly, glancing to his partners. "Had we realized the pockets of the royal family were so deep, we would've come home to Oûros a long time ago. But I have some ideas." He cocked a glance toward King Jasen and the others. "You may want to bring in some of our homeland's famous coffee, my friends. It's going to be a long night."

Thirty-Five

Over the next few days, Fran found herself so distracted, she could almost accept the fact that she was never going to see Ari again.

Part of the problem was her sleeping arrangements. Emmaline now had a gorgeous solo suite near enough to the royal quarters as to make clandestine meetings with Kristos at least technically possible. However, Nicki, Fran and Lauren were grouped in a series of suites with adjoining doors. Doors that stayed open twenty-four-seven. If Fran decided to sneeze on her own, it would be noticed.

Not that it mattered, anyway. Ari hadn't made a single attempt to contact her over the intervening day. Nor should he, she reminded herself now as she leaned into the mirror, applying another layer of mascara to lashes that were already sharp enough to pierce armor. Ari wasn't her no-strings boyfriend, he was the soon-to-be crown prince of an entire country. She'd helped bring him back, yes, which was super impressive. But not impressive enough to merit a check-in.

And she had been expecting a check-in, as pathetic as that was. Which, of course, pissed her off.

"Fran, can you zip me up?" Nicki walked into the room in stilettos that rivaled Fran's eyelashes as potential deadly weapons. Her get-up was so completely un-Nicki that Fran grinned despite her foul humor.

"Stefan isn't going to know what hit him."

"Yeah, well, I hope he gets hit in a hurry," Nicki groused. "I haven't balanced on anything so narrow since I tried tightrope walking in the sixth grade. If I so much as trip, this dress is going to split right up the seam." She glanced down at her cleavage. "As it is, there's no way I'm going to be able to wear a bra. I don't know who designed this thing, but it definitely gets an F in functionality."

"You'll thank me later." Lauren sailed in with a dress that Fran would never have picked for her in a hundred years, yet, somehow, it was absolutely perfect. The lightest shade of pink—almost a creamy petal—it was a soft sheath gown that dropped silkily over Lauren's body like a second skin. She wore her hair down and around her shoulders, secured with a single clip, and the entire ensemble made her seem soft and eminently touchable.

The other thing that tied Lauren and Nicki's dresses together was the word sleek. While there was nothing sleek about Fran's ball gown.

A sick wash of dread pooled in her stomach. "Guys, you both look way more chic than I do. I can barely get through a door in this gown."

"You look beautiful," Lauren said, and Nicki blinked as she nodded her head several times.

"Seriously, girl, you do. Like, I wouldn't know it was you except I know it's you. You were born for that dress," Nicki said. "Even the queen thought so!"

"Yeah, like she was going to tell me I looked terrible," Fran cracked, but as she said the words, she realized they were unfair. The queen had been nothing but kind to them since they'd arrived at the royal palace. She'd welcomed Emmaline with open arms, had pushed Dimitri and Lauren together, and had arranged it so Stefan and Nicki would take off on a grand adventure...an adventure that had ended with them falling in love. Fran was sure she'd even attempted some matchmaking with herself and Ari—at least in a general sense. She'd wanted Ari to have a friendly female face to help him through his transition back to Oûros and, well... Fran had been that for him. She knew the queen was grateful. But she was hardly going to embrace Fran as her bosom friend.

Even if she was wearing a ten-thousand-dollar gown.

"Will Em meet us there?" Nicki asked, then slapped her hands to her ears. "Oh my God, I forgot my earrings. How could I forget my earrings?" She held up a finger. "Talk loudly or come with me."

Fran and Lauren exchanged a knowing grin, then dutifully trooped into Nicki's room, a veritable disaster of clothes, makeup, and shoes. "I put the ones I wanted to wear right over here," she muttered, then she glanced up. "Keep talking, though. Is Emmaline meeting us there? She's a part of the family now, right? She should be meeting us there, going with Kristos and the parents. Don't you think? Oh—here they are. Okay, good. What do you think?"

Fran blinked, trying to follow Nicki's rapid words, but it was Lauren that replied first. "Yes, Emmaline is with Kristos, and no to the other open question. I have no idea if he's planning to propose tonight. Dimitri refuses to speculate."

"Propose!" Nicki's eyes narrowed. "He already proposed."

"I mean propose properly, with a ring," Lauren said. "Kristos gave Em some kind of military pin, which she wears everywhere now and that's darling, but it's not a ring. She deserves to have a ring, and I think Kristos should propose tonight."

Fran thought the same thing. "Is there any chance of that?"

"Well, I think that's why, despite the occasion being so intimate, we're all dressing like Royal Barbie. If there's going to be an official photographer on hand, you might as well show the American girls in a good light, especially since we're all fast friends of the newest princess of Oûros."

"Princess or Queen?" Nicki was shaking her head in the mirror, watching the dangle of her earrings. "Is Ari seriously going to bounce Kristos off the throne?"

"Only if Kristos is really, really lucky," Lauren said. "And those earrings are ridiculous. Wear these."

Nicki scowled as she saw what Lauren had picked up off the dresser. "But those don't dangle," she said.

"Your hair is down and dangling earrings will get tangled in it. They'll also block your neck, so if you were hoping to get any action from Stefan tonight, you might want to keep all available kissable zones obstacle-free."

Nicki's brows went up. Then she grinned. "Okay, you totally win at this. Tiny gold hoops it is."

Fran touched her own earrings, which felt like the size of roller skates. "Should I change?"

"No, but be careful," Lauren said. "Those earrings don't have backs and I don't trust the self-hooking things on them. That said, your bangle bracelets totally rock."

A staff member came to their doors a few minutes later to walk them through the long hallways of the palace to the cars that would take them to the Visitors' Palace, where the royal family held all the country's special events. Due to their dress volume, their original limo was scrapped in exchange for an SUV, and two men helped them step into it, picking up Fran's voluminous skirts as if they were used to handling such cargo on a daily basis.

"There isn't a receiving line, right?" Nicki asked, her knees pressed together and her hands clutched atop them. "I don't think I could do another receiving line."

"There might be one, but it's not supposed to be anything like that first ball, for all the fact that they're calling it a ball, and that we're dressed to impress," Lauren said firmly. "It's family, friends and dignitaries. That's it."

Fran glanced at her. "By all accounts, that's pretty much everyone we saw at the ball last time."

"It's not, I don't think," Lauren said, but her mouth pinched into a frown as the car slowed, and they saw the long line of vehicles ahead of them. She grimaced. "Then again, maybe the guest list got out of hand or something."

"Or something," Fran muttered as they slowly crept to the front of the line. She saw a collection of people at the top of the small flight of stairs, and her heart sank.

"They're waiting for us," she said morosely. "We are going to have to endure a receiving line." She grimaced as Nicki groaned. "I thought once in a lifetime was going to be enough for that."

"Uh-huh. You two have entirely the wrong attitude," Lauren said, opening her clutch to take out a thin compact. She checked her makeup, then critically surveyed both Fran and Nicki. "You both are beautiful. You both have been the source of endless speculation, and you both have been called to make a command performance today. You can totally pull this off, trust me. I've had lots of practice."

Thirty-Six

A ri couldn't believe the circus this supposedly private ball had become...especially since he had far more to worry about than filling his gods-cursed dance card.

The work with the mercenary team of Poseidon's demigods was yielding quick results. Half a dozen monster farms, for lack of a better word, had been shut down along the coast of Turkey in the past 48 hours, the victims of highly targeted storms. Stefan and a few other carefully vetted demigods of Hermes had been on hand in every case to shuttle what creatures survived back to Olympus, the whole operation moving so quickly that the traffickers couldn't react fast enough to move their stock. The rescuers had all been called off for the time being because of this ridiculous ball, but that couldn't be helped. The Crown couldn't breathe a word to anyone about what it was doing. Outside of the group that had met the other night, only Kristos and a few operatives of the ONSF had been read in.

And now he was supposed to chaperone a freaking ball.

"Where are they?" he gritted out as he watched the sinuous line of limos snake its way up the drive to the Visitors' Palace's front doors. "Since when are we supposed to greet guests without them?"

Beside him, Kristos shrugged. "All part of the act, I suppose. You're the next king, remember? You served as primary host for these for the last three months before you—you know. Before."

"I did?" Ari winced as a sudden stab of pain clamored through his mind. He hadn't had one of those flashes in a while, but tonight, every time he turned around, something was setting him off. "And I enjoyed it?"

"Well, I wouldn't go that far." Kristos grinned. "But you didn't complain about it like a ten-year-old."

Ari sent him a withering glance. "Why do I feel like you're rewriting history?"

"Probably because I can." Kristos's smile broadened. "In fact, the more you can't remember precisely, the better my life is going to be, I suspect." His voice dropped to a quieter tone. "Grigori and the wonder twins are circulating through the crowd. They'll let us know if they get any alerts from their watch teams, but we should be good for tonight."

"Because it would be such a tragedy to have to leave a ball and do real work," Ari said with a twist of his lips.

"A tragedy to Mom, anyway." Kristos glanced back to the line of cars coming up the drive and straightened. "Okay, this is where it's going to get a little dicey. Chin up."

"Dicey how?" Ari pivoted as well and scowled as yet another black limousine coasted to a stop in front of the palace. The back doors swung open, and two attractive girls stepped out, their hair and skin slightly fairer than typical Oûrois women, but the thick accents in their bright chatter proclaiming them as natives.

There was no mistaking the next woman to step into the glowing lights of the reception carpet. Edeena Saleri looked resplendent in a ball gown of deep rose pink, the color perfectly setting off her flawless skin and long, flowing dark hair. "Remind me again, there was no trouble between us?" Ari asked. "I get the most incredible headache every time I see the woman."

"She's not the one who gives you a headache," Kristos said, his voice remaining low enough not to carry. "Neither do her cousins, who adore both you, Edeena, and really, anything they lay eyes on. It's him."

The car's final passenger emerged, and it was all Ari could do not to falter back a step. As it was, Kristos widened his stance so that his right leg was right behind him, bracing his hip. "Easy there," he muttered. "Silas Saleri is a snake, but you defanged him once already."

"Explain," Ari said tightly as the three women fussed over the old man, arranging themselves to his apparent preference—the two younger girls in front, himself and Edeena following behind.

"A long, long time ago, apparently, Silas got the idea you should marry Edeena, which was funny since you guys grew up to be friends, but not that kind of friends. More the kind who would knock each other into the ocean and throw dirt at each other."

Ari snorted, and Kristos continued quickly as Silas and his entourage began strolling purposefully up the red carpet. "He finally approached you with his master plan a little over a year ago. You let him know you weren't interested, and neither was she, but there were hard feelings."

"Edeena?"

"Not her so much, pretty much all him. But that's when we learned about the curse."

"Curse?" That was the second time he'd heard of it, but he'd not followed up. "What curse?"

"Caroline and Marguerite, you're here," Kristos announced,

grinning as the two younger women reached them. "I didn't think we'd be able to pry you away from the beach."

"Uncle Silas insisted," the first young woman pouted, apparently Caroline. Ari couldn't place her at first, even though she beamed at him, her entire face lighting up. "And we missed you so much, Ari! It's so much better that you're not dead."

Ari caught her embrace before she bowled him over, her hair smelling like honeysuckle and roses and another flower he couldn't quite place. It was the scent of the flowers that awakened his memory most forcefully, but there was no pain here. He simply remembered the girl.

Marguerite was easier. Her eyes dancing, she didn't hug him but dropped into a proper curtsy, mock-glaring at her sister until Caroline did the same. "Sorry," Caroline whispered, also with mock chagrin, and both young women dissolved into giggles. They were Kristos's age, Ari knew, but seeing their laughing, carefree faces made him feel a thousand years old.

The girls shifted to the side and Edeena stepped up, moving slightly ahead of her father. "Ari," she said, her expression much more tense than he expected and maybe a little desperate. Ari stepped toward her and took her outstretched hands in his, drawing them up to his lips in a formal, almost courtly manner.

"Edeena," he said, allowing his voice to be filled with rich warmth. "You look beautiful, as always."

The relief that flooded her golden eyes gratified him. He'd said the right thing. He had no interest in marrying the woman —he knew that to the core of his being—but he could make her way easier tonight under the hawkish glare of her father.

When he turned to Silas, however, Ari nearly blacked out.

"Count Saleri, thank you *so* much for coming," Kristos said brightly, his words overloud as Edeena's grip on Ari's hands became more urgent. She nearly crushed his finger bones, the pain clearing his head in a sharp counterpoint to his fogged thoughts.

He stared at Silas Saleri.

"Count Saleri," Ari said, and if his voice was several shades cooler, the man didn't flinch. Instead, he peered at Ari almost curiously, his beady eyes dark and piercing in the ghostly pallor of his face. This wasn't a man who spent time in the sun—not enough of it, anyway. His skin was the color of old straw, and his hair a sallow near-white, for all that his body remained whip-cord tight. The man's suit was impeccably cut. Gold gleamed at his wrist and fingers, and everything about him proclaimed old money.

"It's good you are back, Aristotle," Silas said, and his voice sent another shock of urgency through Ari's brain. That was it, he suddenly realized. He didn't feel pain at seeing this man; he felt anxiety, apprehension, anger. Like he needed to be on his guard at all times. "Perhaps now you can attend more intelligently to the business of being crown prince."

"It will be my honor to do exactly that," Ari said, bowing to the man.

"Count Matretti, *welcome*," Kristos's still strained voice announced the next man in line, and Ari offered Silas a polite nod.

"I'll look forward to talking to you further inside, Count Saleri," he said, his voice a little sharper than he intended. "I'm sure we'll have much to discuss."

Was it his imagination, or did Silas pale a little at that?

Then the family moved on and was replaced by Oûros's ambassador to the US, a tall, athletic-looking man who greeted them both warmly. But the car pulling up to the red carpet next set Ari's every sense on alert, and it was all he could do not to bumble the ambassador along so that he could peer down at the newcomers.

"Relax, will you?" Kristos asked, though his tone was wry. "Though I'm not one to talk. I'm honestly glad you missed me making a fool out of myself these past few weeks, trying to step into your shoes. Your job is way harder than it looks."

"Don't you mean your job?" Ari teased, his heart lifting when Kristos coughed a laugh.

"Not if you love me, brother. And now with everything going on—there's more of a need than ever for me to be where I belong."

The doors to the SUV swung open, and the drivers helped down the first of the American women—Nicki. Kristos's chuckle transformed into a strangled cough. "Oh, this oughtta be good. Where's Stefan?"

"Inside," Ari said, but he couldn't keep the humor out of his voice either. He'd never seen Nicki Clark look so utterly feminine and strong at one time—though admittedly, half the time he'd known her, she'd been in athletic gear. Now she looked up and waved energetically at him and Kristos as Lauren Grant stepped down.

"Mom is going to hate missing this," Kristos said, and Ari slid a glance over to the doorway, further up the stairs.

"No, she's not," he murmured back. "Look alive."

Queen Catherine Andris stood slightly separate from her husband atop the upper landing, her face lit with satisfaction as she gazed down at the women emerging from the SUV. Her glance took in Lauren and Nicki with a satisfied smirk, then shifted to the car. So it was that Ari's first impression of Francesca wasn't with his own eyes—but in the lifted brows and delighted expression of his mother.

He turned around as Kristos breathed out a startled "whoa," and focused on the SUV.

"*Francesca.*"

He nearly spoke the words as a benediction, but he couldn't

help himself. Francesca stepped down on the carpet, exuding everything he saw in her every day, but suddenly and fully manifested for everyone else to see as well. She straightened regally in a gown that was absolute perfection. Ari couldn't pick out the details though, because he couldn't stop staring at Francesca's face.

She was as serenely, stunningly beautiful as the sea after a summer storm, and as her gaze lifted to meet his, her smile was bright enough to fill his whole world.

And she *was* his, he realized. She may not know it yet, but he did.

Thirty-Seven

"Yo, who's the old guy staring daggers at you?"

Nicki asked under her breath, but Fran didn't need the warning. She'd sensed the hatred rolling down the stairs from the Visitors' Palace since she'd stepped out of the SUV. "I have no idea," she muttered. "I've never met the man, I swear."

"Silas Saleri, Minister of Tourism," Lauren mused, drawing up beside her on Fran's other side. "Maybe he's decided Americans are bad for business? If so, he's not the only one. Looks like you're not terribly popular among the geriatric nobility."

As Fran groaned, Lauren just laughed. "Welcome to being gorgeous, my friend. Keep your chin up and act like you get glared at all the time."

Nicki giggled and Fran's tension eased as the three of them strolled up the red carpet. "We could have used some cameras," Lauren said, looking around. "This feels positively reclusive without the paparazzi here."

"Well, you know, private party—uh oh. Dimitri's spied you."

That seemed to mollify Lauren, and she straightened and stepped regally up the stairs as Fran took an extra moment to gather her skirts. Fran's dress weighed probably a thousand pounds, but she was pretty sure it could stop a stampede of elephants. Nicki went next, her laughter filling the air as she flung her arms first around Kristos and then Ari.

"You both look so great!" she gushed, her loud voice drawing more curious onlookers from the castle onto the wide receiving porch of the upper landing. Fran glanced to the top of the stairs to see that Stefan had stepped out of the main doorway, and the look he leveled at Nicki was enough to carry Fran for the rest of her days. Fierce, protective, and proud all at once.

With her heart full, she reached Kristos and Ari.

Kristos said something—she was sure of it—and she said something back, their voices brushing against her mind like the patter of rain. But it was Ari that touched her, Ari that drew her hand up to his mouth, his lips a bare brush over her knuckles. Perfectly polite, perfectly formal. But the expression on his face was one of transfixed intensity. His eyes bored into hers as if he was trying to see all the way to her heart, and his grip on her fingers was almost painfully tight.

"Francesca," he murmured, and in that word there were a thousand other words, all of them rich with promises and possibilities. Beside him, Kristos nudged Ari's elbow. He blinked, as if coming out of a daze. "Thank you so much for coming," he said, the stilted phrase so awkward that Kristos burst out laughing, clapping his brother on the back.

The additional human contact seemed to be exactly what Ari needed. He straightened and gave Fran an abashed grin, as if he hadn't just leveled her with a look of total and abject possession. "Thank you," he said again. "It seems far too long since I've seen you. You'll have time to talk inside?"

"Of course," Fran said, nodding to him, then Kristos again. Suddenly feeling painfully awkward, she stepped quickly around the brothers. Car doors slammed below them, indicating the arrival of another limo. But as she moved to gather up her dress, Ari caught her hand again, turning her back to him.

"You're absolutely beautiful," he said quietly, and his heart was once more in his eyes, fairly lifting her off her feet with the power of his gaze. "Thank you for being here."

"Of course—" she said again, though she unaccountably felt like crying...something she couldn't allow to happen, given the amount of mascara she'd layered onto her lashes. Nicki said something further up the stairs and Fran used the interruption to break away from Ari, lifting her skirts and hurrying as best she could to catch up with the other women. Seriously, who got anything done wearing dresses like these? She felt exhausted climbing a single flight.

At the top of the stairs, a second welcoming party awaited—including Dimitri and Stefan. But while she wanted nothing more than to see Lauren and Nicki reunite with those two, she found herself planted in front of King Jasen and Queen Catherine.

"Francesca, I do believe you've quite stolen the show," the queen said. She glanced at Jasen and scowled. "I told you we should have invited the media."

"If you don't think there aren't long camera shots being taken this very instant, you're very much mistaken." Jasen's chiding tone was soft, though, and he looked at his wife with indulgent affection. "Nothing happens outside of closed doors in Oûros that won't get captured on some camera, somewhere. It's the nature of the beast."

Fran was about to move on, but it was Jasen who stopped her, not the queen. "I may not get a moment to thank you later, and so much more than a moment is needed," he said, his voice deepening with emotion. "Thank you for what you did for Ari."

Fran automatically shook her head. She couldn't bear to be

given credit a moment longer for something she hadn't really done.

"Ari's memory was right there on the surface, wanting to re-emerge," she countered. "That would have happened without me being there. He truly wanted to come back, to work—to take care of his family. That was the foremost concern on his mind, that he had to get back to protect you."

Jasen's face creased into a soft smile. "The desire was there, I'm sure. The doctors said as much. But it wasn't the doctors, and there were plenty of them, who helped him take that first step. Who gave him a hand to hold while he took it. You did."

The simple declaration was almost Fran's undoing, but she was saved by the queen linking her arm with Jasen's, the expression on her face shifting to one of adoration as she gazed at her husband. "I knew there was a reason I married you," Catherine said, and her good humor effectively broke the chokehold of emotion that had grabbed Fran's throat.

The king laughed. Fran laughed. Then she was past the two of them, sailing into the Visitors' Palace.

Nicki greeted her on the other side of the door. "Isn't this place *fantastic*?" she enthused, tugging Fran inside. "The main palace is great, where everyone lives, but this place is all for wowing the outside world. It's all glass and flash from the front, and the back stretches all the way to the sea. Well, by way of jagged cliffs, but still."

"The sea?" Fran blinked. "I guess I've never made it back that far."

"Yeah, that's for photo ops and fancy teas with ambassador types," Nicki cracked. "Every time I come here, I can't help but remember you and Emmaline walking around like a couple of tourists, with no idea how much your lives were about to change."

Fran laughed. "Well, I think I had some idea. Emmaline was

clueless, though—which made her face when Kristos appeared one of the best things I've ever seen in my life."

"She's not clueless anymore." Lauren's voice rang with pride as she strolled up to them. She nodded to the front of the room, where Emmaline stood in the center of a small knot of women, talking animatedly. "As soon as she realized half of Oûros seems given over to charitable works, she's been willing to lend her ear to everyone with a cause. She's not even officially married yet, and she's volunteered for half the organizations in the city."

"She has?" Fran frowned, swiveling her head. "But isn't she going back to school to finish her violin studies?"

Lauren shrugged. "Eventually. Northwestern was gracious enough to extend her deferment, given the publicity she's already brought them. Nothing like royalty in America. We can't get enough of it."

A gruff voice interrupted them. "And do you regret that you chose not to fall in love with a prince, but a humble public servant?"

They turned, Fran's breath catching at seeing Dimitri Korba dressed in his formal military uniform. The material stretched over his powerful body like a glove, a row of medals gleaming across his chest.

Lauren stepped toward him, linking her arm with his. The smile she sent his way was radiant. "Who said anything about falling in love?" she teased, and his expression darkened slightly, though it remained fiercely possessive.

"Perhaps I was mistaken. You should explain it to me," he rumbled, and with the barest of nods, he steered her away into the crowds.

Nicki giggled. "I swear to all the gods they can serve up in this country, I never thought I'd see Lauren look so happy to be carted off like that. She's totally doomed."

"And what about you?" Fran scanned the room until she

spotted Stefan, standing with a cluster of expensively dressed men and women she'd never seen before. "Are you and Stefan going to continue to...I guess, date? Are you staying here?"

"He's..." Nicki blushed, and Fran glanced at her more sharply. "Yeah. I don't know how it's all going to work out. I mean, he's a demigod and I'm...I'm just me. But he wants me to stay here, to maybe open a windsurfing school and to live with him in his villa until I figure things out. And he's started asking me about, you know, getting trained in stuff. Ambassador-y stuff. I don't really understand it all, but...the queen's already told me she supports whatever he thinks I can do."

Her expression softened as she watched him across the room. "Honestly, I couldn't imagine being away from him, not anytime soon. So...well, so I think I'm going to take him up on the offer to let me couch surf here for a while. Because I've traveled a lot in the last few years, you know?" She gave Fran a small smile. "I think maybe I'll try staying put, see how I like it."

"You should," Fran said, reaching out to squeeze Nicki's arm. "You should make his life hell for as long as you can—or dedicated to Hades, anyway, to keep up the whole Greek theme we've got going on here. No one deserves it more."

"Hades..." Nicki smiled, looking happier than any one woman should. "I kind of like the sound of that. I really do."

Thirty-Eight

Nicki's laugh drew Ari's attention. He reassured himself that she was still with Francesca, the two of them enjoying themselves as the last of the guests flowed in through the upper entry to the Visitors' Palace ballroom. It was a perfect night for a dance in the solarium-style room, and musicians responded to the queen's nod by striking up the first strains of music—a burst of interweaving violins.

He frowned, looking over at the collection. The violinists were exceptionally skilled, but he hadn't remembered violins featuring so prominently in the musical selections for these events. Something else he'd need to follow up on. So much had changed in the last year.

Edeena strolled over to him as he paused to liberate a glass of champagne from the tray of a passing server. She already had her own glass, half drunk. "Sorry about Silas," she said with a grimace. "He refuses to give up."

Ari couldn't wait any longer to have at least one question answered. "Both my father and Kristos mentioned a curse," Ari said. "What's that about?"

If Edeena was startled by his abrupt statement, she didn't

show it—other than by draining the rest of her glass. Ari handed her his, and she took it without hesitation.

"The family prophecy. I'm surprised I never told you about it. I totally thought you knew," she said, and Ari masked his own grimace. The pockets of his memories were still only about half-full, it seemed. Fortunately, Edeena's gaze shifted to the far wall, as if remembering something told to her a long time ago. When she spoke again, her tone was resigned.

"According to family lore, which he conveniently did not trot out to me until, like, a year and a half ago, if the Saleri family only manages to produce a single daughter in a given generation, then she's destined to marry *either* a prince of Oûros...or a god."

"A god." Ari stared at her. "Are you serious?"

"Oh, yeah." Edeena made a face. "That way, our children will be royalty or demigods, go us. However, if we don't manage to pull off the godly or royal wedding, we're straight up doomed. The family's fortunes will be ruined, the daughter won't marry anyone at all, the line will be destroyed, and..." she frowned, tilting her head. "I think we'll develop boils. I'm not sure. But since there are only two princes to choose from this generation, and gods aren't exactly jumping out of the bushes these days... it's a problem."

"Two princes." Ari winced, then glanced over to Kristos. "I see the dilemma."

"Why do you think Silas has been so obnoxious?" Edeena scanned the room until she located her father. "If mom were still alive, she wouldn't put up with any of this. She didn't believe in those old stories. There's also one about the birth of three Saleri brothers in a single family requiring one of them to marry a princess. Two generations back, a trio of boys was born to the Saleris. Shock of shocks, they didn't transform into frogs when my grandfather decided to marry *my* grandmother instead of yours. Although," she frowned, fixing her father with a glare over the rim of her glass, "their son is kind of a toad."

Ari slanted her a glance. "He's been unkind to you?"

She shrugged. "He's just fixated, and it's gotten worse over the past few years, like he would win some sort of prize by marrying me into the royal family. Then you disappeared and Kristos ran off to hide in the military, so I got a reprieve for a while. Dad's business projects suddenly took off, and your parents turned most of the tourism duties over to him while they were in mourning. Meanwhile, I traveled as much as I could. Silas remarried, if you didn't know."

"Really? Where is the happy bride, then?"

"Shopping in London, I think. She's clearly smarter than the rest of us—and she's quite a bit younger than he is, too, so perhaps his fortunes will increase tenfold. There's an old tale about second daughters, too."

Ari stared at her. "How did I miss that he'd remarried?"

"Happened after you left. And it's fine, as far as I'm concerned. He needed something to distract him. All his dreams went poof the same day you did." She grimaced at her unintentionally cold language. "Sorry."

"Don't be." Ari shook his head, and another thought struck him. "Did he say anything to Kristos about this?"

"Not to his face, but he summoned me home to make a run at the poor guy after the Accession Ball, only to lose his mind when Kristos fell for Emmaline before I could astound him anew with my magnetism and charisma. And frankly, thank God. These old prophecies need to be written out of the history books." She nodded to the side of the room, where he knew without looking that Francesca stood with Nicki. "Speaking of, are we about to lose our second royal cousin to an American? Because that's going to get half of Oûros petitioning the gods again, not gonna lie."

Ari tried to be angry with her for her directness, but he couldn't. Instead, he shrugged. "It's a little too early to tell."

"You think so?" Edeena granted him a condescending look, appearing suddenly as wise as his mother, for all that she was his age. "I think it's pretty clear to anyone with eyeballs."

"I'll take that under advisement."

"You do that," she grinned. "And you better invite me to the wedding, since my failure made your happiness possible." She tilted her head. "You know Silas has shown me the gates to the gods, right?"

Ari went very still. "Why?" he asked sharply. "He's the Minister of Tourism. He of all people knows how important it is to keep knowledge of the gates secret. Why would he put you at risk?"

"Oh, please." She rolled her eyes. "It's not like we took a group of sixth graders with us. It was all very quiet, and he was as respectful as I've ever seen him. Besides, this was years and year ago, right after Mom died. Back then, he just wanted me to petition the gods for better fortune for our family. He hadn't completely gone around the bend yet."

"Then he should have taken you to the Temple of Winds." Ari scowled, watching the grim smile curve her lips. "Let me guess. He did."

"What can I say? You guys chose your head tourism guy well. Silas doesn't just believe the old stories, he lives and *breathes* them. And I mean, it worked, right? He found love, fortune, power—*and* he totally thought he had pole position on the royal race to the altar." She blew out a long breath. "Now, I just have to skip town before he figures out which god to throw me at."

"Stop," Ari begged. "Don't even think about that."

She snorted. "I assure you, it's *all* I can think about. I figure I'll have to head out for a tour of the world or something until he comes up with a second child. If that happens, the prophecy gets scuttled, and we'll have an easy 18 years before we have to deal with baby number two's marital requirements. I'm good with that."

"But where will you go?"

"It's not like I don't have the whole world to choose from." She waved a careless hand. "Mom dabbled in real estate and owned properties all over the world—visiting them should keep me busy for a while. I'm *way* less likely to trip over a Greek godling if I'm outside the country, right?"

Ari nearly groaned. "I'm so sorry you have to go through this."

She shrugged. "I'm sorrier for Silas, in a way. You and I had been friends for so long, he sort of assumed something would work out between us." She took another sip of champagne, her golden eyes glinting with humor. "Now he's stuck with the threat of doom hanging over his head. All because I couldn't bag my own prince."

"Well, to be fair, if you'd really wanted to bag me, you wouldn't have filled my wetsuit full of sand when we were scuba diving."

Edeena grinned at him. "Except you totally had that coming. And sometimes there are more important considerations than a family curse. Like being able to laugh my ass off."

He accepted a glass of champagne from another server and clinked her glass. "It's good to have a sense of perspective."

"I thrive on it," she said. Her gaze shifted behind him, and now her eyes truly danced. "You may need to move a little more quickly, though. Francesca's attracting her own legion of admirers."

Ari pivoted so quickly that Edeena snickered, and he handed his champagne to her. She accepted it readily enough, then nodded to Francesca. "Go get her, Ari. If anyone ever looked at me the way she looks at you, I'd hold on to him with both hands."

It wasn't so easy, of course, to get across the ballroom floor. Ari was stopped no less than three times by well-wishers, glad-handers and distant family cousins. By the time he reached the far end of the floor, the music had struck up in earnest, easing into a traditional Oûrois ballad.

As Edeena had warned, Francesca was surrounded by a half-dozen young men, each of them plying her with questions, their English at various levels of disaster. Ari didn't recognize any of them, but that was just as well. Fewer people for him to kill later.

"Sir." The furthest man from Francesca saw Ari approach and had the good sense to stand back. "Welcome home, Your Highness."

"Thank you," Ari said gravely as the other men fell away from Francesca like autumn leaves drifting from a tree. Apparently, there were greater benefits to being crown prince than he realized. He held out his hand to Francesca.

"If I could claim you for this dance?"

Thirty-Nine

Fran didn't know how to waltz, but she figured no one would be able to see her feet anyway, and she was so grateful for Ari's rescue that she would have agreed to do the Chicken Dance at this point.

He folded her hand into his arm and they moved toward the dance floor. She didn't miss the way heads turned as they walked.

"Is this your first dance of the night?" she asked suddenly. "And is that significant? Everyone is staring at us."

"It is, it is and they are," Ari said, facing her as they stepped onto the ballroom floor. "I expect you'll have to get used to it."

"Have you gotten used to it?" Fran suspected that Ari knew she was redirecting, but she didn't care. She felt like she was having an out-of-body experience, dancing with him on the smooth hardwood floors, the music flowing around them like something out of a fairytale. The way Ari held her, and the decisive way he moved, allowed her to step naturally back and forth, then to the side, as if she'd been waltzing for years. Maybe there was something to these dresses, she thought. They carried a superpower all their own.

To her surprise, Ari answered the question seriously. "I got used to it, as you say, at a very young age," he said. "When you grow up with the scrutiny of others on you, it becomes second nature." He lifted one shoulder. "You learn very quickly not to search for yourself online or on TV. You'll find things you won't be happy about, but the thing that's out there—it's not you, not really. It's the perceptions of others as they see you through their own filters."

"Perception becomes reality," Fran murmured.

"In their minds, yes, but not in your mind. It doesn't have to be that way. Can't be, really, if you plan on maintaining your sanity. You have to accept that there are two versions of you. The one that you are, and the one that someone else thinks you are." He shook his head. "More than two, of course. A hundred thousand versions of you that live in the minds of people you've never met—will never meet."

Fran smiled wryly. "You sure you don't want to take a run at psychology? Because they'd be all over this."

"I think I'll have my hands full with my own occupation," Ari said. When she lifted her brows, he nodded. "The doctors believe it's going to cause no damage for me to take on more responsibility. More importantly, the council is meeting this week, and they're expected to vote to reverse the accession so that Kristos can return to his military commission. They see the value of the increased attention Oûros has received. We'll be welcomed on an international tour in the wake of my return, even if it's mainly out of curiosity. That entrée will give my father plenty of opportunity to discuss the issues that are hampering Oûros's growth. It's a win-win."

"You don't mind?"

"Mind?" he glanced down at her, clearly startled. "No. I don't care how we get through the doors of other world leaders. If I could do it wearing a clown costume, I probably would. What's important isn't how you get across the threshold, but what is worked out on the other side. That's how it's always been." He grimaced. "And it's more important now than ever."

She nodded. "Your parents are so happy to have you back," she said. "Beyond the obvious, I can see why. You'll make a good king one day."

He tightened his grip on her hands, but he didn't say anything more, and Francesca allowed herself to be swept along with the music of the dance. It ended far too soon, and she caught sight of the queen moving forward, another impossibly beautiful Oûrois girl by her side. "I think your dance card is about to get full," she said, and Ari looked up as well. His smile was automatic, gracious, and appeared authentically warm. "Do you know her?"

"I have no clue," he admitted, then he glanced down at her. "My mother knows the importance of optics. She'll have me dance with half the room to satisfy the old families, but she won't force me to see any one of them again."

Fran smiled. "Sounds like a wise woman, then."

"But I don't want to be wise," he grumbled, holding her gaze steadily. "Right this moment, I'd really rather just sweep you away."

"What?" Fran's eyes went wide even as she blushed, hard. "No. Definitely no. That would cause an international incident."

"I suppose for one night, I'll bow to your wishes," he said, and he did bow to her, the movement so graceful and aristocratic that she found herself inclining her head back to him. "You'll be okay while I take care of these dances?"

She nodded, keenly aware of everyone staring at them. "Of course I will."

"Good." And then he leaned forward. Catching up her

hand, he raised it to his lips, kissing it soundly as his gaze bored into hers. "Because when they're all done, I'm coming for you."

Ari stepped back from Fran as his mother and the girl she was tugging along burst onto the dance floor, and the music started up with another trill of violins. Fran's heart was thundering in her ears, her breath fitful, and she whirled around. Her mascara was about to give up the ghost, she knew, and she needed air—needed to breathe! She had to escape this place.

Escape.

She pushed through the crowd as slowly as she could manage, but her mind was whirling. Ari didn't look at her with the gaze of some idiot college student. He looked at her like he was a man in love. She'd seen that expression before. Granted, not on such an impossibly perfect face, and not with her as the target of said affection, and never while she was wearing a gown that cost more than a flight around the world...

She moved into the hallway, scanning right and left. She rounded a corner and noticed a plant stand, perfectly centered down the long hallway. She headed toward it. If there was water in that plant stand, did that mean a bathroom was nearby? There had to be one somewhere close. Why hadn't she just *asked* someone?

And why did she feel so much like crying, anyway? So what if Ari thought he was falling for her? He'd been through a lot; he was probably still reeling. He couldn't be held accountable for his emotions. She certainly didn't hold him accountable. She also didn't expect him to act on them. Not in the cold light of day, not when—

"Francesca Simmons?"

Fran stopped and turned back, but the tough-looking man in the black suit was nobody she'd ever seen before. His accent was thick, his face hard, and she nodded quickly with embarrassment. Clearly, she'd stumbled down the wrong corridor of the Visitors' Palace, and had breached some restricted zone.

"Yes?" She smiled. "I'm sorry, I must have gotten lost. Is there a restroom somewhere around here?"

The man didn't respond verbally, though. He lifted his hand and jerked his fingers upright, and then two other men entered the hallway from the doors facing the corridor. To Fran's absolute shock, both of them were carrying guns.

"What?" She stepped back automatically. "What're you doing—hey!"

Before she could draw a breath deep enough to scream, she backed into a third man who'd materialized out of nowhere. A heavy hand came over her mouth, then a pinch of something hard and sharp flared at her neck. A second later, a bag dropped over her head, surrounding her in darkness.

"No—no!" she tried to bark, but no sound came out. She smelled harsh chemicals caught inside the heavy burlap, and whatever the needle prick had pumped into her system, it did its job effectively. Fran's head swam, and she struggled to keep her focus. She couldn't dump her shoes—they'd see that—but jewelry? Maybe.

She slumped to the floor heavily, feigning a faint that was less of an act than she wanted it to be. She worked off one of her thin bracelets, letting it slide down the heavy folds of her gown. Rough hands reached for her, and she kicked and struggled as best she could—anything for a distraction as she slipped off a cocktail ring and dropped it too. She thought one of her kicks connected with something solid, but then everything seemed to stop and she was floating...floating. She felt herself being lifted, her body going slack with alarming speed, and the men carrying her started moving faster.

Doors slammed, and she could tell by the coolness of the breeze on her feet that they'd reached the outside, but though panic battered against her fading awareness, her greatest fear wasn't realized—at least not yet. She wasn't immediately thrown into a vehicle. If that happened, she knew that far worse would follow.

"No," she moaned again, her voice dying in her throat. Panic surged through her, but she was so...so tired.

The coolness continued, but there was still no vehicle. No car. No trunk. They weren't going far, then. Instead, she thought she heard a bird call out overhead. A second after that, the crash of waves sounded in her ears.

Wait. Waves?

Within another dozen steps, her captors dumped her onto a wooden surface, her fall softened only slightly by her heavy skirts. Her elbows and head banged against the planks beneath and behind her—some sort of boardwalk, she thought woozily. Then the bag was whisked off her head.

The flashlight pointed into her face almost blinded her. She slapped her hands to her face to block the glare, her heart raging so loudly she could barely hear the man's next words. "It's her. Good," a man said, his voice sounding stiff and haughty. "Cover her up again. I can't stand to look at her."

"Another shot?" someone else asked as Fran fought to shake off her drug-induced haze. The bag went back over her head again, but she couldn't protest, couldn't form words. Distantly, she felt her wrists bound together, her ankles too. She no longer really cared, though. Her mind drifted, and she couldn't corral her thoughts enough to generate any real fear.

"No." The first man moved close to her, his mouth all the way to her ear, and she immediately thought: old. "She needs to put on a show, after all. Are the cameras set?"

"Five minutes."

The man chuckled, though the sound was bitter, harsh.

"Get ready, monster," he hissed, as Fran's mind cartwheeled and twirled. "It's almost time for you to shine."

Forty

"Why, Prince Aristotle, I'm sure I've never seen you dance for so well and so long. What *has* gotten into you?"

Ari smiled down into his mother's happy face, his heart lightening to see her deep contentment. "You're enjoying tonight, aren't you?"

"I can't imagine why," she said, not trying to dim her grin. "All the men I love most in the world are under one roof, safe, and for the most part, as happy as I have ever seen them. We've had great success winning over the council to the idea of a national holiday to celebrate your homecoming, There's also been good discussion on expanding the homecoming theme to imply a greater inclusivity of any returning national. The idea is gaining momentum."

"Good," Ari said. "Because an annual event reminding me how I dumped my own plane in the ocean isn't one I'll cherish, I have to tell you."

His mother laughed. He turned her again, scanning the crowd absently as they danced. After so many turns around the dance floor, he'd finally relaxed enough to just accept this night for what it was: a reprieve from the real danger Oûros faced. Nothing was going to happen until tomorrow on that front. So tonight could be for dancing.

Except he hadn't seen Francesca in over an hour. Not that he would have been able to break away to go to her, but still. He liked knowing she was in the room.

The queen caught him looking. "You shouldn't be so obvious, Ari," she said, though her gaze remained merry as he refocused on her. "Francesca knows you have obligations to perform. I had the same challenges with your father when he first asked me to marry him. It was an absolute chore to make myself scarce until he needed me."

Ari lifted his brows. "And you put up with that?"

"Oh, I would have done about anything for that man," she said, her voice going suddenly soft. "Even leave him, if I thought that would be best." When she glanced back at Ari, her eyes were a little misty. "I want someone like that for you too, you know. Someone who would do whatever it took to make sure you were safe."

He grimaced. "Well, if you like Francesca so well, why have you thrown half of Oûros's marriageable daughters at me this evening? Which, by the way, I wasn't aware we were inviting."

"All those girls will be fine, and they need the practice," his mother said blithely. "You've done a credible job not betraying your interest in Francesca too overtly. I think we can probably get three or more official balls out of this if we play our cards right."

He stared at her, horror-struck. "Tell me you're joking."

Her laughter filled the surrounding space, competing with the music. "That's up to you, I should say. If you don't make your move..."

They danced for the remainder of the song, then parted, his mother curtseying gracefully as the crowd applauded with genuine delight. The music shifted then to faster-paced traditional reels, and Ari stepped pointedly off the dance floor. Francesca still had not put in an appearance and that felt...odd to him. Granted, she had no reason to be at his beck and call, and yet it felt strange to have her absent for so long a time.

He spied Dimitri standing by the large French doors leading out to a courtyard and angled his way.

"Finally tired of dancing?" the captain cracked as Ari approached him. Then his face went instantly serious as he caught Ari's expression. "What's wrong?"

"Nothing—it's probably nothing," Ari said, lifting a hand to massage his temple. The jagged knife of pain was back, poking at him insistently. "Have you seen Francesca recently?"

Dimitri frowned. "No. I thought she was with Lauren."

As one they scanned the room, and Dimitri spotted Lauren first. Nicki, Lauren and Emmaline all together, clustered at one of the large banquet tables. They weren't eating but talking to a man who looked like the chef, who was gesticulating wildly, his face beaming with joy.

Dimitri grimaced. "Why do I get the feeling they're planning another party?"

"But if Francesca isn't with them, and they're not concerned, she can't have been gone long, right?" Ari tried to squelch his growing panic. "One of the women's restrooms?"

Dimitri cocked a glance at him. "Her friends could check— and would." He narrowed his gaze at Ari's face. "You're concerned. Legitimately concerned."

"Something about this isn't right," Ari muttered. He stepped closer to Dimitri, keeping his voice low. "The night I crashed my plane—I asked you about it already. You said that nothing was wrong at the airstrip. Nothing out of place."

"Not that I knew of, but I wasn't with you." Dimitri shook his head. "I was tied up on assignment. I couldn't believe it when I'd learned the next day that you'd taken off." By unspoken agreement, they'd started walking through the ballroom, the area a little clearer now that so many people were on the dance floor. "I didn't think I'd ever forgive you," Dimitri said grimly. "I sure as hell didn't forgive myself. I should have been there."

"You did nothing wrong," Ari said, for easily the twentieth time. "And if you had, who'd have looked for me so long?"

Dimitri couldn't argue that point, and they reached the girls a minute later. Within thirty seconds of Ari giving his halting request, Lauren and Nicki headed out to search the dance floor. Emmaline stood with her hand half-raised to her face a moment longer. "There are only two restrooms she could have used," she said. "I need to tell Kristos."

"No—" Ari began, but Emmaline shook her head.

"He'd want to know," she insisted. "You'd want to know. Stefan too." She gestured. "Not your mother, not yet. But the rest of you have worked too long together to stop now. Stefan will be able to tell us if anyone else is missing from the ballroom, too. They've got cameras on it, right? He'll know."

Ari blinked. He hadn't thought of that, but she was right. "Go," he said, as Dimitri touched his arm.

"Through there," he pointed. "Corridors to the back gardens, and easily someplace Francesca could have wandered by mistake. She's not as familiar with this palace."

They strode quickly through the room and entered the hallway, immediately struck by the silence of it. "No one would have seen her leave or come back from here. Too many people focused on the music and dancing."

"And the music dims quickly. Still, she could hear it. She wouldn't have gotten that lost."

"Dimitri." Lauren emerged from another door at the end of the long hallway that ran alongside the interior wall of the ballroom. "No and no, on the ladies' rooms. Nicki is going after Stefan. What can I do?"

Dimitri tapped his ear. "I have Stefan on closed circuit mic, but he's currently with the US ambassador. I don't want to interrupt that if Francesca is simply out for a stroll. But once he gets clear, tell him to hit the cameras. Have him contact me."

"Right." Lauren strode up to Dimitri and, standing on her tiptoes, placed both of her hands on his face and kissed him fast and hard. "Go save people. You're good at it."

Then she swiveled on her heel and was gone.

Ari stared for a moment after her, then turned in time to see Dimitri staring too. "You are never going to get over her, are you?" he asked as they headed deeper into the Visitors' Palace.

Dimitri snorted. "Never in my lifetime."

Ari slanted him a glance. "And does she know that lifetime is about a hundred times longer than normal?"

"Yeah, well, we've been talking about that." Dimitri rubbed a hand over his face. "She's got some misguided idea that she's not worth me giving up my status as demigod for her. She'll figure out she's wrong soon enough."

Ari laughed. "Not if she's half as stubborn as you."

They strode through the hallways, unconsciously picking up speed as each new corridor yielded no Francesca. Ari was ready to start shouting her name when Dimitri held up a hand. "Something's wrong here," he said, frowning at the empty hallway. Two doors flanked the hallway, both of them shut tight. The corridor was empty except for a stand of flowers, molting onto the floor. "Those leaves aren't right, all scattered around like that."

Ari stared at him. "You're kidding me, right?"

Dimitri shook his head. "You haven't been with the queen in the year since you've been gone. The royal palace is only so big, and she spent entire months pacing it and this one as well.

Anything out of place, anything askew, she fixed. It became the standard. Those leaves—that would have been caught, no matter how deep we are in the palace."

"I'll go one further," Ari said, as his gaze landed on something that glistened about twenty feet beyond the stand, next to another set of facing doors. He strode forward quickly and bent down, scooping it up in one motion.

He tossed the thin bracelet to Dimitri. "Francesca was wearing that. She was here." The two of them stared at each other for a long moment, then started moving.

"Rear courtyard," Dimitri said. "Ocean walk."

"Has to be," Ari agreed. Their strides picked up as Dimitri's earpiece crackled, and the captain put his hand to his head.

"Dimitri," he barked. He pulled out the earpiece so Ari could hear as well.

Stefan's cool voice sounded over the device. "Everyone in the ballroom is accounted for, save one," he said steadily, but there was no denying the edge to his voice. "Silas Saleri."

Forty-One

"Sir, everyone's in place. They'll move in on your signal."

"Excellent. Hands and feet first. Then unhood her."

Fran heard the words as if she was in a dream, only it was a dream without beginning or end. It seemed as if she'd always been on this windy ledge, with the smell of the ocean, the sound of crashing waves, and the distant cry of birds all around her. Distantly, she felt her hands being drawn together, secured. Her feet as well.

She should fight. She knew she should fight, but she needed to understand. Needed to fight with her mind even more so than her body. Needed to be smart.

A moment later, the hood was loosened, then lifted away.

She flinched at the bright light shining in her eyes, but this time she saw enough of her captor to identify him. Only, it made no sense. "Mr. Saleri? But—?"

"Count Saleri," the old man snapped, looking every bit as haughty and formal standing there on the boardwalk as he did in his official tourism posters. But he...he was old—he was *rich*. What did he want with her?

Monster. The word slipped and slithered through her mind.

"Count Saleri," she managed, hating the way her voice sounded, thin and pitiful and weak. She sounded like she had when she was a little girl. A little girl who'd gotten backed into one too many corners, a little girl afraid. A little girl who'd finally come out swinging though, who'd finally learned how to fight.

Fran stiffened her resolve a little more, holding onto that thought.

"That's right," Silas said coldly. "Names are important here in Oûros. Names mean something. Ranks mean something. Which you clearly don't understand. None of you Americans do."

Think, think! Fran implored herself. Silas Saleri looked easily close to sixty—and he was part of the inner circle. Edeena's father. A royal. A count, apparently, possibly related to the queen. She'd never even spoken to him before, so what could she have done to upset him so much?

"Why am I here?" she protested, lifting her hands to eye her bound wrists. She should be more shocked about that—more shocked about everything. But whatever they'd injected into her was seriously effective. "What do you want from me?"

"To leave and never come back would be a good start," Silas quipped. "But at least you can be useful to me as you go."

"But I haven't *done* anything to you."

"Haven't you?" he said bitterly. "I've given up on Ari marrying my daughter. She'll just have to accept a god as her consort and be grateful for it. But we can't have the Andris line sullied twice with American whores—even one handed over to me by the great god Typhon himself."

Who? Fran blinked in confusion as Saleri's face twisted into a mocking sneer. "Don't think I don't know what you're all trying to do. The Andris family was weak, broken, desperately trying to recover from their son's death. His *death!*" Silas balled his hands into fists. "He should have stayed dead, if all he was going to do was come back and complete the ruin of his life that he'd started by rejecting my Edeena."

"Edeena." Fran's hands flailed, as if they could grasp some sense from the thin air. "But what—"

Moving was the wrong thing to do. Silas reacted instantly, pulling out a gun so fast that Fran gasped.

"Silence," he hissed and despite herself, Fran froze. The drugs in her system surged to the fore again as she stared at the gun, the gun that wasn't shaking, wasn't wavering, no matter how old Silas was. The count was former military—obviously former military—and he was pointing a gun at her.

And she knew this man, suddenly. Not specifically Count Saleri, martinet of some tiny little hamlet in a kingdom halfway around the world, no. But a grouchy old man who'd let life get the better of him—yeah. She knew that guy. The kind of perpetual victim who'd taken in every good thing and created nothing but bad from it, who'd dragged defeat from the jaws of victory so many times, he was sure life itself was out to get him. She blinked and didn't see Silas Saleri in front of her any more. She saw Bill Lakshi, the drunk at the corner of the peeling counter, blearily taking a swing at anyone who drew near. She saw Mark Hayward and Bob Gutz, leaning over the pool table and cracking up over their own dirty jokes as they spit tobacco juice into glasses she'd have to wash later. She saw Dave Cline, right before he left to go beat up his wife for the last time. The night he later got in a truck and killed himself when he'd run off the bridge.

And not just himself, either.

No, that would have been too much of a kindness.

Silas's voice rose, cutting across Fran's scrambling thoughts. "I said, listen to me, you stupid girl. You don't know anything about nobility. You don't know anything about class. If you really cared for Prince Aristotle, you'd leave him alone to marry someone of his station. Someone who could expunge the shame that you disgusting people have already brought to this country, infiltrating the royal palace like you own it when you are *nothing*. You are *dirt*. After everything I've done to re-instill the magic of the gods into the world, the fear of them...now I have to contend with you. If I didn't have something better to do with you, I'd kill you myself to rid us of the plague you're bringing to our shores."

His smile hardened into a grimace so full of hate, it went a long way toward clearing Fran's fog. "At least you'll end up being a worthwhile abomination. Typhon has been watching you, did you know that? He whispered to me of your existence once you came to Oûros and his scouts caught wind of you, bade me to use you if I could. A reward for all my hard work, he said, and a small way to recoup everything that you and your friends have cost me. Trust me, the corporation who will be buying you is slavering to scoop up every creature I can liberate from Olympus. You're not the beginning or the end of that trade, but you'll be a satisfying sale all on your own. You owe me this, *monster*. You owe me so much for all you've done. And I intend to collect."

Another flash of anger cut through Fran so quick and hot that she shoved away the torpor weighing down her limbs

"You talk a lot of shit, you know that?" she snapped, and it wasn't Francesca's voice talking any more. It wasn't the Summa Cum Laude psychology scholarship earner, the earnest, hard-working student dedicating herself to serving with serenity, composure and compassion.

No. She was Frannie Lambert now, with calloused hands and bitten off fingernails, bruises on her legs and shoes two sizes too small. She was Bert's little girl with the big laugh and the battered knuckles and she shouted back at Silas loud enough to be heard all the way back to that tiny little bar in that tiny little town that had been everything to her. Everything and nothing in the end.

"Big man with the gun," she sneered, and even her voice sounded young—so young, so belligerent, so furious in the face of the senseless tragedy that had changed her life forever. "You try to kill Ari too? When he dumped your daughter and told you to go kiss his ass, that he was going to marry who he wanted? I saw the way you stared at him in the ballroom, and you know what I saw in your face? I saw guilt. Guilt and relief and maybe a sneaking satisfaction that whatever you did to him, nobody's gonna catch you after all. But he is going to catch you. You wanna know how I know? He's going to catch you because he knows something went down at that airstrip. He knows something went wrong that he hasn't quite remembered yet. Wait 'til he finds you you've been trafficking stolen monsters. Bet he'll love that."

"Shut up," Silas growled, but Frannie couldn't shut up. Wouldn't shut up. She'd been shut up for too damned long and she'd *had* it with staying quiet.

"I know you Silas," she said. "I know exactly who you are. What'd you do, spike his gas tank? You were there that night; I'd bet money on it. You were there and you crippled his plane. Crippled it and watched Ari take off, knowing you were sending him to his death—and why? Were you that pissed he didn't want Edeena?"

"I didn't cripple his plane," Silas bit out, waving his gun at her with his own flash of fury that finally broke through Fran's bluster and made her shrink back against the open fence of the boardwalk.

What the hell was she thinking? This man had a gun!

But Silas was caught up in his own memories now. "If Ari had flown like a military pilot instead of like a carnival sideshow, he would have been fine—dropped into the water, yes, injured probably. But fine! And close to home. Edeena is a trained nurse. They'd been friends since they were little. She was perfect for him! Perfect for him and perfect to nurse him back to health until he could see her value, her grace, and her standing and class. And finally the Saleri family would be part of the throne as we always should have been, no longer on the outside, one station less royal, when ours was the older and truer bloodline and has always been!"

Silas pointed his gun at Fran again, more menacingly this time. "Instead, Aristotle didn't have the grace to even die right. He came back with another piece of American filth. Except this one is a monster. And I know what to do with those." He gestured with his gun. "Now."

The two men laid hands on her, and though she bucked and writhed, they were more than a match for her. They used her momentum against her as they hauled her up and, without another moment's hesitation, *threw* her over the short barrier of the ocean walk, still bound up tight.

"No!" Fran shouted, or tried to shout. The wind whistling past her caught the word and wrenched it from her mouth. She hurtled through the night, flipping end over end, and only by some miracle entered the water feet first. At least the shock of the cold water ripped what was left of the drugs out of her system, leaving her brilliantly—brutally—aware that she was going to *drown to death*.

"No!" she gasped again, whirling around. Her arms flung apart, the ziptie bursting somehow, and she stared in amazement at the shreds of plastic floating away from her, drawing in deep lungfuls of...

Wait, what? Fran pushed her hands down in the water, her feet bobbing up. Her eyes nearly bugged out of her head as she realized it wasn't her bound ankles that kicked up in front of her face, but a long slender glistening tail, with purple and blue iridescent scales and a long flapping fin at the end. The appendage just *floated* in the water, attached to her like it was supposed to be there. She jerked her head down, peering at her belly, the effort of her movement sending her ass over tea kettle in the water, a spinning dervish trying to see everything on her body at once. Her arms were long and slender, the fingers now webbed with a gossamer-thin membrane that scooped through the water like a paddle. Her hair floated loose around her, and her beautiful dress now ballooned high above her, floating in the water like a silken cloud.

How in the world had she gotten her dress off? How was any of this happening?

And more to the point, How was she not *dead?*

Or was she dead? Was she?

She spun around in the water, her vision startlingly clear. Though she knew the world was dark up above, cloaked in a canopy of stars, the ocean was layers of blue and teal and midnight and indigo black, and she could see...well, she could see everything.

"Francesca, Fran, Frannie, Francis, Francesca..." she felt the words murmured through the water more than heard them, whispering along her skin, ruffling her scales. She knew that cadence, that music. She'd heard it before when she had dropped into the ocean. The hands. *She had seen hands!* That first time, there had been laughter and teasing, but this was different, this was...

Something drew her attention up, and she stared towards her floating dress, now picked out in sharp relief as a stark light flashed twice and then went out. Something large and dark cut the water high above her. *What the hell?* Was that a rescue boat? Had someone already realized she was gone?

"I'm here!" she cried, straining her gaze upward, bubbling

over with laughter as the sound drifted up, going nowhere. "I'm here. I'm okay!"

"*Fran, Francesca, Frannie, Fran, Francesca, Francesca—FLY!*"

The tenor of the chorus changed suddenly, panicked and fraught. Fran whirled, peering down deep to see the barest flutter of disappearing tails in the distance. Far away, so far away! She curled into a tight ball again, then flipped her tail—she had a *tail!*—high. Still she floated, angling down. She could follow those tails now, she thought. She could go. But go where? And wasn't there a reason to go back to the top of the sea? Wasn't there a man, a purpose, a love up there? She still felt so heavy, so dizzy...

What was she forgetting? What was happening here?

As she puzzled over that, something shifted deep below her —miles away it seemed, but still so clear and true she could see every detail. A light appeared in the depths of the ocean, a sudden burst of brilliant light. A pathway, she thought. A portal. A way home.

And not a single dolphin in sight.

"*Yes,*" she whispered.

Her heart full of wonder, joy shimmering bright, she dove.

Just as a brutally weighted net slammed into her from above, wrapping her tight.

"What the *hell*?" Ari pulled up short at the sound of the Fran's scream, but Dimitri launched past him, grabbing his arm.

"Ocean walk," Dimitri barked. The captain had his gun pulled, and they took off running as more operatives breached the courtyard, pounding toward the ocean.

"Gun!" Dimitri raced in front of Ari, his speed matching that of Grigori Bouras, while the two female agents angled toward Ari. Dimitri and Grigori barreled into the small knot of men racing to flee the boardwalk. One got away, but the other two were tripped up in seconds. Though all the men appeared to be armed, Dimitri and Grigori quickly discarded their guns in favor of hand-to-hand pummeling, while more ONSF guards redirected toward the fleeing third man.

Ari swept the boardwalk with a panicked gaze, but there was no Francesca.

"Over the side," Grigori ordered, looking up from the man he was beating into the ground just long enough to point at his partners. "Go."

One of the sisters, Marta, immediately leapt over the short

fence of the ocean walk, her body flashing in the darkness as she dove toward the water, but Ari grabbed Delia's arm.

"I'm going too," he announced. "With you or without you." He wasn't an idiot. He might be a strong swimmer, but if he entered that water without the help of one of Poseidon's demigods, he would be as much of a hindrance as a help. But there was no way in hell he wasn't going to try. Delia met his gaze, grinned.

"I live to serve, Your Highness. I'll find you down there."

The two of them raced for the boardwalk at a dead run, Ari taking one long, leaping stride to catch the top rail of the fence—and then he, too, was soaring down toward the sea.

"Your Highness, *no*—"

Dimitri's protest was lost in the whistling wind. Then Ari remembered his cliff diving training well enough to flip over in a tight circle, so that his feet were pointing down when he entered the water.

As he did, he saw the dark-hulled craft blasting away across the open water. *Good luck with that, assholes.* The Oûros Royal Navy would make short work of them.

But the fleeing boat was the least of his problems.

True to her word, Delia swam to his side as soon as he cleared the surface of the water again. She carried one knife in her teeth, and she handed him a second then freed her first, treading water. "She's caught in a net," she told him. "She can breathe, but you need to cut her out. There are assholes down there with SCUBA tanks who thought they could haul her off, even with their boat bailing on them. They were wrong."

Before he could protest, Delia clapped her hand over his mouth and spoke words that seemed to flow through him like well, water. When she pulled her hand away, she grinned. "You've got about ten minutes of air down there now. Hopefully a good guy with a really speedy boat is on his way. Otherwise, get her up to the surface and we'll go from there."

Then she flipped away, arching backward to dive deep.

Ari had no choice but to follow after her, shocked that he could see clearly under water, that he could breathe. Was this why so many of Poseidon's agents left military service rather than staying in the Oûrois Navy for longer than a few generations? Earth was nearly three-quarters water, and the ability to explore that...

His wonder was short-lived as he saw the net and the woman inside it. Francesca looked like she was knocked out, but there was nothing over her mouth or her eyes. How did Delia know she was breathing? Had Marta already reached her?

But no, Marta was engaged in hand-to-hand combat with one of the men with tanks, Delia now streaking after the other two. He didn't care about them anymore. They wouldn't get far. But Francesca...

He reached the trailing end of the net, then sliced through the water with his blade. The drag stole some of his force from him, but less than he would have expected. Yet another gift from Poseidon's demigods, he suspected, and one he was grateful for. He slashed through the heavy netting, pulling it away to free Francesca's dormant form. She was naked, he realized with shock and more than a little fury. The bastards had stripped her, and—

Then he stopped. Blinked. And almost in a daze continued cutting the nets until they fell fully away. He gathered Francesca's upper body in his arms, his gaze drifting down, down...to see the long, sinuous tail extending out beneath her. A tail. A sea nymph's tail.

Despite his role as gatekeeper of the gods, despite his work with Stefan and Dimitri, Ari had never encountered one of Poseidon's sea nymphs in the flesh. He'd seen depictions of them, of course—carved into monuments, painted on frescoes, and celebrated in trinkets and jewels. But this...

Slowly, dazedly, he swam toward the surface of the ocean, his demigod-enhanced ability to see underwater allowing him to witness first-hand the wonder of Francesca's body as her tail undulated in the water, propelling her forward even as she remained unconscious. She had transformed into the brightest treasure of the ocean, a glorious creature of myth and magic, but it was her face that transfixed him the most. The curve of her brows, the soft parting of her lips, the angle of her jaw. When she awoke, would she still be able to breathe? Did she know? Did she even realize what had happened to her, or was she in some sort of shock?

That thought sent him kicking harder, and he quickly covered the last few meters to burst through the surface. A cry went up, lights swept the space, and moments later, a speedboat belonging to the Royal Navy purred closer to him, a sturdy ladder dropping over the side

Ari kicked toward it, Francesca still a dead weight in his arms, but he'd be damned if he didn't pull her out of the water himself. He found the base of the ladder with his feet, gripped one side of it with his right hand—his left arm still snug around her—and started climbing.

The moment he pulled himself up above the water line, he could feel the change in Francesca's body. Her lower half lightened, reducing the drag on his arms. A moment later, it was her legs curled up against him, her sweet, perfect ankles dangling past his waist. The sudden change in weight made him bobble her a bit, but not enough to wake her. It also allowed him to make short work of the rest of the ladder, and at last he handed Francesca up into willing arms.

He scrambled over the rail as well, unsurprised to see that

he had just handed Francesca off to Stefan. She now rested in his arms, wrapped up in a thermal blanket.

"You can move pretty fast when you want to," Ari observed dryly.

Stefan waited only long enough to make sure that Ari was safely aboard, then he turned away, carrying Francesca to one of the deeply padded seats of the royal speedboat. "There are benefits to my role as Hermes's messenger. A facility of travel is definitely one of them. Sit."

Ari slung himself into the seat, and Stefan handed Francesca to him. "We had to muster too quickly to get medical aboard, but you'll be checked out as soon as we land. You appear to be in worse shape than she is."

Ari coughed a laugh, the movement causing him to cough more in earnest, and he dragged a hand over his mouth, spitting out seawater. "You're not wrong," he admitted. He caught Stefan's eye. "You saw what happened down there? You know?"

"As we reached your destination, we intercepted video being uplinked to satellite, stopped it at its source. Our data techs are going to need to work it, but we don't think any of it got out. I had it streamed to me. So yes, I saw." He held Ari's gaze. "She's one of Poseidon's."

"She's not," Ari said flatly. "She's mine."

A smile tugged at the edge of Stefan's mouth. "I think, in this case, we can safely say, she's both. Clearly my research into her past was not at all as thorough as it should have been."

"I'll forgive you this time," Ari said, sagging back in the seat as Francesca stirred beneath him. "Thank you for getting here so quickly. If I'd lost her…"

"Ari?"

Fran's quiet question drew his attention down, and he slowly, gently, eased her away from him. Though he was still streaming with water, she'd already dried, it seemed, her hair waving in the wind, her skin warm and unclammy. If anything, he was soaking her all over again.

Had it been that way on the rowboat after she'd dunked into the water not a dozen meters from where they were right now. Was it along this same stretch of rocky shoreline that he hadn't realized was right beneath the Visitors' Palace? Had that really only been a few days ago?

"You just decided that you couldn't stand wearing that dress any longer, and you needed to take a midnight swim?" he teased her gently. "You could have waited for me, you know. I like swimming."

"I..." with a jolt, all Francesca's memories seemed to come back to her, the blood draining out of her face. He held her tight.

"You're okay, you're okay," he murmured as she began trembling uncontrollably. She gripped the edge of the blanket, her mouth working, but no sound came out at first.

"He—he took me, Ari! Took me, said he was—said I was—" She looked around wildly, clearly trying to make sense of her surroundings. "I was in the water! I'm a...a..."

"Hero, in my book," Ari said, and she broke off with a choking laugh. "But—who took you, Francesca? Did you see? Did you know him? Who did this to you?"

"Oh, Ari." She closed her eyes, swallowing, and he could almost see the visible struggle to parse all her memories together, all her thoughts. His disquiet deepened as she drew in a shuddering breath. "They drugged me, in the Visitors' Palace. Propofol, most likely. It's fast-acting and doesn't last long. And apparently, given what they wanted me for, I needed to put on a show."

Who? He yearned to ask the question, but knew she had to get this out in her own way, at her own pace. Hadn't she taught him that?

Francesca continued, her teeth chattering a little. "They

carried me all the way to the boardwalk, and then he said terrible things about you. About me too, but that's to be expected."

She smiled a little shakily and lifted her gaze again to meet his. "It was Silas Saleri," she said quietly. "He wanted you to marry Edeena but I think there's more to it than that. He talked about m-monsters. That the world needed to be afraid of them again, the world needed to honor the gods. I don't know what he's planning but then he, he..."

"It's okay," Ari reassured her again, though she could be excused for not believing him. How had he come that close to losing her? "You're safe now."

"I could *swim*," she said with wonder, startling him. "Did you see?"

He took in her glassy eyes, her quivering lips, trying to gauge how much she knew. Wondering if the trauma of her dip in the ocean and the net crashing over her had stolen her memories. She could be excused, if so. Maybe it would be better that way. He glanced up to see Stefan watching him from across the deck and knew the demigod of Hermes would have had no problem hearing the words carried on the breeze.

Stefan shook his head subtly, sending Ari a message he could understand just as clearly. *Don't push her.*

"You were amazing," he murmured instead. "Braver than anyone I've ever met.

At his words, the softest sob broke free from Francesca's lips, and she swayed. But this time, he was there to catch her. This time, he could keep her safe.

As she sighed against him, so small and fierce, he drifted the softest kiss over her hair. "In the future, though, you really have to do a better job of letting me save you."

She coughed a laughing sigh, and snuggled close.

Forty-Three

ours later, Francesca sat in a briefing room with a heavy blanket draped over her, her new attire of a long, linen tunic and flowy pants allowing her to feel almost normal again. She couldn't stop shaking, but the assortment of tea, coffee, and tsipouro drinks in front of her would probably help with that. Just as soon as she could calm down her hands enough to hold a cup.

She composed herself as the small group descended on the room. The queen entered first, along with her husband, their gazes immediately fixing on Fran.

"Don't you dare stand up," Catherine announced when she shifted. "In fact, we should all sit down. All of us, everyone." She gestured imperiously to the seats around the conference table and everyone seated themselves. Fran also settled back, fidgeting as more people entered. Stefan and Dimitri came first, then Kristos and Ari, then advisor Cyril, and another handful of guards. And then, finally, her friends.

Fran couldn't meet their eyes. Not yet.

Ari strode past his parents to her side, and dropped down to one knee until his face was level with hers.

"How are you feeling," he asked earnestly. "Have you seen a doctor?"

He was so intent that Fran nearly burst out laughing, though she knew that was a sign of nerves as well. "No I haven't seen a doctor, Ari. I fell in the water, not a volcano. I'm fine."

He grimaced, clearly not satisfied with that answer, but moved to the chair beside her. He glanced at his parents. "We should have a doctor in here."

"We will, once he's done examining Silas," Queen Catherine said. Fran jolted at the name, and the queen's gaze fixed on her. Dark shadows lurked below the queen's normally serene eyes, and her face was white and drawn. "He's my relation, Francesca. I am responsible for this attack on you. I had absolutely no idea that he could do anything like this. It's my fault."

From the pained look on the faces of King Jasen and Kristos, Fran could tell that this wasn't the first time the queen had made this statement. "I don't think this is anything you could have predicted," she said gently, trying to ignore the grateful glance Jasen sent her way. Instead she held the queen's gaze. "Silas had a vision for Oûros that I stood in the way of. I represented everything blocking his plan."

"But that makes no *sense*." The queen put her hands to her head. "Ari and Edeena weren't going to get married. They had no *intentions* of being anything more than friends. Nothing was going to change that."

"I know," Fran said gently. She fixedly didn't look at Ari or Stefan. They knew more than the queen did about Silas's abduction of her, and Fran was fine with keeping it that way. "But a year ago, in the first brush of realizing that Ari and Edeena weren't following the script he'd so carefully worked out for them, Silas believed he could push them together a bit. Make Ari see how valuable Edeena could be to him."

Ari scowled at her, looking genuinely surprised. "What are you talking about?"

Stefan's face now lit with understanding, and Cyril's did too, but Dimitri merely looked ready to kill someone. "What did he do to try to achieve that?" the captain asked gruffly. "Specifically?"

"I don't know what, specifically," Fran said. "But he—he did something to Ari's plane that night." She swiveled to look at him, and though she longed to reach for his hand, she didn't. She needed him to recall this moment as it actually happened, taking in the information and judging it on its own merits, not clouded by her leftover panic.

"I don't think it was anything truly treacherous, like spiking his gas tank or whatever," she continued. "Not something that could seriously threaten Ari's life on take-off. He simply did... something, I think to one of the gauges or monitors, to cause them not to function correctly."

"But why?" someone asked, but she couldn't turn away from Ari. Ari, who stared at her with deep and growing understanding, everything falling into place.

"He thought that if Ari dumped into the water close to home, maybe was injured and needed to convalesce—well, Edeena would be there. She's a trained nurse, and the two of them were good friends. If he cast her in a caretaking role..."

"He was there," Ari said slowly. "That night, Francesca's right. He was at the airstrip. I thought it was odd, I remember now, because he hadn't been at the state dinner. Edeena had, but she'd left early with a headache or something, and he'd not shown up at all."

"He was waiting for you there?"

Ari shrugged. "I don't know. I'd told him about wanting to test new equipment earlier in the week, that I was still making installations, but I didn't think I'd fly that night. There was the storm, and I figured it was late—night even. I could fly another day. But then I got to the strip to check things out and Silas was there."

"What did he say to you?" the king's words were sharp, but Fran knew Ari's answer before he gave it.

"I honestly don't remember," he said, wincing as he rubbed his head. "He was excited about the new instruments I'd installed. I—I must have told him about them. He encouraged me to try them out, said the storm was moving east, not west." He grimaced. "Idiot that I am, I didn't question what he said. I listened to the parts I wanted to hear—I wanted to get away from him, and the damn fool wouldn't leave. I got in the plane."

"That's why you felt the leftover threat when you thought about that night," Fran said. "He *was* a threat to your family—to you certainly. But maybe to others too."

Ari scowled. "He was definitely a threat. But he's not going to be one for anyone, any more. And there's more we need to know."

Fran nodded, dread pooling in her gut. It was over, she thought. It was all—finally—over.

Monster. The word shimmered and danced, taunting her on the edge of her hearing. It was time she explained herself.

Forty-Four

Rage knifed through Ari as he saw the misery playing over Fran's face. "He held a gun on you," he seethed. "That gun was loaded. You could have been killed." He shifted his gaze to Cyril. "What's the recourse here?"

"We need to gather more information," Cyril began, ever hesitant, and Ari's temper fractured.

"What additional information is needed? The man abducted Francesca, threatened her, then *threw her into the ocean*. And for what? He couldn't think he was going to endear his daughter to me with that!" He wheeled on Francesca. "What is it he wanted from you?"

Stefan had told him his thoughts on that, and Silas would be grilled accordingly, but what mattered most to Ari was Francesca. How much she'd been damaged by that asshole, how much she knew.

Her gaze held his steadily. "He wanted me to go away, Ari. That's all."

"Go away where?"

"Away from you." She gave him a small smile that made his heart twist. "Silas isn't alone in his prejudices. He saw Kristos falling in love with an American, and here was—well, he thought that here the same thing was happening all over again with you. You were fraternizing with an American woman instead of ideally one of his daughters, but failing that, then one of the daughters of Oûros, someone who understood the class system here, the rank of nobility." She shrugged. "He's not wrong. If he was a true nationalist…"

"He's no *nationalist*." Ari fairly spat the words. "He dared to insult you like that?"

"Ari," Francesca shook her head, fixing him with a gaze that almost bordered on chiding. "They were only words."

"No, they weren't only words, there was a gun as well—and he threw you. Over. The cliff." When Francesca moved to speak again, his father interrupted her.

"Ari is quite right," King Jasen said, to his surprise. His words were chillingly cool. "Silas took you against your will, held you against your will, threatened you and intended you serious harm." He frowned, clearly well aware that Silas could be the thread that unraveled much of what had entangled Oûros of late. "He'll be dealt with."

"His poor daughter, though." Queen Catherine was watching the king too, but Ari knew that whatever he decided, she would support. She'd support anything Jasen thought was in the best interests of Oûros.

Clearly, Francesca was also more concerned with Oûros than her own welfare, but Ari wasn't. Not right now, anyway, perhaps not ever. His country was his life, yes, but Francesca was becoming his every waking breath.

"Edeena won't be forced to carry the burden of her father's inadequacies," Jasen said. "And to some extent, Silas's actions will come out. The country is not so large that one of its noblemen being detained by the royal family will go completely unnoticed. Especially as a relation to the queen."

He shifted his gaze to Francesca. "Was anyone else aware of his attack on you?"

"I don't think so," Francesca said. Her voice remained calm, almost serene, despite what she'd endured. All Ari could imagine was holding her in his arms, yet she seemed so far away from him.

"He seemed pretty certain about the course of action he wanted me to take," she continued. "And I honestly didn't get the impression he waved his gun around for much more than bravado. He didn't shoot me, after all."

"Well, he threw you in the ocean," Nicki repeated dourly, the first of the girls to speak. "That's bad enough."

"But it's done," she said quietly, looking around the room. "Please let me be clear on that. I don't want to drag the royal family into any more turmoil."

Ari started, turning to her in surprise. "Francesca—"

"No, Ari," she said, and there were tears now standing in her eyes. "You—all of you. You have to know who and what I am before you say anything else. You think I'm someone to be protected and—well, you're wrong. I've put off owning this for far too long, and I see now that's been a poor decision."

She visibly swallowed and with a jolt, he realized...

Francesca's hands were shaking.

Forty-Five

Fran felt sick to her stomach, but strangely serene as well. As if she'd been waiting her entire life to endure this firing squad, and now that the rifles were pointed at her, she could finally breathe easier.

Except in this case, the rifles were the faces of nearly a dozen people who knew her better than anybody on the planet.

Which was exactly the point. They didn't know her at all. And now she didn't even know herself.

Monster.

She focused on Stefan. "When Emmaline first attracted Kristos's notice, you ran identity checks on all of us, pulling up information that was readily available, maybe going a level or two deeper, to make sure we were no immediate threat to the royal family. In my case, you found what I wanted you to find."

Stefan's brows shot up, but Fran lifted a quick hand. "I have no doubt that you would've pierced my current identity quickly enough, though that one has served me the longest. The others would have fallen in quick succession."

She forced herself to look at Lauren, then Nicki, then Emmaline. There was no outrage or shock on their faces, at least not yet. There was only confusion. "I wasn't born Francesca, though it's always been a beautiful name to me," she said quietly. "But my birth certificate says Frannie. Frannie Lambert. I was the child of Gus and Maribeth Lambert and I lived about five miles from a bar on the outskirts of Piketon, Ohio. The bar was my father's. It's not there anymore, but Bert's Bar and Grill was known by about every biker in Ohio and all the clubs rolling through as well."

As she talked, Fran could hear her voice change cadence, slipping back into the same rhythm that'd spiked when Silas had challenged her. She knew that voice, and while she didn't welcome it, it added a measure of comfort that she couldn't pull from anywhere else. "Mom and Dad split when I was three, and she remarried and lived in the next town over. I stayed with Dad so she could...I don't know. Focus on her own life or whatever. I spent the next several years of my life on the countertop at Bert's, or playing in the dirt yard behind the bar. It wasn't a bad place. The men were rough, but they respected Dad and they considered me no more interesting than a puppy. I was simply the newest feature in the bar."

As she talked, she could picture it. The faded newspaper clippings and snapshots tacked behind the bar, the dollar bills with markered-in notes on how or why they'd been donated to the "wall of shame." The men—and it had been almost all men, with their long, thinning hair and bulging forearms, most of them bearded or trying to be. The women were few and far between, which was okay because her dad usually employed women as servers and back-up bartenders, and any time a girl came around his staff members complained they got lower tips.

Her dad had run the place, cooked the cheeseburgers and hot dogs and pulled the beer. He didn't serve wine, and he didn't serve hard liquor. You went to Bert's for beer and a burger or you didn't go at all. He always told Fran that going simple cut down on his expenses, but honestly she didn't know if he could cook anything more complicated than cheeseburgers and hot dogs. She hadn't minded, though.

"When I got to be about seven years old, someone reported me as not being in school, so I split my time between school and the bar after that. Dad could never take me and it was another few miles up the road, so I got good at negotiating. I'd get a biker to take me home if it was late and dark, or to take me on to school after Dad opened up the bar. He opened early, six a.m., and there was usually someone sleeping it off in the back shed. Sometimes I guessed wrong about who I could trust, but never so wrong that I got hurt. And as I got older, I found the same kind of kids on the playground. Most of them with more money than I had, but that wasn't saying much."

She shrugged. "Mom eventually wanted custody, though her husband creeped me out. Dad fought it and threatened to take her to court, though that was a bluff. He didn't have any money. Worked, though, and that's what mattered."

The next part was the important part. Fran blinked, trying to keep her voice steady through it all. "We had our share of troublemakers, and one night, one of them left to go...somewhere. When he was done with whatever he did there, he took his truck out of the garage to head back to Bert's. Never made it. My dad had left early that night. I don't know why. He was broadsided by that same man before the guy ran off a bridge." Fran shook her head. "Never saw it coming, they told me. I sure didn't see it coming, either."

She sighed. "I was only fifteen. I wasn't going to live with my mom and her sick-o husband, and I wasn't going into foster care. I looked old for my age and, well, I knew some things. Some people." She glanced over at Ari but she couldn't fix on his face, the pageant of her own memories crowding him out. "I learned new things, too. How to make fake IDs, create disappearing trails. How to turn the internet into an identity factory. I learned how to find out who'd died and who'd simply disappeared, who'd lived and run and lost themselves. I used that information for myself, but..." she swallowed. "For other people too, sometimes. People who needed help, for good reasons or bad."

The tears were falling now, but she couldn't care about her mascara anymore. She'd never told so much at once to anyone. She'd never told all of it, ever. But Ari had to understand, finally. They all did. "I fell into a grifter's lifestyle, became a thief when I needed to, ran some petty cons, but mostly I helped others with forging really...whatever they needed. One life led to the next, and to the next. I eventually faked an older ID so I could get my GED without anyone asking questions, then re-fashioned it with a different age to take the standardized tests and enroll in college. The scholarships came unexpectedly, and that's how I managed such a nice school that no way could I afford."

She flattened her hands on the table, looking straight out at nothing. "Once I managed that, it was a matter of building the new life around me. The blended family in Michigan, the pets. The hot dog parties."

Emmaline's soft voice cut in. "You made up the hot dog parties? We would have had hot dogs more often if I'd known that."

The interruption was so unexpected that Fran blinked, and finally her eyesight seemed to clear. It was no longer her father standing at the end of the bar, her mother's sneering face with her husband leaning too close, or the countless parade of weathered, slow-eyed bikers in front of her. It was Nicki and Lauren and Emmaline, sweet Emmaline, whose face was tracked with tears. It was the king and queen sitting so close together their shoulders touched, their hands firmly clasped as if no storm could ever part them. It was Cyril gazing without any expression at all, Stefan with his eyes on Nicki, and Dimitri grinning at her like she'd given him a favorite birthday present. And beside her, still beside her, there was Ari, staring at her as if she was still his whole world.

"Are you finished yet?" he rumbled and she coughed a startled laugh that came out more like a sob, her voice choking when she could speak again.

"I'm not finished," she said. "Everything about me is a lie. My passport, my high school transcripts, my college application. Grad school wasn't because this ID finally took, this one could finally help me. But I broke laws, I—" Fran stopped, waving a hand at him. "Stop looking at me like that!"

Ari shook his head at her, but he still didn't stop gazing at her with his heart in his eyes, which meant he still didn't get it. But then he started talking, and it was even worse.

"You haven't said anything to me tonight that's a problem, Francesca. Why would you think it is?"

"Because I've broken the law—American law, probably international law. I'm pretty sure I bent a few of Oûros's laws as well, and I've only been here a few days."

Beside Ari, Dimitri snorted. "I want to see some of those IDs you've fashioned. We could use that skill."

"Dimitri," the queen's voice was a warning, but it was still too warm, too loving, and Fran felt the hysteria rise up again within her.

"Stop it," she practically begged Ari, but he simply shook his head.

"I don't know what you want me to say to you, Francesca."

"But I'm *not* Francesca, that's the point!" Her voice was desperate. Then again, so was she. "No matter what identity I take on to show the world, I'll always be the girl with the skinned elbows and worn-out clothes, who learned to fight in the dusty back lot of her dad's bar while bikers cheered her on. You—you forgot who you are, for a while, but now you've remembered and that's truly who you are. A good person. A noble person. I've always known who I am no matter how much I wish to forget it, and I've never wanted to be her." She bit her lip to keep the tears from falling again, to no avail. "I'm Frannie Lambert, while you...you're the crown prince of Oûros."

"I am," Ari said, eyeing her curiously. "Would you prefer I become a fisherman or a net maker? Of did you prefer me as Ryker Stavros, pilot at large?"

"*No,*" she retorted. "That's not who you are, and who you are is amazing."

"Then how can you imagine that I want you to be anything other than who you are?" Ari asked gently. "The woman who looks at me with so much caution in her eyes, whose hands held mine when they were shaking and never let go? Everything you've been through makes you everything you are, and I love every last part of it. I love Francesca Simmons and I love Frannie Lambert and I would love every person that you were in between. Because you've made even the ugly, broken, and painful parts of you more beautiful than anyone else could, simply because they are yours."

"I..." Fran couldn't stop now, wouldn't. No matter what amazing thing Ari had just said, no matter how he stared at her. "There's something else, too. I'm a—"

"Miracle," the queen announced, cutting her off.

The room as one turned to Queen Catherine, but she only had eyes for Fran. "Wasn't that what you were going to say, dear? That when you dropped into the water, the strength of who you are, who you really are, finally got a chance to shine?"

Lauren, Nicki, and Emmaline were staring wide-eyed, but everyone else in the room clearly knew her secret—and were equally shocked that the queen did, too. Which begged the question... "How did you know?"

"Know what?" Nicki demanded. "What are you talking about?"

"Do you mind, dear?" Catherine asked, gesturing to the wall. Fran blinked, saw the screen, and knew instantly what she meant. So it wasn't enough that she was a criminal, she needed to show the world she was some kind...some sort of freak, too?

"Francesca," Ari said, and she turned to him. His eyes were still so full of love, of wonder, that she knew she had to go through with this. He had to see.

"Go ahead," she said, swallowing. She moved her hands, just a little, and Ari instantly reached out to cover them with his. He held them tight and kept his gaze steady on hers as the screen powered on.

Nicki burst out of her chair. "What in the—wow!" she announced, striding toward the screen. "That's *you*?"

"Oh my god, Fran," Lauren's voice was hushed and awe-struck. "You're *beautiful*."

At Lauren's damned near reverential tone, Francesca finally glanced up—and Ari saw the moment her gaze saw, really saw the images on the screen. A goddess of the sea twirled and floated in the deepest depths of the ocean, caught by some underwater camera whose technology Ari applauded, even though the intention was for the foulest purpose imaginable.

Francesca's hair floated around her head, her webbed hands lifted and drifted through the water, and below her subtly shifting body, with all its soft curves, flapped a long, sinuous tail of iridescent purple, blue, and green scales. An enormous glittering pair of fins stretched out from the tip of the tail, imposing enough that it made Francesca look like she could swim around the world and back without stopping for a snack.

"Are you freaking kidding me right now?" Nicki put in again, still staring gape-mouthed at the screen. "You did this?"

"You are this," Emmaline said, and the words weren't a question. Francesca glanced at her, seeing her friend stare back with wide, adoring eyes. "You've always been someone who could recreate yourself, Fran, you just told us that right now. It looks like you've leveled up the skill."

"Well—I mean, um..." Francesca blushed furiously, for once seeming at a loss for words. "It's not like I thought any of that was going to happen. And now—I mean, I don't know what it means. I have to leave, I think, but I don't know where I'll go."

"You don't have to do a single thing you don't want to do," Ari corrected.

Even as he said the words, Ari could sense Francesca rejecting them. This was all so new to her—too new. It was new to him as well, but at least he'd been taught from childhood on that the magic of Oûros was truly boundless, and that the gifts of the gods could take you by surprise at any moment.

He quickly scanned the far side of the table. Emmaline, Nicki and Lauren all gazed at Francesca with nothing but love in their eyes—love and perhaps a few more tears. She'd get no judgment there.

His father and mother watched from the end of the table, but his father's face seemed more strained than his mother's. His gaze rested not on Ari, but on Francesca as she so painfully tried to convince an entire room of her unworthiness, when she'd already proven herself over and over in their minds without even trying—simply by becoming who she was always meant to be.

Finally, he glanced at Cyril, whose opinion he wanted not for any reason that would stop him, but to guide how he should proceed. Of all the Crown's advisors, Cyril was the most shrewd. He had the ear of the council and he had the pulse of the people. He would know exactly how far Ari could push the acceptance of the nation, and when he should pull back. Ari knew he couldn't live without Francesca—not now, not ever. But neither would he subject her to any scrutiny that would cause her to cry such tears again. Never would he ever permit her to be in such danger again as she'd faced from his own countrymen. If Cyril disapproved...

His mentor gave him the slightest nod. He could proceed however he wanted.

Ari's heart expanded in his chest and quickly he turned back to Francesca. He reached out and quieted her hands, which were shredding the tissue she'd pulled from the box to a fine pile of snow.

"What do you want, Francesca?" he asked, and her eyes met his, blinking in confusion.

"I don't know what you mean."

"I think you do," he said, shaking his head. "This isn't simply a question of me choosing you. If you were to come to Oûros and live with me, your life and your identity would change, again and again." He smiled as she furrowed her brow. "To one set of constituents, you would have to be a loving mother figure, helping them to teach their children to grow tall and strong, the pride of Oûros. To another you would have to hold their hands like you held mine, in sickness, in loss, and in the sorrow they would feel when their children or their husbands or their grandmothers die. To one set of diplomats you would be laughing and filled with joy at the event of a wedding or an anniversary. To another you would be serious, for their country is at war. You would have breakfast with your enemies and dinner with your allies, and they might be the same people on any given day. And to another group—a new group for us both—you would represent Oûros royalty to the gods...as one of their own."

"Ari, what are you *saying*?" Francesca whispered, but he wasn't finished yet.

"It's not a life that many could manage. It is a life perhaps best led by someone who knows the value of understanding who people most need her to be. And then there would be the obligations you would face with me, handling my work, my position, the demands on my time. I would travel—sometimes with you, sometimes without. I would tell you all that I could, but that wouldn't always be everything. Yet I would need you to be that same woman who sat next to me on the wind-swept ridge, not saying anything, not doing anything, but simply allowing me to suffer, allowing me to heal, allowing me to become the man that I have to become in order to be successful in my work. It's a great deal to ask of anyone, but I'm asking it of you, a total stranger to me before this week—yet someone I feel I've known my entire life. I want you to be my wife, Francesca. If you'll have me. If you'll have us."

He smiled as gently as he could. "And I'd so love to take you to Paris one day."

By this point, Francesca was staring at him. "You can't possibly be asking me...you can't possibly be," she protested. Her voice was barely a whisper, so low that no one else would ordinarily be able to hear her, at least not if the entire room wasn't sitting forward in their seats, hanging on every word.

"I'm not asking you, Francesca," Ari said. But before she could glance away, he tightened his hold on her fingers, lifting them to his chest as he dropped to one knee. "I'm begging you. On bended knee, I'm pleading with you to live your life with me, to be my wife, the princess of Oûros. Then one day, I hope you will be her queen, and the mother of our children, should we be so blessed. I want nothing more than for us to hold each other's hands in sickness and in health and never let go, never let each other face the world alone again, but always be by each other's side. I want us to bring each other laughter in times of sorrow and peace in times of pain. I'm asking you to let me care for you, too. To love you with my whole heart, to protect you with every force at my disposal, and to help you be the woman you most want to be. To show me each broken, hurting part of you and let me try to help make it whole. To accept who and what I am as I accept who and what you are, both of us imperfect, but together...together, something more. Something more that I want to explore with you, Francesca, you and only you."

Francesca tried to speak, she really did, but her mouth was trembling so much that it seemed she couldn't form any words. Ari took pity on her and squeezed her hands again, letting her catch her breath. "I'm asking you Francesca Simmons, Frannie Lambert, newly minted sea nymph and anyone you have ever been, anyone you will ever be—I'm asking you if you'll marry me," he said softly.

"Yes," Francesca said, the word far more than a half-sob now, and one that was echoed by other sobs, deeper in the room. "Yes, I will, Ari. If—If you'll have me."

His heart seemed to slow its beating, the moment transfixed in time. "I'll have you, Francesca," he whispered. "And I'll never let you go."

He leaned down to softly kiss her trembling lips, then rested his forehead against hers. When he looked up again, the girls were all leaning together in some kind of complex group hug. His men were grinning—even the stoic Stefan. His parents were no longer looking at him, but caught into an embrace all their own, their arms wrapped around each other so tightly it was as if they were fashioned from birth to be a matched set.

When he glanced again at Cyril, he found himself unaccountably tensing again, though the advisor had already given his approval.

But Cyril was watching Francesca, an expression on his face unlike any Ari had ever seen. He positively beamed, staring at her, and in that expression Ari realized that of everyone in this room except his own parents, he'd known Cyril the longest. The curmudgeonly counselor had been there when he'd been three years old and had helped him ride his first pony. He'd been there when Ari had fallen off the church wall—where he shouldn't have been playing at all. He'd stood by silent and watchful through every step of Ari's life, from childhood to rebellious teen to junior statesman, and he'd never ever smiled... not like this. Not ever like this.

Cyril, sensing Ari's focus, shifted his gaze to him and tempered his expression only slightly. "You've chosen well, Aristotle," he said in Oûrois. "When the time comes, the people of Oûros will stand with you both. Your beautiful, extraordinary Francesca will make a most excellent queen."

Forty-Seven

Ari stood with his hands clasped behind his back, wondering how, in the space of only a few weeks, everything in his life could have changed so much. From being held in a cage without a clue of who he really was, to waiting with his family to greet the gods to whom they'd dedicated their lives. He hadn't just come full circle, he'd leveled up dramatically. More than that, the audience due to enter the receiving room of the gods was unlike any that the royalty of Oûros had experienced in well over a thousand years.

And the amphitheater had changed dramatically to accommodate it.

Gone was the comparatively simple row of thrones with the gallery of bleachers behind it. Instead, a wide deck extended through the whole of the space, terminating before a shallow pool that marked an entry way to the deepest reaches of the oceans.

An entry way where Poseidon was due any moment.

"You think he'll show?"

Ari was glad that Kristos displayed the show of nerves

before he did. He glanced at his brother gratefully, knowing that he only spoke aloud what was on all their minds.

"The others are waiting on it," Stefan began—only to be interrupted by a long, indolent laugh—followed by a burst of doves that exploded into the room, their bodies transforming into puffs of glittering smoke as Hermes, the messenger god of Olympus, strode into the room from some totally unseen door. He wore a pair of long, baggy shorts, a white wifebeater tank top, and a ballcap he'd positioned backward on his blond locks. His feet were shod in scuffed black high-top basketball shoes.

"Don't flatter him, Stefan. He doesn't deserve it." Hermes lifted a negligent hand and twirled a finger. "Still, I can't say I don't love what you've done with the place. Who all are we anticipating? And oh, ho, ho! If it isn't Windsurfing Barbie. Well, this is a special day! Bet I can guess who one of the attendees will be, eh?"

Ari felt Stefan tense as Hermes sauntered up to Nicki, who was clearly doing her level best not to overreact at being approached by a god. As brash as she was, she was far more comfortable in a fight than in a dress, and there was something about being in the presence of the Olympians that tended to knock the breath out of you before you could speak. Even one dressed in early Justin Bieber.

"What, you don't have anything to say?"

"I do," Nicki piped up, clearly startling Stefan and causing the queen to tighten her mouth in a half-buried grin. "I'd like to thank you for being such a good boss that Stefan hung around working for you as long as he did. If he hadn't, I never would have met him. And I would never know how much life is worth living, and how much love can knock you over, even when you're standing still. So thank you. You mean the world to him, and he means the world to me."

Clearly surprised, Hermes stared at Nicki a long moment,

then a slow easy grin creased his face. "I like her," he said, turning back toward Stefan. He poufed out of view and appeared again at the far end of the room, leaning against the largest of the repositioned thrones. "I like her a lot."

"So do I," Stefan gritted out.

"And why am I not surprised at your choice, Dimitri?" The voice that echoed through the room was heavy, imposing, but nothing compared to the figure who appeared on the throne Hermes leaned upon. Easily eight feet tall, Zeus had chosen Armani as his clothier for this assembly, the silky suit echoing the color of his thick, slate gray hair. He gave the messenger god a sharp glance that didn't move Hermes an inch. "Lauren Grant, you should know he's petitioned me to release him from service."

Ari glanced Lauren's way, completely unsure how the composed American heiress would take this announcement. To his surprise, she merely inclined her head, as regal as Zeus in her long simple, toga-styled gown. "Then you know how difficult he is when he makes his mind up about something."

Zeus snorted, and Ari shot a look at Dimitri, who merely grimaced.

Then the father of the gods leaned back on his throne, folding his arms. "Jasen, Catherine, your sons honor you. It's good to know the next generation of Oûros is assured. Now, can we get this moving? If Hera realizes I've left her out of our chat, I'll never hear the end of it, but we didn't want to draw too much attention. Brothers!"

In response, the floor of the receiving room blackened and fell away, fire licking up and around the hole. The swarthy, dark-haired Hades, deceptively graceful despite his bulk, glided up a staircase that spiraled into the hole. Nicki gasped, and Stefan suddenly looked stiff again.

Hades, for his part, ignored them both, turning instead to

Zeus, and offering his brother a brief bow. He was a god who knew how to bide his time, Ari knew. Stefan had told him about Hades's interest in allowing Nikki to represent him on earth, but for now, he was content to let her be curious.

But there was one more god they waited on, a proud god. A god that, Ari knew, they had ignored too long.

"You knew he was going to do this," Hades supplied, and Zeus rolled his eyes.

"Ari?" At his elbow, Francesca looked up at Ari. "You thought this might happen, too," she said softly. "I don't mind, truly."

He sighed, but she was right. If Poseidon wanted an honor guard to escort him into the receiving room, you couldn't get a better one than a sea nymph come home.

"Go," he murmured.

Forty-Eight

Francesca swallowed, trying desperately to manage her nerves. Though she had prepared for this moment, dressed for it even, in a gown of iridescent green the color of the Aegean on a calm day, she still couldn't quite believe that this would work.

In the intervening days since Ari had plucked her out of the ocean, she had replayed the video footage of her transforming into a sea nymph no less than a dozen times. She and Nicki had even tried out the transformation process on the sly, Nicki strapping her into a life jacket before commandeering a sea kayak one dark and starlit evening. Nikki had paddled them out just far enough for Fran not to be able to touch bottom, then she'd helped Fran half-fall into the water.

The change had been instantaneous. The moment Fran had been fully submerged in the Aegean, the life jacket and her swimsuit had simply shucked off her like an unwanted blanket, and her body had transformed into the powerful, beautiful figure of a sea nymph. She'd stared at her long purple and green-scaled tail for so long that Nicki had begun slapping an oar on the surface of the water, demanding proof of life. Fran had been happy to give it, bobbing out of the Aegean like a cork, spinning and twirling around.

They'd spent over an hour in the open sea, one of the silliest hours of Fran's life. Afterward, they'd snuck back into the royal palace, knowing they'd been watched, shadowed, and kept safe by people who loved them.

And they always would be.

But this—this was something different.

Ari had warned her that Poseidon might not be willing to come without proper veneration, that he might demand tribute. The demigods who served him had already left on assignment, but they weren't necessary here, anyway. This meeting was only for the closest members of the royal family. Her family, she realized, or as close to it as she would ever get.

She stepped forward, pausing as the queen fell into place behind her, smoothing her hair over her shoulders, straightening her gown. "You are a goddess of the sea in your own right," Queen Catherine murmured to her quietly. "Never forget that."

Francesca nodded quickly, but she'd only moved forward a few steps when the waters of the tidal pool started bubbling, and a bare moment later, Poseidon, god of the sea strode forth.

She nearly stumbled, but instead stood stock still, lifting her chin to keep her gaze on the impressive god's face for as long as it took to unscramble her brain.

Poseidon was breathtaking. His long silver hair flowed over his shoulders, his sun-bronzed skin stretched taut across a powerfully built upper body. Alone among the gods, he was dressed in more traditional wear, with a toga of deep greens and blues draped over his shoulder and cinched at the waist. He carried his trident in one hand and what looked like a glass sphere in his other. As he stepped out of the water and onto the ledge of the receiving room, he stared around the space with beetling thick brows, taking it all in as if he needed to get used to seeing the world through the lens of air rather than ocean.

Finally, his gaze rested on Fran a long moment, then he nodded.

"Welcome home, child," he said gruffly. "This is for you."

He held out the glass orb, and, not knowing what else to do, Fran stepped forward, her mind racing. Child? Did this being, this deity or ancient alien or whatever in the world he really was, genuinely consider her to be one of his own? A child, however many times removed?

"Thank you," she managed, lifting her hands to accept the misty blue orb. When she touched it, she drew in a sharp breath as the swirling patterns on the sphere began to move and shift. It was a globe, she realized, a depiction of Earth covered by clouds. But as she stared at it, the clouds shifted and parted, revealing broad swaths of ocean broken up by land masses. At various points in the ocean, along certain shorelines or near tiny islands, fairy lights glowed.

"No, it is I who thank you for coming home." Poseidon gestured to the orb. "Your family awaits you, whenever you wish to find any one of us."

"Oh..." The full import of the gift landed on Fran like a crashing wave. What she held in her hands was a map, a map of all her long-lost relatives. The family who wanted to claim her, and who wanted her to claim them. She blinked up at Poseidon, meeting his storm-gray eyes as she struggled to keep new tears from falling. "I will," she said. "I would be honored to meet them all."

"And so may it be done." Zeus's voice boomed out over the room, making Fran jump. "And may we *finally* turn to the matter that unites us all—Land, Sea, and Underworld. This war council to defend Earth against all those who would fail her, god and mortal alike, shall now begin."

Epilogue

A lone woman climbed the marble steps of the Temple of Winds, then crossed swiftly toward the far edge of the building, breaking off only briefly to trace the path of the ancient maze to the eternal flame. When she emerged, she continued her journey almost breathlessly, forcing herself to slow down enough that the taper didn't gutter out. She always forgot how temperamental firelight could be up here. Then again, it *was* called the Temple of Winds. There was obviously a reason for that.

Edeena Saleri stopped in front of the three bowls, blindly reaching into her pouch for the dried petals, herbs, and coins that her petition called for. Gratitude, first and always. "May the world be at peace with the gods favor, and all that occurs find delight in your eyes," she murmured, setting the first pyre alight.

The second vessel was more important. She filled the bowl full, the turbulence of her own emotions evident in the wild mixture of offerings. Daffodils, roses, lilies, lavender and hyacinths here, and yet more coins. "Forgive me, that I wasn't stronger, that I didn't see what he was doing. That I ran away instead of taking up my responsibility to keep him safe, to keep all of Oûros safe," she whispered. "They'll treat him more fairly than he deserves, but if there is a burden for retribution, let me pay it. He is an old and foolish man."

She glanced briefly at the third bowl, but she didn't have the heart to look ahead. Not right now. So much had happened over these past few weeks. Worse, what little she'd been able to glean from her father's files, the private records and papers that she'd pored over before consigning them to flames, had shown her that his businesses had profited through some very dark investments. Her best recourse was to leave Oûros and not come back for a very long time. That would be easier for everyone.

The winds of the Aegean lifted up just then, the crashing waves below sending forth a mournful cry that tugged at her heart. She loved it here on this lonely promontory. She had since the first time her father had urged her up the stairs and across the mosaic floor to give thanks for her mother and beg the gods for a way forward after her death. A way forward for him, she remembered, not for her, but she hadn't cared. She'd been happy to have a reason to reach out to her mother, happy for a connection, no matter how frail. She'd had no idea what her father had been planning at the time—but she could have figured it out if she'd just tried. She *should* have figured it out.

"I'm so sorry," she said again, bracing her hands on the marble ledge and sagging forward, allowing the tears to fall, finally. Tears she couldn't—wouldn't—shed anywhere else. A few dropped on the burning pyre, making the flame sizzle. Would that honor the gods, she wondered? Or simply piss them off anew? You never knew with them.

Pulling herself back together, Edeena fished a linen kerchief out of her bag, dabbed at her eyes, then dropped it beside the vessels as she pushed the pyres around with her taper, watching until her offerings burned low. The sun was setting now. It was getting late. Her flight away from Oûros would leave early the next day, and there was still so much to do. As she studied the dying flames, her mind filled with details, logistics, plans, tasks. She had so much to do—too much! It was too much.

With a final muttered prayer she stepped back, then walked quickly through the temple and down the stairs. She'd go forever and far away from Oûros, she thought, as day bled into night. Forever and far, far away.

A minute passed.

Another.

Then a new figure stepped out from the rocks and wildly flowering bushes that choked the path, and mounted the short stairway to the Temple of Winds. A fresh, jaunty breeze made the pyres spring back into life in the offering vessels. There was no need for additional flame, of course. All that was necessary was to pick up the precious scrap of tear-stained linen, catch it alight, and drop it in the third bowl, along with a scatter of dried lilies, roses, and even a few morning glories. What followed then was a simple murmured wish upon the wind to follow the disillusioned, golden-eyed girl out into the world. To follow her, keep her safe, and—perhaps—to bring her home again.

For even gods could dream.

Thank you for reading CROWNED! The adventures of Oûros will continue, and if you'd like to be among the first to know about Edeena's star-crossed romance with a very grumpy Greek god, sign up for my newsletter at www.jenniferchance.com

(look for the signup at the bottom of the page!) or drop me an email at jennifer@jenniferchance.com. You can also find me online at Facebook!

I appreciate your help in spreading the word about my books, including telling a friend. Reviews help readers find books! Please leave a review on your favorite book site.

Acknowledgments

Thanks to my editor Holly Thompson, who took this majorly rewritten book and made it better at every turn, and to Judi Soderberg, who was willing to take on a mushy book and proofread it like the boss she is. Any remaining errors are definitely my own. To Sabra Harp, thank you for being with me on this crazy journey—I couldn't do it without you! And thank you to Dar Albert for my absolutely stunning covers this entire series through. I could not love them more.

And to those readers who have continued the journey with the gatekeeper royals of Oûros, thank you. And keep on dreaming.

Also by Jennifer Chance

Gatekeepers of the Gods

Courted

Captured

Claimed

Crowned

Boston Magic Academies

Touch of the Mage

Blood of the Mage

Heart of the Mage

Soul of the Mage

The Hunter's Call

The Hunter's Curse

The Hunter's Snare

The Hunter's Vow

Witchling Academy

Teaching the King

Tempting the King

Taming the King

About Jennifer Chance

Jennifer Chance/D.D. Chance are the pen names of Jenn Stark, an award-winning author of paranormal romance, urban fantasy, and contemporary romance. Whether she's writing as Jenn or D.D., she loves writing, magic and unconditional love.

Thank you for taking this adventure with her. If you're feeling social, you can find her online or visit her on Facebook!

www.ingramcontent.com/pod-product-compliance
Lightning Source LLC
Chambersburg PA
CBHW050528110726
47899CB00005B/1641